Being Greta

Visit the author's blog at https://maxinesinclair.com

Written with thanks to all my D/deaf friends and the wider Deaf Community.

Being Greta

Greta pads to the bathroom in their pokey one bedroom flat and spots the letters on the mat. She doesn't mind not hearing the postman – although it does annoy her when she has to traipse to the post office for missed parcels – but having been born deaf she's had twenty-six years of not hearing stuff.

Bill, bill, junk, bill, she flicks through the pile until one buff envelope catches her eye. Her heart beats through her pyjama shirt as she slides down the wall – right, here we go…

Dear Miss Palmer,

Thank you for your application to participate in the new Channel 8 documentary, 'The Art of Being Disabled'. We have received an overwhelming response and after careful consideration we would like to invite you to The Broadcasting Hub on Friday 9th September for an interview.

Please find information relating to the day enclosed.

Should you not wish to pursue your application further please contact us at your earliest convenience.

We look forward to meeting you shortly.

Yours sincerely,

Jenni Fields.

Head of Production.

Blowing a lock of blonde curly hair from her face, she stares at the letter shaking in her hands. She remembers how this started, and how she had honestly believed it wouldn't go any further, and for that, she blames Mia.

'Gretaaaaaaaa,' her best friend had slurrily signed, the other

side of two bottles of red. '*C'mon – live a little! Or just live!*' Greta had shaken her head as emphatically as a drunken person can. '*Gretaaaaaaa, Gretaaaaaaaa – you know you want to, it'll be fun.*'

'*Nuh-uh.*'

'*Come on! I won't tell anyone about that night in Majorca.*'

Greta had collapsed into giggles and Mia took this as her acquiescence. How they'd then gone on to navigate the online application is still a mystery.

She feels the floorboards vibrate underneath her signalling that Olly is up. She quickly folds the letter and instinctively shoves it into her dressing gown pocket. Will Olly approve? She doesn't know, but as he's not a morning person, now is not the time to find out.

'What you doing down there?' Through his sleep-contorted face she reads his lips.

'Just haven't got the energy to stand and read at the same time,' she responds light heartedly. He shrugs his shoulders, scratches his bottom and heads for the kitchen for his usual strong coffee.

She gets up to follow him, and patting her dressing gown pocket, she finds an unusual spring in her step and a tremor of excitement in her belly, both of which she hasn't felt in quite a while.

•••

Mia opens one eye and sees him pulling up his boxers and heading for the bathroom.

Oh My God! Quick! Memory kick in! Who is he? What happened? Mentally racing through the night before she recalls The Jolly Sailor's monthly gathering of deaf people, vodkas with lime and soda, signing with a group of out of town deaf folk, more vodka, playing 'Hot or Not' with Jazzy and Amber, an unnecessary whisky nightcap and then her legs buckling and big arms picking her up…but who did they belong to? Mr Boxer Shorts?

She rearranges the covers and tries to smooth her wild afro into some kind of symmetry when he appears at the door. He smiles.

'*Morning,*' he signs. She raises her thumb, taking in his dark blonde dreadlocks, pierced eyebrow and suntanned physique. '*I have to get to work. You got any milk?'*

Mia knows for a fact that the fridge is bare – she buys food on a 'need to eat' basis and applies the same principle to cleaning; if there's any danger of her mother visiting, she'll trot round with the hoover.

'Sorry, don't think so,' she signs.

'Black coffee then?'

'Not sure there's any of that either.'

'Ah.'

She inwardly groans that he must be thinking she is a complete flake. She gets blind drunk, brings him, a complete stranger, back to her flat (which is an almighty tip) and now can't even offer him a coffee. At least she can't see judgement in his eyes.

'Right, well, thanks for a great night. It was fun!' he signs with a cheeky grin.

'Was it?'

'Ouch.' He holds his heart with a mock pained expression.

'Sorry, it was just too many vodkas. I'm sure it was fun...er...?'

'Jerry.' He spells out his name on his long fingers.

Nope, she thinks, wouldn't have remembered that in a million years...

'Jerry, right.' Instinctively Mia sits up and holds out her hand. Jerry looks at it, then up at her, laughs and shakes it.

'Nice to meet you, Mia,' he signs, spelling out her name.

'Yeah, you too, Jez.'

'Yeah, don't call me that – I hate it.'

'Right. Sorry.'

'OK, like I said, gotta get to work. Hope to see you again sometime.'

'Sure. Absolutely.'

Jerry lifts his coat from the chair piled high with most of Mia's wardrobe and with a final wide smile, and a slight shake of his head, he makes for the door. Reclining back, Mia ponders how they will meet again – as far as her patchy memory goes, they didn't exchange numbers.

Ah well, she thinks, – another notch on my multi-scored bedpost.

Pulling out the shake awake alarm clock from beneath her

pillow, she checks the time. Eurgh, she really needs to get up! Tossing the clock that bounces and lands on a strewn blanket on the floor she then flops back onto the pillow and snuggles back down for just another ten minutes.

Chapter 1

Grasping a skinny cappuccino as if her life depends on it, Greta runs for the lift at Bridgewell County Hall. Actually, standing in the marble foyer and awaiting the next lift is infinitely preferable to dealing with social services matters, but she runs nevertheless. She shares the lift with the usual blank faced workers who determinedly avoid eye contact on their silent journey to the fourth floor.

Passing the matching rows of desks to arrive at her workstation, Greta finds Joy and Joanie, her forty-something, twittering colleagues deep in conversation.

'So, it got to the early hours and we had to call the police,' Joy, with a drawn expression says to Joanie who listens intently. 'I just don't know what we're going to do with her.'

What are they talking about? Greta attempts to piece together the story by following their flapping lips. Has Joy's wayward teen has been out on the razz again? It wouldn't be the first time.

Interrupting their flow, Greta asks, 'Everything OK?'

'Sorry, what?' Joanie asks. Greta's voice is that of a deaf person, it holds a certain throaty quality, but having worked with Joanie for so long it's incredible that her colleague still doesn't fully understand her. Most others do.

'I asked if everything is OK.' Greta gesticulates.

'Oh I see,' Joanie says. 'Joy's dau-ghter has been in a lit-tle trou-ble a-gain.' She does that thing that people do: mouth and exaggerate every word very slowly - it reminds Greta of a goldfish she'd once owned. Joanie finishes with a patronising little smirk, signalling that their exchange is done; she clearly doesn't want to elaborate – that would be far too much effort.

Greta pulls a sympathetic half smile and asks no more, opting instead to start up her computer and attack her bulging inbox. Around ten o'clock the 'out-of-the-blue-but-it-happens-every-week-without-fail' fire alarm sounds out. Clocking the barely visible flashing alarm she follows her colleagues to the crowded stairwell where they inch their way to fresh air. Taking micro steps she dreads to imagine the carnage if it were a real fire.

Once outside, she is perched on a low brick wall in her designated area in the car park when she sees Mia heading towards her.

'*Gotta love fire practice*,' Mia signs.

'*Sure do!*'

Mia reaches in her bag for chewing gum. '*So, how's life?*' she asks, offering her a stick.

'*Okay, ta*,' Greta replies, taking one. '*Hey, guess what I got.*'

'*Herpes?*'

Greta rolls her eyes.

'*A marriage proposal from Olly?*' Mia grins.

'*Very funny, but no. Look.*'

Greta pulls the letter from her bag, and as Mia reads it her hazel eyes widen and her white-toothed smile dazzles.

'*Greta, I'm so proud of you! Of us!*' She enthusiastically hugs her friend, rocking her back and forth and jumping up and down on the spot. '*This is so exciting!*'

'*Yeah, yeah, get off me*,' Greta laughs. '*I haven't told Olly yet. Didn't even tell him I'd applied. I'm just not quite sure how he's going to feel about it.*'

'*Oh sod Olly! He loves you so he should want what's best for you*,' Mia signs with a shrug.

'*I also need to get Dodgy Roger to agree to me having time off.*' Greta signs.

'*You'll ask that miserable git and if he says no then you'll throw a sickie and go anyway!*'

Greta smiles at her feisty friend. '*It must be so easy being you! I can't pull a sickie after I've asked for the time off!*'

'*Yes you can, this is a great chance for you. You might even earn a little respect from Moanie-Joanie and Joy-less.*'

'*Mmm, hadn't thought of that.*' Greta grins and gets up. '*OK, is this done yet?*' She looks around at the orange-hatted fire wardens attending to their clipboards.

'*It takes forever – but it's a damn sight better than working!*' Mia signs.

'*Ha! Not enough people complaining about potholes in the*

road for you today?' Greta laughs and Mia pulls a face.

'I was late in this morning as well,' Mia sucks in her cheeks.

'Oh yeah?' Greta's eyebrows rise.

'Yep, guilty as charged.'

'Oooh who was he?'

'Jerry' apparently,' Mia signs with a mischievous expression.

'Jerry eh? And where did you meet this poor unfortunate?'

'Hey! It was deaf night at The Jolly Sailor.'

'Oh, of course.'

Mia tugs on her friend's arm. *'I do wish you'd come again.'*

Greta scrunches up her face. *'You know what Olly's like, he doesn't really enjoy it. And you can't blame him with loads of deaf people all signing and he can't understand any of it. It means I have to interpret all night too– it's no fun.'*

'He could always learn to sign…'

Greta pulls a face that says 'you know I've tried to convince him before and you know that he won't'. *'Next month I'll try and make it there, Mia, I promise.'*

They turn to see one of the orange hats signalling for people to return to the building.

'Here we go then,' Mia signs, as they begin to shuffle back towards the building. *'You know, Greta, I really think it's a great opportunity for you. I mean how many girls like us get this kind of chance, eh? Deaf power!'* She giggles, raising her fist in solidarity. *'Hey, can I be your stylist?'*

'Ha! Like you did when we were fourteen and you dyed my hair orange?'

'Told you before, belisha beacon was bang on trend back then!' Laughing, Mia links Greta's arm. *'I'll make a star of you yet!'*

'Haven't got through the interview yet,' Greta says, biting her lip.

'Yeah, but you will.'

Chapter 2

Greta knocks on the door of her parents' large nineteen thirties detached house in the leafier part of town, steps back and reviews the text she'd received earlier; *'do you remember us?'* her mother had asked. 'Huh, yes,' Greta thinks, 'and I remember exactly how our relationship is.'

Her mother appears at the door, all twin set and pearls, every inch the well-bred, wealthy woman of leisure.

Greta purposely signs and speaks the word, 'Mother,' and then sees the familiar look of disdain flash across her mother's face.

'Darling,' she says, reaching for Greta's hands.

Mmmm, a sign of affection or intentional restraint?

'Sorry it's been a while, I've been busy,' Greta says.

'Never mind, dear, you're here now. Well come in, don't stand there on the doorstep like a stranger.' Greta follows her mother through to the lounge where they take seats on the cream floral suite. 'Daddy will be down in a moment, he's just got in from the golf course,' Sylvia continues, smoothing a stray hair and pursing her shimmery pink lips. 'He's just taking a shower.'

'Did he win?' Greta asks.

Sylvia lowers her head to brush some cotton from her skirt as she answers. Greta sighs. Despite giving birth to a child that has never been able to hear, her mother has never grasped the simple notion that a deaf person, in order to understand, has to read lips.

'Mum, what did you say?'

'I said he was up against Dirk so you know how that goes...' Sylvia laughs whilst recounting the tale which only serves to distort her lip patterns further.

'Mum! What?'

Sylvia's laughter fizzles to a sigh. 'Ah don't worry, dear, it's not important.'

Greta feels the heat in her blood rise. If she had a penny for every time someone had told her that 'it's not important' she would be exceedingly rich. Mia reckons that it actually means 'you're not important enough to take the time to repeat it to,' and, in Sylvia's case, Greta thinks it fits perfectly.

Greta sighs loudly and looks away, avoiding a quarrel (she has only just got here!) and denying her mother any further opportunity for small talk. After a few uncomfortable moments of silence, Sylvia crosses the lounge to look out at the neatly cropped higher and lower lawns. Completely silhouetted by the evening sun behind her, Greta squints at her and takes a guess at the next question

'How's Oliver?' her mother asks.

Bingo. 'Fine. He's busy work.'

'*With* work, darling, busy *with* work.'

All her life Sylvia has been the echo on her shoulder - her home-grown speech therapist. Greta has always been told that she speaks well considering her hearing loss, (and learning to speak when you can't hear is jolly difficult,) but this doesn't stop Sylvia chipping in with corrections.

'WITH work,' Greta sighs.

'Ah yes, it's a good solid job, banking, isn't it? He's a young man who's going places, that one. You definitely need to hold on to him.'

'I need to hold on to him?!' Shouldn't her mother believe that *he* should want to hold on to *her?* Greta takes a sharp intake of breath to reply but at that moment her father enters the room.

'Ah, here's my favourite girl!'

Her dad's soft dark grey crinkly hair and crystal blue eyes give him a distinguished look many would envy. And Greta stands to be enveloped by his warm hug. He pulls away and holds her at arm's length to look her squarely in the face.

'You're looking gorgeous, Gretsy. How's life treating you?'

'Good. In fact, I have some news..'

'Do you, darling? What's that?' His eyes light up.

'Well, -'

'Right, sorry dear, dinner's almost ready,' Sylvia interrupts. 'You two go through and I'll serve. Chop chop.' Greta and her father exchange raised eyebrows and little smiles and obediently follow Sylvia to the dining room.

Sitting down to starters on the family china, her mother fiercely dominates the conversation. It's a one-woman monologue covering the bridge club, Mrs Hoffman's new Cockapoo and whether or not Henley Regatta is out of the question this year due to the hideous weather of last year's. Greta and her father nod and chip in occasionally. When Sylvia pauses to breathe, her father taps the table to get Greta's attention and leaning forward, he smiles.

'So, Greta, what's your news?'

'Well,' She looks to both of them. 'A few weeks ago, Mia came round and we had a couple of drinks.' Greta can feel her mother bristle. 'And we were messing about on Facebook and saw this ad for a TV show they're making and I don't know how it happened but she talked me into applying!'

Her mother's bristling turns to earthquake shaking.

'What's it about?' Sylvia questions through tight lips.

Greta's brow furrows and she looks to her father.

'Mum asked what it's about,' he clarifies.

'Oh, right. It's called The Art of Being Disabled. It's a new series about disabled people who are involved in the arts. And this morning I got a letter inviting me to interview -'

'Darling, you're not exactly 'involved in the arts', are you?' her mother says.

'Sylvie, our little girl is a great artist, as well you know,' her father defends. He turns back to Greta. 'That's marvellous – when's the interview?'

'Next Friday.'

'You go for it. I've always said you're the star of the show, my darling.'

Her mother rises with a face of thunder and Greta worries for the china plates that her mother is forcefully stacking. Seeing his wife disappearing into the kitchen, her father pulls an apologetic face, rises and chases after her. Greta quietly snorts. John Palmer, the easy going loving father that he is, although rumoured to have a spine, knows his place with his wife and spends half his life smoothing things over to keep the peace.

Greta remains in the wood-panelled dining room, playing with the silver cutlery and imagining the conversation in the kitchen. Her mother will be close to tears exclaiming how she'll 'never understand' her daughter, and her father will be hushing her and trying to find a middle ground that she can accept. Greta sighs. When did she become the source of her mother's constant disappointment? Or has it always been like this?

Carrying tureens back into the room her father reappears bright and breezy whilst her mother has red eyes and a downturned mouth. He tops up the crystal glasses with red wine while her mother serves the coq-au-vin.

The conversation hardly flows.

'Your mother and I are thinking of getting the hall decorated,' her father starts. 'In time for Christmas.'

'Really. What colour?' Greta asks.

'Not sure, are we, Sylvia?'

'No dear.'

Three minutes later.

'Did you hear that your brother bought a new car?' her mother asks.

It's on the tip of Greta's tongue to say, 'no, I don't hear…'

'No, what did he get?'

'A beautiful Range Rover. Brand new. Lovely and spacious.' Her mother's eyes beam with pride.

'Is that for when they start a family?' Greta asks.

Sylvia face drops. Mikey's fiancée fell pregnant last year but sadly lost the baby. By all accounts they had planned the pregnancy but her mother doesn't like to believe that - babies out of wedlock don't happen in Sylvia's world. And so it is with anything that doesn't match her mother's ideas of propriety: it is simply brushed under the carpet. Safe to say Sylvia has a very large carpet.

'No darling!' Sylvia says. 'It's so he can put all his snowboarding gear in there.'

Right.

As with many relationships there's an unspoken agreed pattern to the evening that Greta now mentally ticks off: dinner, coffee in the lounge, more clipped conversation followed by brief goodbyes. Hugs are cursory and her parents are not ones to linger or wave from the door.

Heading home on the bus, Greta takes her favourite upstairs seat at the front and stares at the pink and orange blotchy sky. She half smiles that the only saving grace of an evening with her mother is that it's usually all done and dusted in an hour and a half. And sometimes, when the conversation is well and truly stunted, like tonight, it's only an hour and fifteen…

Chapter 3

Letting herself into the flat she sees Olly sitting in his usual end seat on their white leather sofa watching the football on the wide screen television.

'Hiya,' she says, knowing it's always risky interrupting. 'Another beer?' He raises a thumb without taking his eyes from the screen.

Heading for the kitchen she opts for tea, and whilst waiting for the kettle to boil she idly smiles at the framed art hanging on the wall. Her charcoal outline of a person holding two fingers to his ear – the sign for 'deaf' – looking downcast in a windowless room triumphed in a local competition with the judges saying she'd 'depicted the isolation of the character perfectly'. She and Olly had celebrated her first ever cash prize with a Chinese takeaway and a bottle of plonk and Olly was so proud that he'd suggested they hang her work in the kitchen. She'd been hoping for the lounge but he was quite right when he explained that it wouldn't match the décor in there.

She feels a thump on the floor and turns to see Olly standing in the doorway.

'You gonna be long with that drink?' he says.

'Sorry, I'm making a tea.'

'Don't worry, I'll get it myself,' he says, heading to the fridge. As he brushes past he kisses her lightly. 'Game'll be over in ten, Switch.'

She pours boiling water into her mug and smiles at her nickname that started early in their relationship. In a jokey moment he'd called her 'Sweet Cheeks' but, reading his lips, she'd got 'Switch.' It had been weeks before she was brave enough to ask why he would call her that and then it had been weeks of him laughing at her mistake. Needless to say, it stuck.

Joining him on the sofa, he looks at her. 'So, how's your day been?'

'OK.' Greta says. 'Dinner with the folks was the usual.' They exchange small grimaces. 'But I got through it relatively unscathed. Bit of a bust up with Sylvia when I told her my news…'

'Oh yeah? What's that then?' He frowns.

'Er….you remember that evening you were out with the work crowd? Mia came over and we hit the wine?'

'That could be any number of nights.'

'Oi!' She playfully punches his arm. 'Well, anyway.' She swallows hard. 'Mia talked me into applying to be in a documentary. It's called The Art of Being Disabled…' She sees a darkness cover his face. 'It's kind of a fly on the wall thing about people with disabilities who are involved in the arts.'

'Babe, you work for the council.'

'Yeah, I know that - but it's about my art!'

'Oh that, yeah, yeah that's great…' He trails off.

'Well,' she tries to remain upbeat. 'They want to interview me. And you never know, someone might see it and like my work and commission me or offer me an internship or something?' She feels a small lump forming in her throat.

'Yeah, course. It's great, Grets. I'm stoked for you.'

'Really? You don't look it.'

'Look, I just don't want you getting your hopes up. You know the art world – it's jammed with talent and only the top few really make it. I've seen you disappointed before, I just don't want to pick up the pieces when you've had your hopes and dreams crushed. I love you too much, babe.'

'I know. But maybe this is a great opportunity?' she says in a small voice.

'Course, course. You go for it. Fly on the wall eh? They gonna be filming here?'

'Would you mind if they did?'

'I don't wanna be in it if that's what you mean. It's about you, babe, not me. You go for it though. I'm right behind you, you know that.'

'Thanks, Olly.'

She leans across, kisses him and snuggles up. He slightly pulls away to face her.

'Hold on, sorry Switch – just remembered there's boxing on.'

He reaches for the remote and her heart sinks a little. Catching her expression, he pulls her back in. 'It's not on for long. Why don't you trot off to bed and put your sexy gear on and I'll be in in a bit.' He tweaks her nose and then turns his attention back to the TV.

Moving to the bedroom, Greta sits on the edge of the bed, feeling that with the exception of Mia no one is particularly enthused about this TV programme. Hmph, should she forget it and 'keep her head down and earn a sensible wage at the council' like her mother would prefer?

She looks up to see Olly in the doorway. 'Where's the sexy gear?'

'Sorry, seriously not in the mood. Blame the parents,' she lies. He sits next to her on the bed and putting his arm around her, she rests her head on his shoulder. He takes her hand and writes 'OK' with his finger on her palm.

'I wish you'd learn some sign language!' she says.

He writes 'OK' again, only this time with a kiss. She laughs and turns to him.

'Go on, you'll miss the boxing.'

'You OK?'

'Yeah course.'

He kisses her lightly on the lips, gets up to walk away but turns back, 'Oh that's what I came to say – you haven't forgotten we're invited to Ronnie and Jill's this weekend? Just the old gang together again.'

'Your old gang, not mine,' she thinks uncharitably. Ronnie and Jill are nice enough, not really her kind of people, but they're better than some of the others who'll be there. As if reading her mind, he says, 'It'll be a laugh.' And with that he disappears back to the lounge.

Greta sighs. Yes, she knows it'll be 'a laugh' for him – they're his friends – but as is the way with old friends, people talk over each other, old jokes are recounted and laughter punctuates half stories; she won't stand a chance! She hopes that, as usual, Olly will try to interpret for her…well – at least until he's had one too many. Her phone's vibration interrupts her thoughts. She lifts it to see his name.

Night Switch. Love you x

Their home texting softens her heart – he never lets her go to sleep without texting his love. She runs her finger over the screen thinking how lucky she is to have him - he may not sign, be overly expressive, or particularly domesticated, but he looks after her, is one hell of a good-looking guy and more importantly, out of all the girls he could've chosen, he chose her.

Night, Geezer. Love you too x

Chapter 4

Eventually the end of the working day rolls around and Greta is sitting on the bus, relishing her Wednesday bag of chips, happily anticipating the two and half hour art class when her phone buzzes.

Are you out tonight, babe? O x

She sighs. How many years has she been going to the art class on a Wednesday night? And how many times does Olly send her that text? She half wonders if he's just double checking so he can do whatever it is he does when she's out – sit on the sofa in his underpants and watch TV, go out for a drink with the lads, play Fifa 16, browse the internet...

Art class AS USUAL! she writes, but hesitates to send, as she's not sure he would appreciate her capital letter exasperation.

Art class 6.30 – 9.00pm. See you later. Love you xxx

Arriving at black-beamed adult education building she finds only one fellow student, Richard, already there in the classroom.

'Evening! Where is everyone?' she asks with surprise. 'Usually 'The Magnificent Seven' are here catching up over a cuppa.'

'Hi there, I don't know, maybe we're early? How are you anyway?' he half signs with a smile. A wave of gratitude washes over her as she returns his smile. At the advent of the art classes Greta had told her fellow students that she was happy to lip-read them, but unbeknown to her they all enrolled onto the basic sign language course. She thinks it's kind of funny that they only learnt to say their names, favourite colours, what the weather's doing and that they're sorry – but it's the collective thought that counts.

'I'm fine, thanks.' she speaks and signs slowly to him. 'How's your wife?'

'Getting better. It's not much fun getting old but her hip is mending nicely. How's that decision coming along?' he smiles devilishly.

'Richard, it's such a big thing – I don't know.'

'Greta, all my years in Ear Nose and Throat and those aids you're wearing are positively prehistoric!' he laughs. 'A cochlear implant isn't a cure but it could give you greater amplification.'

'It's tempting…but someone cutting into my head…'

'I told you it's a tried and tested op now. The surgeons are truly magnificent.'

'I just can't imagine the headache afterwards – is it worse than a couple of bottles of Rioja?' Greta winces and Richard laughs.

'My girl, you do so well lip-reading one to one, don't you?' he says kindly. She nods. 'Well the CI could give you a better shot of understanding us all in a group when we're gabbing away.'

'Or you lot could go and do the next level of sign language and we could all sign?' she teases.

'My dear girl – have you seen the quality of our signing?'

Greta chuckles thinking about two of the group who just can't grasp the necessary hand-shapes and expressions, and then, right on cue, the pair of struggling signers, Joan and Nigel, walk in.

'Hi, how are you?' Greta signs to the identically dressed couple.

'Yes, thank you,' Joan signs.

'Sorry,' signs Nigel.

Greta looks to Richard who winks back at her with a grin.

'Let me hang up your anorak,' Joan says to her husband. He dutifully takes it off and passes it to her, smoothing his jumper down over his round tummy. Greta smiles, thinking that all their years together really have morphed them into the same person: even their home-cut hair is greying at the same rate.

'What are you working on this week, Greta?' Nigel speaks more than signs.

From her portfolio she produces the bare bones of a charcoal drawing depicting a few characters in the corner of a room and a mass of stick figures over the other side. She hasn't yet decided what's to feature in the area between.

Richard leans over, clearly not finished with his cochlear implant propaganda for the evening.

'You know, a CI might give you a new direction in your art? Maybe the theme of isolation could be transformed into acceptance, integration?'

'Oh Richard, now you're really pushing it - I'd have to use colour and everything!' They both laugh.

'I'm only teasing you. What's the sign for 'teasing'?' he asks.

She shows him and then returns her attention to her work. She wonders if he's right. Has she got herself into an art cul-de-sac? Her themes are consistently despair and isolation and Mia often says that Greta's art, if it were the written word, would definitely be more along the lines of Emily Bronte than Bill Bryson.

'We're a little low on numbers tonight,' their tutor, Malcolm, says, entering the room and shrugging off his herringbone jacket. Joan, ever eager to please, notices that Greta missed what he said and waves to get her attention and attempts to interpret. None the wiser, but ever grateful, Greta nods, smiles and raises her thumb.

'OK folks, let's get started. Anyone needing help right now?' Malcolm asks.

Greta catches Malcolm's lips perfectly (he even trims his beard for her) and looks around the room at her fellow students. Nobody raises a hand, but Greta idly wonders whether she should. She sighs thinking how she could certainly use a little help. For starters, should she change her direction in art? Ditch the charcoal and use bright colours to draw rainbows and unicorns? And what about the cochlear implant? If she goes for it, will it change who she is? Will her identity become a hybrid of a deaf and hearing person? And more pressingly should she go on TV against the wishes of her nearest and dearest? (It strikes her again that her nearest and dearest should want her to go on TV!)

Greta shakes her head and keeps her arm by her side. Malcolm may be an inspiring art teacher, but as far as she knows he doesn't deal in life advice. She sighs, takes the charcoal and starts drawing soft smudgy lines and with that all thoughts of cochlear implants, family strife and art directions begin to drift away. With no distraction from her classmates' chatter she is absorbed by her drawing. She creates lines and then uses her finger to shape them into the characters. The smaller group in her picture, she decides, are the deaf people – isolated but happy in their unity, bound together by their deafness. The mass of stick figures on the other side represent the rest of society – those who can hear. But what goes in the middle? What is the bridge? What can link the two groups? Love?

Mutual respect? Communication? Hmm, she thinks, if communication is the key than maybe she does need to seriously consider the cochlear implant.

Chapter 5

Contrary to popular belief Greta doesn't live in a world of silence, and 'brrrr er er er ay it' is all she hears from the back of Olly as he heads out of the front door.

'What did you say?' she yells, frustrated that without reading his lips she is scuppered – a fact he knows only too well.

He stops in his tracks with his shoulders dropping in what she assumes is irritation or exasperation. He turns.

'BRING OUT THE RED CASE, SWITCH,' he mouths patronisingly.

'OK alright! You know I can't understand you when I can't see you.'

He sighs. 'Sorry babe, but come on, we're gonna be late.'

'Wouldn't want that,' she says under her breath.

Returning to the bedroom she picks up the case. In her heart of hearts she really doesn't think the mammoth trek up to Ronnie and Jill's in Ashbourne is worth it. When Olly's pals visit their flat she can disappear to bed when her eyes are hanging out on stalks, but up there, there'll be no escape. She imagines the exhaustion of all those lips she is going to have to read. On one particular visit she'd decided to knock back the drinks, telling herself it would improve her communication skills, and consequently ended up head down the toilet, and in bed for the following day. She smiles at the memory, still wondering if the sore head was worse than the lip-reading hell she was trying to avoid.

With Olly's Audi TT jammed with cases (she always tells him it's really only a one-and-a-half-person car) Greta sinks into the leather bucket seat and prepares for almost four hours of his erratic and sometimes downright frightening driving. She wonders what it is with him being 'stuck' behind a lorry. He will inch out continuously, nudging the car's nose into the on-coming traffic, impatient for that moment to nip out and get round. It makes her smile as guaranteed the same lorry will be the vehicle behind or beside them at the next traffic lights.

Despite a few under passes, many honks of his horn and a near collision with an equally zoomy Audi, they arrive in Ashbourne unscathed. As they sweep up the long winding drive to Ronnie and Jill's large Edwardian property Greta considers how beautiful it all is. The autumn sun casts beams on the surrounding open fields and she thinks how a place like this would be perfect for when Olly has popped the question and she has popped out their sprogs. It's idyllic.

As they climb out of the car Ronnie and Jill race out to greet them.

'Olly, Olly Olly, oi, oi, oi! You old bastard,' Ronnie says as he slaps Olly on the back and attempts to pick him up.

As they continue with their play fighting male bonding ritual, Jill grabs Greta firmly by the shoulders.

'Greta, lovely to see you,' she mouths without using her voice. Greta dearly wants to explain that miming just distorts lip patterns but, considering how many people don't even try to talk to her, this is a lot better than nothing. Besides she doesn't want to hurt Jill's feelings.

'Lovely to be here.' Greta smiles.

Jill gestures to follow her into the house. 'Let's leave the boys to their horsing around,' she says, shaking her head in mock despair.

As they enter the ornate reception hall Greta is once again reminded of the grandeur and timeless elegance of this home, and how it could easily house a few families. Jill and Ronnie don't have any children and when Greta once asked Olly why that was, he said that Ronnie would have to leave childhood first before that could happen. Glancing over her shoulder at the two men now wrestling she thinks that Olly has a point.

'Tea or something stronger?' Jill mouths.

From the flush in Jill's cheeks Greta can tell that her hostess is already on something stronger, but Greta is not going to repeat her past performance.

'Tea would be lovely, thanks.' A look of mild disappointment flashes across Jill's face before she disappears off to the kitchen. Olly and Ronnie enter and, without asking, Ronnie hands Olly a beer. Greta glances at her watch – two o'clock – this doesn't bode well.

'How was the drive up?' Jill asks.

'Smooth,' Olly says.

'Fast,' Greta says at the same time.

Jill and Ronnie laugh.

'What did you say?' Greta turns to Olly.

'Same as you.' He grins.

Judging by the laughter Greta knows this isn't true and feels a little at sea; why does he make her the unwitting butt of the joke?

'You know sometimes it's a good thing not to hear,' Jill says directly to Greta. 'The other day at the gym, this fellow was making all these grunting noises and a woman complained to a member of staff who asked him to be quieter!' She turns to the others. 'Can you believe that?'

Greta is mentally patting herself on the back for getting every word of that when all eyes turn to Olly and they all laugh.

Aaaaargh – what did he say?

He repeats it for her benefit.

She's still not sure. Now, if she's got it wrong and adds something she's going to look a right idiot. She remembers too well the boarding school matron glowering over her, demanding that she hand over her (strictly forbidden) 'straighteners' and Greta scurrying off and returning, in a state of confusion, with her 'trainers'…

She gives a wan smile but opts to say nothing. Pulling her feet up underneath herself she thinks how it's going to be a very long weekend. Over the course of the next two hours she pulls facial expressions pretending to follow conversations and when Jill leaves the room and returns with more of the gang, Greta steels herself further.

Now what *are* their names? she thinks, as she lip-reads them. Tina. Jack. Daniel. Heme?

Heme? That's not even a name!

As Greta watches them hug and greet each other she becomes transfixed by their mouths. They open them so wide to laugh that their tonsils are on full show, and she thinks that if a fly were in the room he would be lucky to escape…

When the sun is finally over the yardarm, Greta figures that taking a drink will either boost her lip-reading prowess or leave her not giving a flying fig. 'Yes, a large one please,' she says from there on in whenever she is offered.

The minutes tick by, the hours drag and the alcohol soothes her into a comfortable fuzzy focus. The roaring open fire with its vibrant orange flames hypnotises and makes her drowsy in equal parts, and by eleven, unable to keep her eyes open any longer, she decides to call it a night.

'Hey guys, I'm exhausted. I'm going to head up,' she says, rising from her seat.

'Oh no, Debby, don't go,' the red head in the bodycon dress slurs.

'Greta! It's Greta,' Olly says to her.

'Oh shit, sorry babe,' she says to Greta. 'Anyway, don't go – the fun's just starting. We're gonna play Cards Against Humanity.'

Having drunk the county dry Greta seriously doubts any of them are sober enough to make the relevant decisions, or for that matter even read the cards.

'Thanks, but I've got a headache, I'll just go and sleep it off,' she says, raising a hand to her forehead.

They all mumble agreement. Greta looks to Olly who gets up and crosses the room.

'You OK?' he asks, placing his hand on her arm.

'Yeah, yeah just tired, that's all.'

'OK, I'll be up later. Love you,' he says, kissing her on the lips.

'You too. Night.'

Greta bids goodnight to everyone else and closes the door behind her to a raucous laugh that even she can hear. Well, that's enough to make anyone paranoid, she thinks, as she treads the spiral staircase to their room.

After luxuriating in the ensuite's roll top bath until the water goes cold, Greta puts her best pyjamas on and slides into the majestic four-poster bed. She pats the crisp white bedding and admires the gold and red swirling patterned canopy and heavily embroidered counterpane. She feels like a princess – albeit a princess who buys her pyjamas from Primark. With all the strain of communicating and the large glasses of wine she goes out like a light.

It's pitch black in the room when the bed jolts, disturbing her. She reaches for the light to find Olly hopping around trying to get out of his jeans. Eventually with his limbs at odds to his body he falls on the bare floorboards with a huge thud.

'Sorry babe.' He looks up with bloodshot eyes and a smirk. 'Can't get these buggers off.'

The irritation she feels is only softened by the thought of the enormous hangover he'll suffer tomorrow.

'Yeah, I can see that,' she says, getting up to help.

He smells like he's been dipped in a vat of whisky and knowing his penchant for drunkenly peeing in inappropriate places, she guides him to the toilet and sits him down. Minutes later he wobbles into the bedroom and collapses into bed. He reaches for her.

'I love you, Switch,' he says, his tongue hanging out like a drooling dog.

'Ha ha – course you do, Olly.'

'Come here my little sex kitten.' He fumbles for her beneath the covers making her give out a little shriek. 'Shhhhh,' he says, aiming to place his fingers over her lips but missing and catching her chin. With stifled giggles they disappear under the duvet only for Greta to surface two minutes later when it becomes evident that Olly's ambitions are wildly unachievable.

•

Awaking with the sunlight glinting in through the gap in the curtains, Greta turns to see Olly, passed out and looking as dreadful as he should. He is emanating alcohol sweats with his face scrunched into the pillow and his mouth gaping open. He is completely dead to the world – what does she do now? Should she go downstairs and try to interact with whoever might be there? Or hide up here with the lingering smell of whisky and bad wind? She opts for reading her book…and opening a window.

After an hour or so, from the comfort of the bedroom chair, she looks up to see Olly regaining consciousness. His normally sleeked back brown hair is standing to attention and heavy bags line his watery red eyes.

'Urgh, Greta, get us a glass of water. And paracetamol.'

Obligingly she puts down her book and crosses to the ensuite.

'You're a doll,' he croaks as she returns. She stands watching him down the tablets with needy gulps of water and thinks how he makes a pitiful sight. 'Come here,' he says, holding out his arms. His puppy dog eyes still having the desired effect despite being glassy and red rimmed and she plonks herself next to him. He wraps himself around her.

She feels the vibrations of his chest and looks up.

'I said, I love you,' he repeats.

'Me too, Olly, me too.'

'Sorry I drank too much,' he says, brushing a stray hair out of her eyes. 'I'm an arse.'

She purses her lips. 'Hmm, you're an arse with a massive hangover, so I'd say that's payback enough. It's nature's finest karma.'

Flopping back on the pillow, he winces. 'And we all know karma's a bitch.'

•

Eventually, showered and dressed, they join the rest of the guests around the large scrubbed pine kitchen table where Jill is producing a never-ending supply of bacon, sausages and eggs. Seems everyone is in need of the universal hangover cure.

'How's your head?' Jill mouths.

'Better than a lot of people's,' Greta says breezily provoking scowls from the majority of guests.

The girl who was in the bodycon dress says something and people seem to agree. Greta looks to Olly.

'Sadie suggests we take a walk to blow away the cobwebs.'

'Oh yes, that sounds like a great idea,' Greta says, wholly grateful for the respite of not having to follow conversations all day. The great fry up and copious cups of tea and coffee are consumed before people disappear to their rooms to prepare for the walk.

The sun is shining brightly as they leave the house and head for the hills. Some of the females totter along in heels whilst Greta plods in her trainers, and although they set off as one large group, fairly quickly they stroll in groups of two or three. Greta finds herself with Olly and Jamie, an ex-colleague of Olly's, whom she's never particularly warmed to. They discuss how Arsenal is doing in the league and, although Greta isn't interested, both men keep turning to repeat their conversation to her. Eventually she decides to spare them their efforts.

'Guys, it's OK really, I don't mind not knowing,' she says. Immediately she is perplexed to see Jamie's eyes widen and more than a hint of annoyance cross Olly's face.

After another ten minutes or so Jamie leaves Greta and Olly to catch up with his girlfriend. Greta goes to slip her hand in Olly's but he glowers and yanks it away.

'Really Greta, what is with you?' he snaps.

'What? Me? What have I done?'

'Saying that to Jamie!'

'I was just saving you guys the trouble of repeating everything for my sake – I really don't mind not knowing about the footie!'

'Yeah, but he was telling us about his mum dying last year!'

'What? Oh crap! Well I didn't catch that, did I?' Olly looks away and Greta pulls his arm. 'I'll apologise to him, Olly. I honestly didn't know the subject had changed.'

He takes a deep sigh and then reaching for her hand, entwines his fingers in hers.

'It's always tricky when we're around folk isn't it?' he says. 'I just want you to fit in and for you to like them and vice versa.' He pulls her close.

'I know, but it can only happen if they make the effort with me.'

'That's what Jamie was doing.'

'I know, I know. I'm sorry. I can't just suddenly hear.'

He takes another sigh. 'So, what about the cochlear implant, then? Your man in the art class raves about it, doesn't he? Wouldn't it help you in situations like this?'

'Possibly.'

'Well, I don't understand why you don't go for it?'

'Would you like a surgeon's hands in your head? Supposing something goes wrong? An infection or something? I could lose the little hearing I have. I do okay most of the time, don't I?'

'But it could give you a better quality of life, Switch. I tell you, if it was me, I'd go for it like a shot.'

Olly's attention is drawn to someone up ahead calling for him.

'They want me,' he says, looking for permission to leave.

Greta nods, lets go of his hand and watches him stride off to join his friends.

She considers turned tables; if he were deaf, would she

happily give consent for him to go under the surgeon's knife? She guesses she would follow his lead – if it was what he wanted. He's so keen for her to consider it… She wonders if this operation would help her to hear more? Allow her to join in? Make her an equal participant? And what if it could prevent her from making blunders like the one she's just made? For the second time in as many days she wonders if it is time to seriously consider it…

The rest of the day passes in mass hangover lethargy. Conversations are thankfully sporadic and Greta is relieved when they end up spending the afternoon watching an old 80's movie that even has subtitles. After scones, biscuits and mugs of strong tea, Olly and Greta are waving goodbye to their hosts. Once on the road they drive in silence until Olly reaches across and takes Greta's hand. (The desire to firmly place it back on the wheel is strong but she doesn't want another row.)

'Switch, we're OK, aren't we? You and me?'

'Yep, of course.'

He squeezes her thigh and returns his hand to the wheel.

'Olly,' she continues. 'I will consider the CI.'

He beams. 'That's my girl.' Enthusiastically he leans over to kiss her and in doing so they swerve into the middle of the road. As he pulls back into lane the oncoming car passes, honking loudly. Olly raises his middle finger in the rear-view mirror and throws his head back laughing. Greta exhales slowly.

'…That's if I live long enough.'

Chapter 6

Sitting in the plush reception at The Broadcasting Hub, Greta isn't sure if it's from the two-shot coffee she drank on the train or if it's just plain old-fashioned nerves, but whichever it is, she's wired. Her trusted friend, Mia, who was more than happy to accompany her for moral support, is surveying the scene.

'*Wow! I love the brick work and look how high those ceilings go,*' she signs, her eyes wide with amazement. '*How many famous people d'ya think are in this building right at this moment?*' Just then a young presenter, with a-symmetric hair and low hanging hipster trousers sashays past. '*See?*' Mia signs, beaming with delight. '*I have no idea of his name, but he is definitely famous.*'

'*Oh God, Mia, I'm so nervous, I think I might throw up.*'

'*No you won't – but if you do, don't do it on this carpet, it looks like it cost a fortune,*' Mia signs, brushing it with her foot.

'*I need the loo.*'

'*You went about fifty times on the train!*'

A tall woman with glossy blonde locks, flawless makeup, dressed head to toe in designer apparel approaches. 'Greta Palmer?'

'That's me.' Greta holds up her index finger.

'I'm Jenni Fields, nice to meet you,' she says, extending her hand replete with perfectly manicured French nails. Shaking her hand, Greta cringes at her own clammy palm. Jenni smiles. 'Would you like to come this way?'

'Sure,' Greta says with a mini curtsey. Mia disguises her giggle in a cough.

Greta glares at her friend. '*See you later.*'

'*Good luck*,' Mia signs.

Greta follows Jenni along long corridors into a glass-panelled office. Chrome and splashes of purple fill the room and Jenni invites Greta to sit in a chair so large it could house three of her.

'So, are you OK at lip-reading?' Jenni asks.

Oh, she hadn't even thought of that! Of course she can cope, but for important meetings like this she likes the safety net of an interpreter.

'I'm a fairly good lip reader,' Greta says hesitantly. 'But I do like to have an interpreter as well, just in case – but I can try my best,' she says, thinking that a programme about disability really should've booked one.

'Well, we did book one for you, but he's just called to say he's going to be late; stuck on the train. I don't mind waiting if you'd rather?'

Greta relaxes a little. 'No, really, that's fine. I'm happy to make a start.'

'Wonderful. For the first part I just want to get to know you a bit, find out more about you; think of it as a chat.' She smiles warmly, revealing beautiful white straight teeth. 'Then we'll be joined by the series producer, Mike Drayton, and our HR lady, Gracie McKenzie, for the formal part. Is that's OK?' Greta warms to Jenni's perfectly symmetrical easy-to-lip-read mouth. 'So, before we get started, would you like a coffee or tea?'

Fearing a caffeine overload, Greta says, 'Just water, please.'

'Back in a mo.'

No sooner has Jenni left the room when a handsome face appears around the door.

'Church fields?'

Greta frowns, fairly positive that that's not what he said.

The man steps into the room. '*You deaf?*' he signs.

'*Ah, yes,*' she signs back. '*You the interpreter?*'

He holds out his lanyard showing his registration details and a rather dodgy photo from when he'd visited an over-zealous barber and sported an ill-advised moustache. Greta is stifling a giggle as Jenni reappears.

'Hi, you must be Connor, you made it then,' Jenni says, shaking his hand.

'Jenni Fields?'

Ah that's what he said…

'Yes, pleased to meet you.' She flashes a huge smile.

'Sorry I'm late,' he says, matching her smile.

They chatter on, but being placed at the wrong angle, and even after turning this way and that, Greta gives up and flops back in her seat. 'Charming,' she thinks, 'he doesn't apologise to me for being late and now isn't even signing so I can follow!'

'Right, shall we start?' Jenni eventually says, turning back to Greta. Connor sits and raises his hands, ready to start interpreting. 'So, Greta, tell me a bit about how you got into art.'

'When I was young and all the kids that could hear were out playing,' Greta says, her eyes fixed on Jenni. 'I'd be sitting somewhere with a sketchpad, it's just what I've always done.'

'I was the same only it was all things to do with media – television, radio – they fascinated me,' Jenni says.

'Great to discover your passion young, isn't it?'

'Not sure my parents thought so when they were trying to kick me out of the house on a sunny day,' Jenni laughs.

'Oh, don't get me started on what my mother didn't like about what I did!'

Connor, who by now has lowered his hands, sits watching the two women naturally bounce off each other. With his services being surplus to requirement he completely phases out of the conversation and mentally drifts to his to-do list. Even when Mike and Gracie join the room he is only vaguely aware.

'We just have a few questions each and we'll take it in turns, OK?' Jenni says. Greta nods. 'Over to you, Mike.'

'Greta,' Mike, a large middle-aged man with a balding head, starts. 'First I'd like to ask you about the en fer eeh ur…'

Oh no! Greta panics; his buck teeth dash any hope of lip-reading! That interpreter needs to stop staring at that wall and spring into life! With the room falling into complete silence, Connor, suddenly aware that all eyes are on him, jolts to attention.

'Sorry,' he signs and speaks at the same time. 'As my client didn't use my services for the first part of the interview I assumed I wasn't needed. Yep, I know,' he says, holding up his hands. 'If you 'assume' it makes an 'ass' out of 'u' and 'me'.'

They all laugh except for Greta who fidgets uncomfortably in her seat. Through her life she has met many interpreters and whilst many are model communicators, quite a few have been like this one; conceited, cocky and unprofessional.

'Sorry, really, my bad,' Connor continues as their laughter dies. 'Please could you repeat your question, Mike?' Mike waves away the apology, smiles and starts his question again. With what appears to be a half smug expression Connor lifts his hands to sign.

Through burning cheeks Greta plasters on a smile and tries to focus on the question at hand…

***

'Right, if you don't have any further questions,' Jenni says to Mike and Gracie who both shake their heads. 'I think that wraps it up.'

Greta sighs with relief.

'We've got more interviews on Monday,' Jenni continues. 'And then we should be in a position to make a decision. If you're selected, filming will start in two to three weeks. Is that OK?'

'Absolutely fine. Thank you.'

Greta shakes hands with all three interviewers, thanking them all for their time.

'I'll walk you back to reception,' Jenni offers.

'I'm going that way,' Connor chirps up, smiling at Jenni. 'She can walk back with me.' '*She*?' Greta thinks, 'who's that - the cat's mother?'

'Oh, OK, thanks, if you're sure,' Jenni replies, replacing a stray hair behind her ear. 'And don't forget to mark your invoice to the attention of Jenni Fields.' She flashes him a smile.

'I won't forget that name,' he says.

Greta surreptitiously rolls her eyes…

Walking together in silence back to the reception Connor suddenly stops and puts his hand on Greta's arm.

'*What's with the talkie talkies?*'

'*What?*'

With an earnest expression he asks, '*Why do you use your voice?*'

Greta swallows hard, feeling the heat returning to her cheeks. '*It's my choice, and I prefer to speak. Why do you care anyway?*'

'*Can I be honest?*'

'*Can I stop you?*'

'*Your voice is good – but it's still a deaf voice. Your signing, on the other hand, no pun intended…*' Greta doesn't laugh. '*…is lovely. Just something for you to think about for the next time.*'

'*Next time?*' Greta signs.

'*Oh there I go again, assuming – don't you think they'll book me again? For the programme?*'

'*Well, I have to pass the interview first,*' Greta signs.

'*I think they liked us, don't you*?'

'*Us?*' Greta signs, fully aware that if she were using voice she'd be shouting by now. '*It's not about them liking **you**!*' She jabs a finger at him. '*Are you always this…confident*?'

'*Er, well, no, I'm not, I just meant that they seemed to like…*'

'***You**, yeah, got it. They liked you. You're not the one applying though.*'

'*No. Right. OK.*' He awkwardly glances at his watch. '*Better get off. It's been lovely meeting you.*' Giving a twitchy smile, he turns on his heels and walks away.

Well – if they want me as part of the programme, Greta thinks, the first thing I'm going to do is request a different interpreter!

'*Hey, how did it go*?' Mia asks, getting up.

'*Hmmm,*' Greta says, watching the back of Connor leave the building. '*It would've been a whole lot better without him.*'

Chapter 7

Connor arrives at the Deaf Signs office ready for supervision with his long-standing boss, Maggie.

'OK, Connor, you ready?' she asks, passing his desk to the interview room.

'I'm right with you, Mags'

Seated at a small round table they begin the fortnightly session of reviewing Connor's work, what went wrong, what went right, identifiable training needs and any other business.

'So, let's start with anything that's gone wrong,' Maggie says. 'Not usually much to say on this one is there, my little star interpreter,' she teases.

Connor respects and likes Maggie a lot. She has a clear blue-eyed smile, short grey Judi Dench hairstyle and is all in all a great manager. He feels comfortable around her, but, saying that, telling her about Friday's assignment isn't going to be easy.

'Well, actually Mags, I've had a bit of a blip.'

Her eyebrows rise.

'It was that job last week at The Broadcasting Hub. It started badly as my train was delayed and when I got there, the client wasn't even bothering to watch me and insisted on using her voice. I know that kind of thing happens, but it really irked me and…I wasn't entirely professional.'

'Oh?'

'I let my feelings show and I think, in trying to hide my embarrassment I buddied up to the hearing folk and disempowered her. I didn't behave well.'

'Okaaaaay.' Maggie looks at her watch, realising that this is going to be a longer session than she'd anticipated. 'C'mon then, tell me all about it.'

'Like I said, I was harassed getting there, and then, when I saw her I thought she seemed nice enough, but as soon as the interview started she just didn't look at me or use me at all. I suppose I felt shunned – male ego eh?' Maggie nods. 'So, when she did need me I had completely switched off and felt like an idiot so I made light of it and got the panel on my side…but distanced her even further.'

'Connor, how long have I been supervising you?'

'Forever?'

'And has this ever happened before?'

'Never.'

'And why do you think it happened with this person?' Maggie asks.

'Err. She pushed my buttons?'

'And why do you think that is?' Connor looks dumb. 'Oh for the love of God, Connor, do I have to spell it out?' She sighs. 'Perhaps you 'liked' this client a little too much?'

Connor blushes. 'No, I don't think so. She's not even that pretty – I mean, don't get me wrong, she's got something, but no, I don't think so. I mean, she's not my type and I can't see myself with a deaf woman – no offence, but it's my job, not my love life – blurs the boundaries too much.'

'Connor,' Maggie says kindly, 'I think you might find that your boundaries have already blurred.'

'Really? Well, if that's right, I'm certainly going to learn from this experience. You won't book me for her again, will you?'

Maggie pauses to think. 'You know, normally I wouldn't but I think this could be a real learning curve for you. I think you need to go back and work with her again so you can purposefully separate your personal feelings from your professionalism. I feel a bit like the Mother Superior sending Maria back to the Von Trapps…' She trails off with a small cough.

'OK, Mags, no idea what you're talking about now, but I understand what you mean. Can we agree that I work with her again to see if I can exercise my professionalism – but if I stuff up again you'll pull me out?'

'Sounds like a plan. Just remember though, Connor, you're an interpreter, but you're a human first and although we don't encourage relationships with clients, you should be able to handle all different types of feelings towards the people you work with. I remember starting out and this deaf man infuriated me - I couldn't stand him, but my boss sent me back to work with him week after week. I learnt to control how I felt and I ended up quite liking him – I got to see another side.'

'Please don't tell me you went out with him.'

'Ha! No I did not! He was double my age.'

They laugh and fall silent.

'I suppose, Mags, the thing that really bugs me is that I wasn't myself, you know. I turned into 'Cocky Connor' – and that's just not me. I think I came across as an arse both professionally and personally.'

'Oh dear. Well, that confirms that you need to work with this client again and present yourself in a better light.'

'That's if they book me again.'

'Yes, indeed.' Maggie turns to the supervision template on the table. 'Right, let's look at what's gone well in the last couple of weeks.'

Connor thinks for a minute.

'Pretty much everything…except that job.'

Chapter 8

Mia exhales deeply.

'Uh, how did I end up in this job!' she thinks, surveying the multiple emails from the public complaining about potholes, missing manholes and cracked tarmac. Her finger hovers dangerously over the 'Delete All' button when the title 'Cuts to Deaf Services' catches her eye. The email turns out to be from The National Deaf Organisation warning that local sign language interpreting services are to be cut as part of austerity measures. Mia digests the missive and then rapidly reads it again. She quickly forwards the email.

> *Hey Greta – have you seen this?*
> *WTF? What happens when we need to go to the doctors? What about job interviews? (for when I decide to leave this hell hole.) What about having access?? How can the council cut interpreters? We don't have enough of the hand-flappers already! There's a protest on Saturday outside City Hall – you up for it?*
> *Love Mia.*

Hitting send, she returns her attention to an email from a disgruntled member of the public claiming a pothole on a petrol station forecourt was the cause of his buckled car wheel. 'Mmmm, don't think you can pin that one on us, Mister,' she says under her breath. Just as she's typing a response, an email from Greta pops up.

> *Nope – hadn't seen it, but yep I'm with you! Let's go campaign! Solidarity sister! Oh – must tell you my news – trumpet fanfare – The Art of Being Disabled wants me! Yay! And I'm definitely going to do it! Still wanna be my stylist? Filming starts next week. They sent me a timetable and it looks like it'll be over a couple of weeks. It's here first, then my flat and then the art class. At least they don't want to film me with the fam! Can you imagine Sylvia?! You still up for being my wingman for my brother's*

birthday bash chez Palmer tonight? D xx

Oh Greta, my matey, I am so pleased! Yay – go you! And I wouldn't miss Mikey's birthday and an evening with Sylvia and John for the world! Meet in the lobby at 5.30pm. xx

***

'Greta, darling, Mia, come in, come in.' John greets them at the door.

'Hi Dad.'

'John,' Mia says, playfully punching him on the shoulder.

They hug and kiss and make their way into the lounge where they find the rest of the family.

'Hey there, Fartface,' Greta's brother, Mikey, says, getting up to give her a bear hug.

'Get off!' Greta struggles to free herself. Mikey laughs and, letting her go, tousles her hair. Greta wonders why brothers always have to be so annoying. 'Happy Birthday to you too!'

'What is he like?' Elizabeth, his Oxbridge lawyer girlfriend, says, smiling. Greta hugs and kisses her soon-to-be-when-they-finally-set-a-date sister-in-law.

'Mia,' Elizabeth says, 'lovely to see you again.'

The door swings open for Sylvia's grand entrance. She moves to Mia.

'How lovely to see you,' she says, continuing to talk as they embrace. Pulling away Mia nods in agreement to whatever Sylvia just said over her shoulder. Greta receives the obligatory hug from Sylvia that offers fractionally more warmth than she'd get from an ironing board.

'Dinner will be ready at eight,' Sylvia informs the room.

'Great, that gives us time for Greta to tell us all about what she's been up to,' Mikey says with a devilish grin. Greta sighs and pulls a face. 'Come on, tell us about Big Brother!'

'You know full well it's not Big Brother,' she scowls at him.

'Some other kind of in-depth social experiment crap show then?'

'Language, darling,' Sylvia chips in.

'Mikey, leave your sister alone!' Elizabeth defends.

'Oh c'mon, I'm only having a laugh. Seriously sis, tell us about it. I'm genuinely interested.'

He's her brother and he's a pain, but underneath it all Greta knows that deep deep down, really deep down, deeper than deep, he cares for her.

'It's a Channel 8 documentary, The Art of Being Disabled, and I'll be in one episode. It's kind of a day in the life of me…and my art – hence the title.' Bafflingly she feels bashful - is it because Mikey is the one who usually sits in the limelight?

'Impressive,' Mikey says, downing the last of his sherry. Greta looks at him, waiting for the punch line. He looks back up at her innocently.

'What?'

'No sarky comment?'

'Nope. I think it's kinda cool.'

Well this is a first, thinks Greta, and judging by Sylvia's face it's not what she expected to hear either. Sylvia is more of a divide and rule type and this kind of sibling solidarity triggers the earthquake ripple of her agitation again.

'Right, I'll check on dinner,' she says, bustling out of the room. In the silence left behind everyone looks to each other, scrabbling to find a new topic of conversation. Her father stands.

'More sherry?'

Greta takes a sip of wine and surveys the dinner table. In the main it is a table of two halves; the people who talk and those who sign. Obviously the talkers dominate, leaving Greta and Mia feeling like they have to be invited to the conversation; to be thrown a lifeline in.

'So, what does Wally-Olly think of your impending stardom?' Mikey asks.

'Greta pulls a face. 'He thinks it's good for me.'

'That's good. Now then,' Sylvia says, turning to Mikey. 'What else did you get for your birthday, dear?'

'Lizzie bought me a red-letter day – white water rafting,' Mikey answers. 'Apart from that, not much.' He takes a mouthful of food and turns back to Greta. 'So, when is this programme going to happen?'

'Darling,' Sylvia says to Mikey. 'Pass the gravy, please.'

He shrugs his shoulders to see the gravy boat at the opposite end of the table and nods to his father to pass it.

'Filming starts in a couple of weeks,' Greta says.

'And when can we expect to see you grace our screens?' Mikey presses on.

'Er, I think...' Greta starts only to see her mother talking at the same time. 'Sorry?'

'Your mother was just saying about the time Mikey was on television, do you remember?' her father says.

Greta nods. 'So, as I was saying, it should be on...' Once again Greta finds all eyes have turned to Sylvia. 'Mum, is there a problem?'

'Greta, darling,' her father says, putting his hand on hers. 'Nothing's wrong.'

'No Dad, Mum's clearly got something she wants to say as she doesn't want me to talk,' Greta snaps.

All eyes turn to Sylvia.

'Very well,' her mother starts, choosing her words carefully. 'Look, I know you want to do this – but do you really know what you're getting yourself into? How do you know they're not going to set you up as a laughing stock? You know how unscrupulous some of these TV people are – they'll put unwitting participants in all kinds of ridiculous situations to boost the viewing figures. How do you know you can trust them? And before you accuse me of being over protective or whatever - I am just looking after your best interests - I just want what's best for you.'

She wants 'what's best for me', Greta thinks. Mmmm, isn't that what Olly says too? If they truly do, then why don't they ask ME what I want? Are people with ears that function better at knowing what is best for me? And are these two people who are supposed to love me really offering protection? ...Or just clipping wings?

A huge lump sits in Greta's throat, so large she fears it'll block her airways and stop her breathing. Mikey gives her a look and, much to her surprise, speaks up.

'Hey Mum, your little girl's going on TV – isn't that something to show off to your friends? How many of their kids have a documentary made about them?'

Sylvia bites her lip. Defeated by the majority, she lowers her eyes and collects the plates. The rest of the table exchange glances except for Greta who remains close to tears. As the dining room door closes behind her, John stands, coughs and leaves the room. Sometimes Greta thinks that her father deserves the Nobel Peace Prize.

Her parents reappear minutes later with birthday cake and the party mumble their way through a half-hearted rendition of 'Happy Birthday'.

And all the while Greta keeps her eyes on the clock and wishes the minutes away.

Chapter 9

Greta, sporting a new crisp blouse, sharp pencil skirt, a full face of make-up and a spritz of hairspray, arrives at County Hall to find the TV crew waiting in reception.

'Ah Greta! Hi, how are you?' Jenni kisses her on both cheeks.

'I'm fine. Excited.' Greta chews her lip.

She glances over Jenni's shoulder. Oh no! With all the primping and preening for the filming she overlooked the one thing she was supposed to do – request a different interpreter! It's him – Connor – looking expectant and smiling.

'Just got to sign in and then we'll come up with you to your office, OK?' Jenni says.

'Sure.'

Jenni moves over to the desk leaving Greta face to face with him.

'*Hi, how are you doing?*' he signs.

'*Great thanks.*'

'*Sorry, would you prefer me to talk?*'

Greta rolls her eyes. '*Seriously, are we going to go through this again?*'

'*No, no, really, I'm sorry – I just meant is it easier for you to lip-read than to get my signing?*'

'*Shall I explain my communication needs?*'

'*I wish you would.*'

Greta takes a deep breath. '*If I feel comfortable with someone I use my voice. If the person is easy to lip-read then I do. If I'm stuck, I rely on my natural preferred language – sign language.*'

'*Got it.*' He raises his thumbs and smiles.

Having signed in, they all board the lift with the crush of council workers. Jenni and Connor are packed in at the back, nose to nose, talking and laughing. To her surprise Greta begins to prickle with annoyance. Does she want to be nose to nose with him? Is that the problem? The man who irritates her every time he opens his mouth or lifts his hands? She bobs her head to catch a glance of their lips, but all she can see are the corners of their talking, grinning mouths.

In what seems like an age the lift doors finally open to reveal Dodgy Rog hovering, hopping from one foot to the other, wearing an ill-fitting brown suit. They all pile out of the lift.

'Jenni, this is my manager, Roger,' Greta says.

Taking in Jenni's appearance his eyes bulge and Greta thinks she sees a trickle of drool from his lips.

He takes her hand. 'Pleasure to meet you,' he says, using his telephone voice.

Greta notices Connor hovering, waiting to interpret. As he pierces her with his gaze she silently curses the tiny beads of sweat that are forming on her neck.

'OK,' Jenni says. 'Could we convene to a quiet area so I can lay out the agenda for the morning?'

'Certainly.' Rog gives a smarmy smile. 'Please, this way.'

'First of all,' Jenni says, taking centre stage in a small room off the main office. 'I'd like to thank Roger, for allowing us to film here.' He nods and give a 'no problem at all' shrug. 'We'll only be here for the morning, hopefully, and we'd just like some general shots of Greta at her desk and then a piece straight to camera. We'll try not to get in anyone's way -'

Roger says something that Greta misses, so she reluctantly turns to Connor who nods and then starts interpreting. Jenni introduces Colin and Paul, the cameramen and Matt the soundman. She then goes on to give broadcasting information that Greta already knows. Idly, Greta tunes out but remains fixed on Connor. His dark curls are tighter to his head and his green eyes seem even deeper than she remembers. Casually dressed in dark jeans and a plain t-shirt that keeps riding up, he inadvertently keeps flashing the lower part of his belly. She starts to wonder if someone is playing with the room's thermostat control. She shakes her head to refocus and reprimands herself that she is an attached woman...but after only a few seconds Connor's wide hands and the hair on his forearms have her mesmerised again...

She's jolted from her reverie by realising that the whole room is looking to her expectantly. What was the question? Oh shoot! She's clueless – this'll teach her to perv at the interpreter.

'Is there anything you'd like to say before we start?' Connor repeats the question.

'No, that's all perfectly fine, thanks,' she says coolly.

Phew! Got out of that nicely.

Whilst everyone starts leaving the room to set up, she mouths a silent, 'thank you' to Connor.

'No problem.' he signs back and smiles.

Moving to Greta's workstation Jenni directs her, 'OK, Greta, if you could just sit at your desk and pretend to be working.'

'Like you usually do,' Rog says, looking around for laughter that doesn't come.

Greta focuses on her computer and tries to appear natural. She does this every day and yet, with cameras pointing at her, it feels so wrong, so false.

After the first take Colin shows her the playback screen. 'Oh My God! I look like I'm constipated,' she blurts.

'OK, let's do it again.' Jenni smiles. 'I know we can't use your real work in case the camera picks up confidential info but could you create a mock up? Just type an email.'

'OK, I'll give it a go.'

She taps away at her keyboard, still painfully aware of the camera…and Connor.

'OK, much better, we've got that,' Jenni says, with one eye on the playback. 'Let's do a piece to camera now. I want to ask you about your work here, and a little about how you see your future, OK?'

'Fine.'

Connor pulls up a chair next to Jenni and Mike clips a microphone to Greta's shirt collar.

'So, Greta, tell us a little bit about your day job.' Jenni starts. Greta's eyes quickly shift to Connor's interpreting to double check.

'I administer social services referrals,' she says. 'I've been here for five years – it's a good job, but my passion lies in art. I suppose it's a bit like a struggling actor, you have a job to pay the bills and hope that one day your acting will pay them.'

'Of course. Is your disability, your deafness, a barrier to working here?'

'Actually, the council are really good, if I need an interpreter they'll pay for one. Here at work I have access to communication.'

'But not outside of work?'

'Er, well, I suppose social situations are trickier. You can't really book an interpreter for a night out, can you?' She giggles nervously.

'Does that make you feel isolated in social situations?' Jenni asks.

'Yes…sometimes it can be hard, I mean, sometimes people leave you out of things, they don't mean to or anything…' Greta trails off as totally out of the blue a large lump now restricts her throat. Feeling the colour rising in her cheeks and her breath racing, her panicked eyes dart in search of help.

'Really sorry guys,' Connor interjects. 'I need the toilet.' Jenni looks to him and smiles and tells everyone to take five.

For the second time today he's saved her and for the second time today she mouths, 'thank you.' He nods, smiles, signs, *'you're welcome'* and walks away.

'That's a wrap, folks,' Jenni says to a ripple of self-congratulatory applause. Connor and Greta exchange smiles. 'Right, Greta, we've got all that we need for today,' she continues. 'So, tomorrow eve, is it still OK to come to your flat to film? Would your partner do a piece to camera with you?'

'Mmmm, not sure but I'll ask him.' 'Again,' thinks Greta.

'Right see you then. OK guys,' she says to the cameramen and soundman. 'Let's leave these good people to their day.'

As they start to pack away Connor approaches Greta.

'Right – they've booked me for all the sessions so I'll see you tomorrow and at the art class – I'm looking forward to seeing this artwork of yours,' he says, his eyes gently teasing.

'Ha, don't expect too much.'

'Why? Aren't you any good?'

She tilts her head to one side. *'What do you think?'*

'I think you're probably very good.'

'Then I guess all will be revealed next Wednesday.'

'Whoa there, we've only just met!' He laughs.

Greta's cheeks turn redder than an old-fashioned phone box. *'You know what I meant!'*

They are holding each other's smile when Greta becomes aware of another pair of eyes on them: Mia's

Greta turns back to Connor and nervously coughs. *'OK, see you then and thanks again for your help today.'*

'No problem.' He gently smiles. *'See ya.'*

He turns to walk away and exchanges nods with Mia, who, with a huge grin spreading over her face, sidles up to Greta.

'Anything you wanna tell your best mate?'

'Like what?' Greta signs, adopting a look of innocence.

'Look, I'm not a wizard at these relationship things, but I can recognise mutual attraction when I see it and that is exactly what I just saw.'

'No, Mia, you didn't. He's just the interpreter.'

'Really?' Mia puts her hands on her hips and raises her eyebrows.

Greta sighs. *'Did it really look mutual?'*

'Ha ha! Knew it! You like him!'

'Well he is a bit gorgeous.'

'I'm not disagreeing – but have you forgotten one little thing? Olly?'

'Hey, I'm not going to do anything about Connor!' Greta signs, her defences rising. *'God gave me eyes so I could look – no harm in it.'*

'If you say so, Greta. I mean it's not like Olly will see you two together. Oh, wait a minute – yes he will – on national TV!'

Greta groans. *'It's not that obvious, is it?'*

'Oh Greta, you'd better start practising your acting.'

***

'Hey Olly,' Greta calls, putting her keys on the small table and hanging up her coat.

The smell of frying onions greets her and she feels a wave of happiness that he's cooking. She always says he's the better cook when he can be bothered – which unfortunately isn't often. She puts her arms around him and snuggles up to his back.

'Ooh someone's happy,' he says, turning around.

She kisses him hard, fleetingly wondering if she's over compensating.

'Wanna skip dinner?' he asks, half joking.

'Ha, no, I'm starving, what've we got?'

'Fajitas.'

'Fabulous! Let me go and get changed and I'll perch and watch.' He smiles as she wanders off to slip out of her work clothes and into sweatpants. Returning to the kitchen she jumps up onto the kitchen stool.

'Get this down your neck,' he says, passing her a glass of red.

Contentment washes over her as just the two of them, here in this flat, is when it really works. This is what the outside world doesn't see.

'So, filming went well today,' she says, taking a swig of wine.

'Did it, babe?'

'Look, Olly, I know we discussed this before, but they want to film here tomorrow evening and would really like to interview you. You won't be alone – I'll be next to you.'

'Argh Greta, we talked about this.' He looks up, resting the wooden spoon in the pan. 'This is your thing, babe, nothing to do with me.'

'But it is to do with you - you're my partner. They want to show all parts of my life and you're a big part.'

'No Greta, I told you, I don't want to do it.'

'Please Olly. Please.'

He flashes her a dubious look and continues stirring the sauce. Greta jumps down from the stool.

'Pleeeeeeaaaase my gorgeous man, pleeeeeeasse.' She smothers his neck in tiny tickling kisses.

'Get off.' He bats her away, trying not to laugh.

'Come on, you know you want to. Say yes and I won't tell your mum the real reason her plant died.'

He puts down the spoon. 'Right! That's it, you're in trouble now.' He chases her out of the kitchen and catches her in a rugby tackle in the lounge. They land haphazardly on the sofa, laughing and groaning.

'You will never tell Vi how that bloody plant died.'

'Her prize plant!'

'It could've been the dog - they pee on plants all the time.'

'Not indoors they don't!'

They both laugh. Olly tilts his head and pulls a lock of her hair. Watching it boing back into its corkscrew curl he says, 'Love you.'

She strokes his face. 'Enough to do the programme for me?'

He sighs and smiles, takes her face in his hands and kisses her gently.

'OK Switch, I'll do it. But you owe me.'

Chapter 10

'*Hey Mum,*' Connor signs, kissing her on the cheek and placing the flowers on her side table.

Her face flickers recognition and she smiles.

'*Connor*,' she signs a C shape with her fingers – her sign for him since he was a baby. '*Have you seen your dad?*'

The truthful answer is that Connor hasn't seen his father for five years, not since he died of cancer, but his mother forgets that on a daily basis.

'*No Mum, not today.*'

'*He's a good man, your dad.*' She frowns. '*Have you had your tea?*'

'*Yes Mum.*'

'*Have you seen your brother?*'

'*Yes Mum.*'

'*Met any nice girls lately?*' Her fingers shape the words perfectly and Connor smiles at the predictability of the question. He tells her the same tale that he told her yesterday and the day before.

'*I have met someone, Mum. She's a nice girl - you'd like her. Guess what? She's deaf, just like you.*'

'*That's marvellous, dear,*' she signs and then folds her arms across her stomach with a broad satisfied smile.

'*Yeah, I thought so too until I found out today she's not single. I'm working with her again - *'

'*- Have you seen your dad?*'

Connor sighs. He gently lifts his mother's hand and rubs it. Her eyes glaze over and she closes them. He looks around at her small room, filled with photographs of family and friends; mementos strategically placed in the hope of reconnecting her to reality. He even put up the bright flowery curtains that she's always loved in the hope they would give her comfort. He sometimes wonders whether his mother would realise if he didn't visit every day, but it's irrelevant as his conscience wouldn't allow him to stay away.

He appraises his mother. Where once was a spritely woman with a wicked sense of humour is now an ever-diminishing soul, plagued with confusion and repetition. Eyes that were bright stare vacantly and Connor knows that day-by-day he is losing her. Without the nurses' prompts she'd forget to bath and wouldn't choose fresh clothing. Looking at her resting with her eyes flickering he is only strengthened in his resolve to live every day like it's his last – to absolutely seize that day. Life is too short not to.

But what *is* he going to do about Greta?

He's in a pickle, personally and professionally. He shouldn't be thinking of his client this way, especially as she's not even available. He also shouldn't be talking about his work to anyone other than Maggie – confidentiality is a big deal in his profession - but the one guarantee in talking to his mum is that, by this time tomorrow, she will have forgotten every word.

Chapter 11

In anticipation of Jenni and the crew's arrival Greta rushes home to tidy up and spray air freshener throughout. The thought of Connor being in her home adds to her already jiggling nerves, and what makes it worse is they'll all be here in ten minutes and there's still no sign of Olly. She reaches for her phone.

Hiya. Hope you haven't forgotten the filming tonight? Love you, xx

She hits send and then checks her appearance in the bedroom mirror for the umpteenth time. Satisfied that she looks more bohemian than council worker, the flat lights flash on and off alerting her of an arrival.

'Hi!' Jenni smiles.

'Come in, come in,' Greta beckons them all in. The last to cross the threshold is Connor.

'*Hi*,' he smiles brightly.

Don't blush, don't blush, don't blush.

'Is your partner here?' Jenni asks.

'Not yet – but he's coming.'

'OK, we can get started with some general filming,' Jenni continues. 'We want to show you doing ordinary, everyday chores – cooking or washing up or relaxing watching television. It'll be used as background footage with a voice over.'

'Gotcha.' Greta raises her thumbs.

Cooking with a camera pointed at her feels weird and Greta's concentration is further tested by being continually drawn to the clock wondering where on earth Olly is. At a break she checks her phone. No reply.

As they are setting up for the next shots, Colin and Dave turn to look to the door. Craning her neck, Greta sees Olly, tie askew and wide eyes focussing in opposite directions, leaning against the wall.

Oh no!

'I'm ho-ome!' he sings, grinning.

Jenni looks to Greta.

'This is Olly,' Greta says quietly, lowering her head.

'Oh sorry, babe, did I miss the TV programme?' he slurs. Greta frowns, struggles to read his lips and turns her eyes naturally to Connor. Olly follows her gaze. 'Well I'm here now,' he adds, carefully placing one foot in front of the other to cross the room to her. Once there, he puts an arm around her.

'Why don't you go and lie down?' she whispers to him.

'What's that babe?' he asks loudly. 'I thought you wanted me here, to be a part of your big show.' His attempt at jazz hands fails and he loses balance. The crew all look anywhere but at Olly.

'Olly, please,' Greta says.

'Look, sorry I'm late, Switch,' he says lifting her chin. 'But I'm here now. Come on – I'm ready.'

'Hi Olly.' Jenni steps forward, extending her hand, smiling. 'But we've got enough footage – so thank you for offering but we're finished here for tonight.'

'Oh right. No problem, love. Hey mate,' Olly says, switching his attention to Connor who is still diligently interpreting.

'Olly...' Greta interjects.

'Mate – you don't need to do that.' Olly waves his hands around, mimicking sign language.

'Olly please!' Greta tugs his arm.

'Not for me and my girl, OK? We're fine.' Olly pulls her in closer.

Connor looks quizzically at Greta who gives a meaningful nod to stop; as much as she needs his interpreting she doesn't want him getting punched.

'Right, if we're done here...' Olly says. And then, turning to Greta he plants a beer-soaked kiss on her lips and staggers out of the room.

Greta wants the earth to swallow her up. Why did they have to witness Olly at his very worst? Why did Olly have to come home steaming drunk? Was this his way of getting out of the show? She is mortified and can't bear to look at anyone. Out of the corner of her eye she sees Connor lift his arms.

'We'll call it a night, OK?' he interprets for Jenni.

'I'm so sorry,' Greta says.

'Oh, don't worry,' Jenni says, smiling reassuringly. 'It's

funny how people respond to the thought of being on camera – we've seen it all before. It's not a problem – we can film parts we haven't got later. The important one is the art class next week.'

As the crew pack up, Connor crosses the room to Greta.

'You OK?'

'Apart from wishing I could erase the last ten minutes of my life, I'm fine.'

'Jenni's right – maybe he just didn't want to be in the show.' Connor nods to the bedroom. *'Do you think he's okay?'*

'He's probably passed out, but I'd better check.'

As she opens the bedroom door she finds Olly fully clothed, on top of the covers with his mouth open, drooling a puddle of saliva onto the pillow.

May you wake with the mother of hangovers...

Returning to the lounge, Jenni and the crew bid their farewells, and as the front door closes Greta looks to Connor and feels the tears rising.

'Aw, don't do that – it wasn't that bad,' he signs.

'Connor, he humiliated me in front of everyone. And I'm so sorry he was like that with you.'

'Don't worry – I've got broad shoulders. And you're worth it.'

She catches his eye, unsure if he's joking.

'Do you fancy a coffee?' she asks.

'Yes, but as brave as I've just implied, I'd rather go out for one just in case your boyfriend comes to.'

'Ha ha ha! What are you? A man or a mouse?' Connor puts his fingers to his head as ears and squeaks. She laughs. *'Come on then, Mickey Mouse, let's go. I like that late-night café on Grafton Street with the art on the walls.'*

'Lead on,' Connor signs and gestures to the door.

Greta grabs her coat and bag.

At the sound of the door closing Olly opens one eye. He lifts his head and as the room spins around him, he throws up all over himself.

'Urgh,' he groans, as the last of the vomit trickles from the corner of his lips. 'Greta...Gretaaaaaaa!'

***

'This table OK?' the pretty waitress asks, pointing to the round table in the corner.

'Perfect, thanks,' Greta replies, taking a seat.

Connor looks around at the huge abstract coloured canvasses that adorn the walls and the shadows cast by the table tea lights.

*'Cosy **and** arty,'* he signs.

'You've not been before?'

'Nope. I'm a View Café virgin,' he signs with a smile.

Greta blushes and laughs. *'Well not any more you're not.'*

The waitress hovers.

'Could I have a cappuccino please?' Greta asks.

'And I'll have a mocha with whipped cream.'

'Excellent choice,' she says to him, smiling and lingering a little too long before walking away.

'Whoa – way to go Connor!' Greta laughs.

'What?' He frowns and waggles his index finger in the sign for 'what'.

'Did you not see her flirting with you? The big eyes? The held smile?'

'No, really?' He looks over his shoulder to locate her. *'Sorry, Greta, excuse me a mo.'* He starts to get up.

'Oi!'

Connor laughs and sits back in his chair.

'Quite the joker,' Greta signs.

'Thought you might need cheering up after -'

'- After Olly?'

A small silence passes.

'Is he always like that?' Connor tentatively asks.

'What? Drunk?'

'Behaving like that.'

'Er, no, not really. He's a good guy – but for some reason he didn't want to be in the programme. Guess I forced him and I shouldn't have. My fault really.' She sees Connor's eyebrows rise. *'What?'*

He hesitates. *'Why do people do that?'*

'Do what?'

'Look, it's really not my place to say, but he comes home blind drunk, creates an unpleasant scene in front of people you're

working with, and you blame yourself?'

'*Well, I did talk him into doing it when he really didn't want to,*' she signs quickly.

'*Greta, he's a grown man – he could have said no.*'

'*But he loves me and wanted to please me.*' She feels defensive tears threaten.

'*OK, OK, look sorry, I didn't mean to upset you. I'm sure he does love you. Sorry. It's really none of my business. Let's just have a nice relaxing cup of coffee. OK?*'

Greta takes a deep breath. '*OK.*'

The waitress returns, places the coffees down and, passing Connor a teaspoon, she brushes his hand. She flashes him a big smile and then sashays away. Connor and Greta's eyes meet and they erupt into giggles.

'*You might be right about her,*' Connor signs.

'*Women's intuition,*' Greta laughs and taps her nose.

'*That's better,*' he says. '*That smile is far too pretty to be hidden.*'

Greta's cheeks pink. '*Thank you.*' They both load their coffees with sugar and stir. '*So,*' she signs. '*In a profession that's mainly filled with middle aged women, how did you get into interpreting?*'

'*I like middle aged women,*' he deadpans.

'*Ha ha – seriously.*'

'*I come from a deaf family. Both parents and brother are deaf and grandparents were too.*'

Greta takes a mouthful of coffee. '*Are your parents still alive?*'

'*Father, no. And my mum has dementia.*'

'*Oh, I'm sorry.*'

'*Me too.*'

In the easy silence between them Greta looks at the light beams crowning his curls, giving him a halo effect which, when she considers her first impression of him, seems a touch ironic. But where once she saw arrogance, she now sees vulnerability. It's all she can do not to reach out and touch his hand.

'*What's your mum's name? You know how most deaf people know each other.*'

'*Minnie Walsh.*'

'No, I don't know her, but I'm not really in the Deaf Community anymore.'

'Why not?'

'Er, I don't know. I used to love The Jolly Sailor on the deaf nights –'

Connor leans forward. 'Yeah! I used to go there too,' he signs.

'But, I suppose living with Olly I've become more part of his world. You know – the 'hearing world.''

'Ah, yeah. How's that working out for you? You feel more comfortable there?' he asks.

'I like both,' Greta states, winding a curl around her finger. 'In fact, I'm thinking about a cochlear implant...'

'Really?'

'Yeah – I mean, I know it won't make me hear like other people, but it could really help. Olly's keen...' she trails off and sees Connor swallow whatever it is he was about to say. 'I'm not committed though – too nervous about the actual op,' she adds.

'I've interpreted at a few post op appointments and the bandages aren't desperately attractive but they hide all the mirrors from you.'

She mock wipes her brow. 'Phew!'

'And they give you lots of painkillers.'

'Ha! I like the idea of the drugs! I might sneak in my own drug of choice – a nice Rioja.'

Connor laughs. 'Ah – I like your thinking. I'm sure it'll go nicely with the morphine, you'll be nicely laid back.'

'Would you have one?' she asks.

'A Rioja?'

'No! An implant, you fool.'

He laughs again and then furrows his brow. 'Oooh tricky question. I love music, and my brain knows how to hear so if I woke up tomorrow deaf I probably would. But it's a different question for you. You have to do rehab after the op, train your brain to recognise sounds. If you want to put in the work then, why not?' He leans across the table and sweeps her blonde curls to one side. Wondering what on earth he's doing, she holds her breath.

'Do you wear two?' he asks.

Ah - hearing aids! Greta nods dumbly. Him being so close

sends her nerve endings into overdrive and, as she's never quite sure about hearing people, she wonders if he can actually hear her heart pounding.

'Would certainly mean you wouldn't have to be sticking those in your ears anymore,' he signs.

'Yep, they're really old.' She fiddles with the aid, trying to regain her composure. *'I reckon a cochlear implant will make me hear much better.'*

'Yeah, you'll still be deaf, just with a powerful hearing aid in your head. Doesn't change who you are.'

'Yeah, I get that,' Greta signs. *'But...'*

'But?' He looks expectantly as she hesitates. *'Hey – I'm an interpreter; confidentiality is my middle name.'*

'Ha! Is that so?'

'No, it's Sean.'

She laughs and then taking a deep breath, she thinks how surprisingly natural it is to share personal stuff with this relative stranger. *'Well, I seem to have a mother who is in constant denial of my deafness and a boyfriend who's dead keen for me to get the op – I just worry they're expecting me to end up being hearing like them.'*

He nods slowly. *'They're going to be disappointed then.'*

'Mmm.'

Connor studies his cup for a moment and then looks up. *'There is one thing I don't get - why would they want you to change?'*

'For an easier life.'

'For you or for them?'

Greta bites her lip, knowing that he's just hit the nail on the head. *'You don't think I should have it done, do you?'*

'Oh no no no – I'm not answering a loaded question like that. We could end the night as not even friends!'

'You really are a mouse!'

'Yep, we already established that.' They both laugh. *'Let's say I uphold your right to make your own decisions and, as your friend – I am your friend, right?'* She nods, smiling. *'I will support you come what may.'*

'How's your bum for splinters there?' She giggles.

'Oi! Sitting on the fence is my happy place.'

As their laughter subsides they are left grinning inanely at each other.

'Thanks Connor. I really appreciate it,' she signs gently.

'What?'

'This.'

'You're welcome.' He gives a sweet smile. *'Anytime. Come on,'* he signs, looking around. *'Let's get the bill.'*

'Anything to get that waitress back, eh?' Greta mock rolls her eyes.

'Damn right, woman, damn right!'

Chapter 12

Standing on the steps opposite City Hall, Greta cups and blows into her hands. Being cold and tired are two of her top three states of unhappiness – add hungry and it's a full set – but two out of three still isn't good. She puzzles over what made her so restless last night; Olly's drunken display? That strong coffee? Enjoying Connor's company a little too much? All the above? And talking of strong coffee, she could use one now, before this demonstration gets underway. Feeling a tap on her shoulder she turns.

'*Hiya.*' Mia signs and gives Greta a hug. '*How's my big star?*'

'*Huh! Wondering why she signed up for it in the first place.*'

'*Oh no! Why?*' Mia pushes her afro curls back from her eyes.

Greta takes a deep breath. '*I told you Olly wasn't keen on the whole thing, right?*'

'*Mmm.*'

'*Well, I had Jenni, the crew and Connor all there last night, in the flat, filming, and Olly comes home late - completely ratted.*'

'*Oh no he didn't.*' Mia winces.

'*Yep, he sure did. He embarrassed me and was rude to everyone, especially Connor.*'

'*How?*'

'*It was a bit territorial really – 'stop interpreting between me and my woman' type thing.*'

'*Urgh.*' Mia shudders. '*How did it all end?*'

'*Olly puking up on himself in bed and me going out for a coffee with Connor.*'

Mia's eyes shoot wide. '*Sounds like a cracking end to a rotten evening to me,*' she giggles.

Greta screws up her nose. 'I *still had to go home and clean up Olly.*'

'*Well you didn't have to...*' Receiving warning eyes from

Greta, she quickly adds, *'How was he this morning?'*

'I left him snoring. Anyway – before we start protesting against our own council I need some coffee.'

'Me too,' Mia signs. *'Let's nip to Café Charlotte. Ooh let's do pastries as well, or muffins, yes, let's do muffins!'*

'You know, Mia, if you had food in your flat you wouldn't have to buy all this stuff.'

'Yeah, but then I'd be like an adult.' She pouts.

'Oh God forbid!'

With laughter and linked arms, they head over to the pastel coloured café where they buy coffee, muffins and sticky buns as sustenance for the protesting hours ahead.

Slowly the crowd gathers; deaf people, workers with deaf people, relatives, professionals and some inquisitive passers-by.

'We're here to do a job!' the enigmatic Owen Carter, head of the National Deaf Organisation branch, signs, from the top of City Hall steps. *'We, as deaf people, are being denied the right to services. We must fight back! I remember, and some of you might too, the days before we had interpreters; when we had to rely on our family and friends to 'help us out'. Is that what we're going back to? Being a group in society who have to rely on others for help? Lose what independence we have? I say no! I say we need to....'*

Greta looks around. Interpreters are out in force today – most of them positioned at various points in the crowd, relaying Owen's speech from whoever is voicing it on the microphone. Greta wonders if that voice might be Connor's. Not that it matters, of course…

'Hi.' Greta turns to see a tall dreadlocked man addressing Mia who has turned all shades of awkward. Mia raises her thumb to him.

'How are you?' he signs.

Mia looks at the NDO badge pinned to his dark pink corduroy jacket. *'You work for the NDO?'*

'Yep. Have done for years.'

'Did you tell me that?' Mia signs.

'Erm, not sure we had in-depth conversations,' he chuckles. He then turns to Greta and back to Mia.

'Ah, yes, sorry,' Mia signs. *'This is my friend, Greta. Greta this is Jerry.'*

'*Nicely remembered,*' he signs, grinning.

Greta gives him a knowing smile. '*Nice to meet you, Jerry.*'

'*So, what exactly is your job?*' Mia asks.

'*Membership Officer. You two members?*'

'*I am,*' Greta signs.

'*I used to be. It kind of lapsed,*' Mia signs.

'*Can I sign you up again?*' As she nods he continues, '*OK, well it's a lengthy form, so why not, after the demo, I buy you a coffee and we can fill in the form?*'

'*Erm, or you could email or post it to me?*'

'*Mia – you're not doing anything for the rest of the day.*' Greta interjects, enjoying watching her friend squirm. '*Allow the kind Membership Officer here to help you.*' She is repaid with Mia's reproachful look.

'*OK then.*' Mia concedes.

'*Demo should be done by noon. Wanna meet in Café Charlotte?*'

Mia lifts the muffins bag she's still clutching and nods.

'*Great, see you then. And lovely to meet you, Greta,*' he signs.

'*You too.*'

They watch him walk away, approaching other potential members.

'*Wow,*' Greta signs. '*If he has to have coffee with everyone he signs up he's gonna have one long and expensive day.*' Mia whacks her friend with the muffin bag. '*You know,*' Greta continues. '*I think he rather likes you. Can you remember anything of your night together?*'

'*It's all a bit hazy, but the bits I do remember make me smile.*'

'*There is something about him, isn't there?*' Greta says as they both watch him signing with a crowd of people.

Mia tilts her head. '*Yeah, I think it's his bum.*'

Laughing, the two friends reluctantly turn their attention back to the protest.

As the crowd disperses, the speakers leave the steps and the organisers start packing away the equipment.

'*Right, I'll love you and leave you.*' Mia kisses Greta on the cheek. '*I'm off for coffee and form-filling with The Bum.*'

'*Have fun, my lovely!*'

As Greta watches Mia cross the road towards the café she decides to wander around the dissipating crowd just to see if there are any familiar faces. She wouldn't say that she is especially looking for Connor, but after fifteen minutes and with no sign of him she can't deny the twinge of disappointment. As the last of the demonstrators pick up their placards to leave she is left chiding herself for being ridiculous – a silly crush is all it is - Olly is her boyfriend and the man she chooses to be with. Nothing has changed.

With that thought in mind Greta heads for the bus to see how things are back at the homestead. And exactly what kind of state Olly is in.

***

Jerry drums his fingers on the distressed vintage café table, willing her to turn up. He was certainly pleased with the numbers that had turned out for the demo, but having so many people around meant he couldn't keep his eye on her, and he didn't want her skulking away. He looks up to see her crossing the road, the wind shooting her wild dark curls out at all angles, and he smiles a little sigh of relief.

'*Hi,*' she signs, taking the seat opposite him.

'*Hi.*' He grins. '*Coffee?*'

'*Yes please. Um, actually, no, can I have a hot chocolate, just straight, hold the crap. Please.*'

'*Sure.*' He gets up.

She idly watches him stride to the counter, all dreadlocks swinging, heavy-duty boots and broad shoulders. Placing his order, he's cool and confident and the young female server blushes under his gaze. Returning a few minutes later he brings the drinks and places a plate with three mini cakes on the table between them.

'*Three? How do we divvy them up?*' she asks.

'*Mmm.*' He rubs his chin for effect. '*One each and the last one has to be won.*'

'*Won? What's the competition?*'

'*All in good time. First things first, let's get you signed up.*' He pulls out the application form and a pen.

'Yes sir!' Mia salutes.

'I like that attitude – keep it up. Right – shall I ask the questions and fill it in?'

'Shoot.'

'Name?' he asks, looking up.

'You mean you don't remember?'

He widens his eyes at her. *'Second name!'*

'You slept with someone not even knowing their second name? What kind of a man are you?' she teases.

'Hey, Missy – at least I knew your first name!'

'Fair point.' She shrugs. *'Gregory, Mia Gregory.'*

'Address?'

'You were there and you don't remember?!'

He gives her a warning look. *'Mia – the sooner we get this form done, the quicker we can fight over the cakes.'*

'OK, OK, keep your dreads on. Lancing House, Flat 4b, Staithe Lane, SB12 1TU.'

He flicks a dreadlock back over his shoulder and laughs. *'Mobile number?'*

'07888 255478.'

'Age?'

'Twenty-five.'

'Place of birth?'

'London.'

'Deaf school or mainstream?'

'Deaf school.'

'Name of school?'

'Janey Finch School for the Deaf.'

He rests his pen. *'Oh, bet we know a lot of the same people. Which year were you?'*

'I was with Brian Green, Imelda Cotling, Joe Thorne, Holly Jones, my friend Greta, Greta Palmer.'

He nods. *'I used to play football with Brian and Joe, good blokes.'*

'Yeah, I still see them from time to time. Joe got married last year. To Imelda.'

'Did he? Ah, good for him. Right, back to the task at hand.' He looks back down to the form and picks up his pen to continue. *'Present occupation?'*

'Council worker.'

'Years of employment?'

'Too many. Five.'

'Number of lovers to date?'

'*What?!*' she squeals, grabbing the form. '*You Jerry, are a fraud! This form wants my name, contact details and signature!*'

'*Hey! Can't blame a guy for trying.*' He holds up his hands and then throws his head back with an infectious throaty chuckle. Shaking her head, she quickly signs the form, slams the pen on it and shoves it back across the table.

'*I think I just won that extra cake!*' she signs, picking up the mini raspberry cheesecake and popping it into her mouth whole.

He smiles as she struggles to chew it into smaller pieces, her cheeks puffed out like a hamster.

'*Oooh instant karma,*' he signs. His phone buzzes from his back pocket. '*Oh sorry, hang on a minute.*' He pulls it out and reads the message.

'*Everything okay?*' she signs, still trying to break down the cake.

'*Yeah, sorry, it's my brother. Gotta split.*'

'*Oh.*'

'*It's been fun. Hope to see you again sometime,*' he says, getting up and throwing his coat on. He gives a quick smile and heads for the door, leaving Mia with her cheeks still bulging.

Hmm, strange, a man is walking out of the door and she has an unsettled feeling; is it disappointment? Hmm, she may have spent a night of unrecollectable passion with him, but she hardly knows him. No, shaking her head, she presses her palm to her chest and thinks how this little tugging twinge is definitely heartburn and nothing more.

Chapter 13

The second he'd opened his eyes the faint aroma of vomit had hit Olly's nostrils. 'Ugh, my head' he'd muttered, as the pain of dehydration kicked in. 'And what the ..?' Peering under the covers he'd found he was wearing his old Metallica t-shirt – he definitely hadn't been wearing that the night before. With pounding skull and eyes throbbing in their sockets, both of which accompanied by a churning stomach, he'd wondered why hangovers have to be so brutal. He'd gingerly turned his head to Greta's side of the bed and found it empty. A vague flashback of throwing up over himself explained the faint whiff of puke and dry acid taste in his mouth, and with that thought, he'd closed his eyes and slept for most of the day.

Now, sitting on the sofa, feeling slightly more human after two large bowls of Cheerios and copious cups of tea, he envisages the kind of mood that Greta will be in when she returns. She was going into the city for a demo – something about deaf rights – and he expects her home anytime now. He flicks on the TV and his eyes grow heavy again.

When he opens his eyes again he finds Greta leaning over him. 'Hi,' she says.

'Uh, hi! Must've dosed off,' he says, shaking himself awake. 'I didn't hear you come in.'

She says nothing. He eyes her warily and rakes his fingers through his hair.

'Greta, I'm sorry about last night.'

'Which part?' she says. 'Rolling in blind drunk and embarrassing me in front of everyone or puking on yourself which I then had to clear up when I got in?'

'Both, I suppose.'

Greta exhales deeply. 'Why Olly?'

'Go easy, Switch,' he says, rubbing his eyes. 'To be fair, I did tell you I didn't want to do the programme.'

'Yeah and then you said you would. Getting drunk to get out of it is a bit lame and childish, don't you think?'

'You know me, I don't always think.' He shrugs.

'Mmm.'

They fall silent.

'Hang on,' Olly says, looking up. 'You said 'when you got in' – where did you go?'

'Damn it,' she thinks, 'he's not going to turn this one on me.'

'It doesn't matter where I went – what matters is I came home to find you covered in your own puke and guess who had to clean it up? Who broke their back trying to get you changed? Yes, me, muggins!'

'Yeah, well I said I'm sorry. Where did you go?'

'I went out for a coffee. Thought it might be more entertaining than watching you passed out!'

'Coffee huh? Who with?'

'It's a pity you weren't more interested in that last night rather than being sparko.'

His eyes bore into her. 'Who with, Greta?'

She feels her cheeks burning. 'The interpreter, but don't you dare start accusing me. You have no right! You're the one in the wrong here, not me!'

'Is that so? OK, I stuffed up, I got drunk – but at least I didn't go sneaking off with handy-pansy boy!' He waves his hands mocking.

'Don't you dare!' Tears sting behind her eyes.

'You're all so smug with it,' he continues, 'Signing in silence, knowing no one understands you. You moan about people not including you, but what about me?'

'What? What about you?'

'When I'm with all the deafos –'

'DON'T CALL US THAT!'

He bats her away. '- you don't include me.'

'You *do know* what the difference is, don't you, Olly?'

He glares at her, his temples pulsating.

She draws a deep breath. 'YOU CAN LEARN TO SIGN – I CAN'T LEARN TO
HEAR!'

An angry silence fills the room.

'You never used to be this militant,' he says matter-of-factly.

'What? I have no idea how I'm being militant. I was deaf when we met -'

'-Yeah yeah,' he says barely disguising his disdain. 'I knew what I was taking on…'

'*Taking on?* That sums it up, doesn't it? You arse.'

'Oh, insults now, very mature.'

Greta's voice is low and cracked. 'Sometimes I don't think I know you.'

'Well, bingo! Something we agree on, 'cos I definitely don't know you!'

Greta moves to the armchair and dropping into the seat she puts her head in her hands and sobs. Being barely able to catch her breath between the juddering cries she wonders how he can just sit there and watch.

Olly hangs his head wishing she would stop crying. Eventually he rises and goes to the bathroom, rips off some toilet roll and returns to the lounge. He waves it under her face and she takes it.

She looks up and wipes her nose. 'What's happening here, Olly?' He shrugs, his tired hungover eyes conveying a mix of sadness and anger. 'Sometimes I'm not sure if you still love me,' she says, the words choking her throat.

'Of course I do,' he shoots back.

She shakes her head. 'It doesn't feel like it anymore.'

'We can't be all hearts and flowers all the time – that's not how relationships work. We get by okay, don't we?' he says.

'But I don't want to just get by.'

'What are you saying?'

'Maybe we need a breather?' she says, surprising herself.

His eyes widen. 'As in split?'

She nods her head gently.

'Is this to do with him?'

'No! No Olly, it's nothing to do with him. This is to do with us. You and me,' she says quickly.

'S'funny that you're out for a coffee with him and the next minute you're wanting,' He uses apostrophe fingers. ''A breather'.'

'Well you're just going to have to believe me that it's nothing to do with him. Look, we just seem a bit lost at the moment.

A bit of time might help us focus on what's important.'

'I know what's important. I don't need a breather,' he says.

'So what is important to you?'

'Oh God, Greta! You know I can't do this 'talk about your feelings' bullshit.' He runs his fingers through his messy hair.

'Then how am I supposed to know how you feel?' she asks, her insides quivering.

'You have to trust me.'

'Like you trust me?' she counters.

'That's different. I do trust you – it's that interpreter I don't.'

'That's a cop out. If you trust me then you'd know I wouldn't be unfaithful.'

'I do trust you.' He pauses. 'But you seem different – you've changed.'

'How?'

'You're more militant…'

'Aaargh, Olly – this is just going in circles!'

He chews his lip and his shoulders sag. 'OK,' he says slowly, his eyes meeting hers. 'If we do take a break, what are the rules?'

'I don't know. I wasn't planning this.'

'OK, well, what kind of time do we put on it?'

She exhales deeply as her voice cracks. 'Er… I'm not sure…a month?'

He thinks for a few moments and nods in agreement. 'OK,' he says, his lips curling.

'OK?'

'Yep. Oh and Greta,' he says, rising to leave the room. 'My name's on the lease so good luck living with Sylvia.'

Chapter 14

'OK, in the words of Pink, 'I'm In Trouble' Mags,' Connor says, tapping his fingers on the desk.

'What've you done now, Romeo?' she laughs.

He groans. 'I really like her! Like, *really* like her.'

'Connor, these supervisions are turning into agony aunt sessions.'

Connor pulls a face.

'Alright,' she exhales. 'Does she like you?'

'I have no idea. She's in a relationship with a right tool, he turned up blind drunk the other night 'cos he didn't want to be part of the filming – how immature is that? She was really upset and we went for a coffee. Nothing happened…'

'But?'

'If she were single it would have.' He rubs his face. 'You know, Mags, I don't need this right now. I'm busy with my mum -'

'- how is she?'

'Not great – good days and bad.'

Maggie pulls a sympathetic face.

'Argh, I can't do this to myself. I could really fall for this girl.' He winces.

'Right – let's separate the personal from the professional.'

'I wish I could.'

'Do you want to carry on working with her?'

'I do, because I want to be around her, but she's attached and I'm supposed to be professional, so…I don't think I can.'

'OK,' Maggie sighs. 'Let's check the diary.' She opens the slim laptop and pulls up the timetable. 'Right, you're down to do all the appointments for the TV programme. Let's see if I can swap you with anyone.'

'I kind of want to be with her 'cos I want to protect her from that idiot she's with - it's that hearing control over a deaf partner thing that really ticks me off.'

'Connor, you're an interpreter, not a knight in shining armour,' she says without looking up. 'Right, there's no one else for that one or that one.' She runs her finger down the screen. 'But I could swap you with Jane for the last appointment at the Broadcasting Hub. You'll be doing Jean Paige's endoscopy.'

Connor weighs up the thrill of television filming against a camera down the throat and ensuing retching. *Mmmm, tough choice.* But, hands up, he has to accept that being around Greta is ultimately not going to bring him joy.

'OK, I'll swap,' he sighs.

'Fine. I'll tell Jane.'

'Thanks, Maggie. I definitely owe you one.'

'Yes Connor, you do, and you can start by getting me a coffee before we get down to proper supervision – to talk about interpreting issues.'

'I'm on it,' he says, jumping up.

'And don't forget the sugar.'

He chances a grin. 'I thought you were sweet enough.'

'Coffee, now!' She shakes her head laughing.

Connor heads to the kitchen thinking how this is for the best. He watched his cousin suffer the hurt and indignity of being 'the other woman' and listening to her tales of broken dates, guilt and remorse he is adamant he is not going through all of that. Being single is fine – no one else to worry about, one set of feelings to keep in check and just himself to answer to – why would he relinquish that for a relationship that already has the odds stacked against it? As endearing as Greta Palmer is with her tousled blonde locks, cute smile and wicked giggle, him and her are not going to happen. Not in this lifetime anyway.

Chapter 15

Greta awakes with a start, slightly disorientated, and looking across at the untouched side of the bed the full force of the night before floods back. After their 'agreement' to take a break, Olly had disappeared to the bathroom and reappeared half an hour later dressed in a fresh white shirt, newest jeans, and a liberal dowsing of aftershave.

'I'm off,' he'd said, standing in the doorframe.

'Where you going?'

'Out.' His eyes were cold.

'OK. You coming home tonight?'

'I don't think you get to ask questions like that now.'

'Olly!'

'I'd really appreciate it if you moved out as soon as possible. OK,' he said, flicking his keys around his fingers and into his palm.

After that Greta had sought consolation in a pot noodle and wine dinner before sinking into bed and crying herself to sleep. And now, after a restless night, she hugs his pillow, breathes in his scent, and a solitary tear rolls down her face. This is going to be hard. As much as things haven't been running smoothly recently, they share three and a half years of history. The beginning of their love affair was filled with unquenchable passionate desire. They'd met through a mutual friend and in those early heady days they'd hated being apart and had spent days and nights enthralled by the other. Romantic nights, weekend trips away and Olly turning up unexpectedly at her work to whisk her out to lunch were all commonplace. He didn't talk about how he felt - she knew – she didn't need to be told. So, what happened? When did the cosy dinners stop? The surprise gifts for no reason disappear? When did the look in his eyes change from lusty love to veiled irritation? Her solitary tear turns into a torrent until his pillow becomes a soggy mess.

Dragging herself from the bed she goes to the kitchen and

makes a strong cup of coffee. Eschewing food, she traipses back to bed, grabbing her phone on the way. OK, Greta, she braces herself, this is where it's going to get really tricky.

Hi, wonder if I could stay with you for a while please? Hope all's well. G x

She hits send to both parents, takes a sip of coffee, sighs and rests her head back on the headboard. Only a few seconds pass before her father replies, '*Of course you can. Everything OK?*' swiftly followed by her mother's reply of '*Why?*' Thanks Sylvia, as caring as ever.

Nothing serious. Olly and I just taking some time apart. OK if I come over later today, please?

We're out until 4pm so best to come after then. Mum x

Mmm, Greta thinks, not having a key to the family home means waiting for Sylvia and John to finish their weekly trot around the garden centre; you'd think a key under the potted bay tree wouldn't be too much to ask, wouldn't you? Ah well, she sighs, at least I have somewhere to go.

Hey Mia, Long story but Olly and I are taking some time apart. Not good. Haven't cried this much since...ever. I'm moving back with Mum and Dad for a while. Definitely had better days. You around for a chat? Xx

When Mia doesn't immediately respond Greta abandons her phone and grabs a chair to retrieve the suitcase from the top of the wardrobe. Tears prickle as she remembers the last time this case was in use: last year, Greece. They'd had ten days of sunshine lazing by the pool, evenings in the twinkly lit tavernas and only one major row when she inadvertently offended a waiter by not understanding him. (And in her defence he did have a thick Greek accent.)

Methodically placing clothes in the case, she wonders where he is. Whose floor will he have slept on? Clarkie's? Rocco's? Stubs'? One of those reprobates' no doubt. She doesn't even want to consider the hi-jinx he will have got up to; how many beers he will have consumed to blur reality. Beer is the panacea to Olly's problems – rather than talking things through, he drinks things away. She silently scoffs at how that's working out for him.

She checks her phone. Still nothing from Mia. Where is her best mate when she needs her? A coffee and chat with Mia would be so beneficial before she heads out to suburbia and back in with the parents. In fact, a stiff drink might be more the order of the day. Just then her phone buzzes.

Oh Greta, I'm so sorry. Yes, of course I'm around. Wanna meet in Café Charlotte? I'll buy lunch xx

That's my pal, Greta thinks, smiling for the first time today. She quickly replies, *See you there in 20 mins. Thanks xxx*

I'll be there x, Mia responds instantly.

Throwing the rest of her belongings into the case she scouts around the flat one last time looking for anything she might've missed. She puts on her coat and shoes, picks up her case and heads out, closing the door behind her.

Meeting in the café, placing their orders and grabbing a quiet side table, Mia signs.

'*So, what happened?*'

'*We had a big row about him getting drunk and me going for the coffee with Connor. I don't know what happened, but the next thing I knew I was suggesting a break! I really didn't plan to say it - it just came out. And before I know it we're spending a month apart.*'

'*Did he just agree?*' Mia asks with surprise.

'*Well, not at first. He was suspicious it's something to do with Connor. But it's really not... He said some horrible things...*' Greta shivers.

'*Oh Grets.*' Mia leans forward and squeezes her arm.

'*He said all this stuff – really hurtful - about deafness and me having changed and how I'm militant.*' Mia doesn't reply. '*It went round in circles until I said that we should take a breather.*'

'*I see.*' Mia takes a sip of her drink. '*So how come you're the one moving out?*'

'*His name on the lease.*'

'*Ah.*' Mia's eyes fill with concern. '*Stupid question, but how are you feeling?*'

'*Heartbroken. Actually.*'

'*Oh Greta.*' Mia moves around to put her arms around her friend who breaks into sobs again.

'*I still love him, Mia,*' Greta signs, pulling away.

'*I know. But maybe this is right. I mean, somewhere in your mind you must've been thinking it for it to come out? Maybe a break is what you both need? Timeout, hit the reset button.*'

'*Supposing he doesn't want to reset? And I've forced him to take this break? It'll be all my fault.*'

'*No, Greta, it won't. It takes two. You wouldn't have suggested it if things had been fantastic, would you?*'

Greta sniffs and scrapes her hair back. '*I suppose not.*'

'*Look at it as an opportunity.*'

Greta eyes her friend keenly. '*Hmm, you're very wise today. Tell me how I'm going to cope with Sylvia.*'

'*I have wisdom, not super powers.*' They both giggle. '*Look, Grets.*' Mia reaches forward to touch her arm. '*Give it time for both of you to realise what you want.*'

Greta pulls a face. '*I know what I want: Olly…well…if I'm honest, I want the Olly from three and a half years ago. The one who would kiss me like it was the last kiss he'd ever have. The one who'd slay a dragon for me. That one.*'

Mia blinks softly. '*Maybe that one will come back.*'

Greta looks up, knowing that her friend doesn't believe that…and, deep down, neither does she. It feels like that version of Olly disappeared some time ago.

Mia continues. '*And if that Olly isn't available any more then it gives you the chance to look for your next dragon slayer.*'

Greta nods her head, tears springing freely. '*One day, maybe.*'

'*Yep. One day, maybe.*'

Chapter 16

Greta leaves the café and jumps on the number twenty-seven bus across town to her family home. She stares at the seemingly suspended white-grey clouds and contemplates her explanations for Sylvia. Does she make it sound more Olly's fault than her own? And if she does, what then happens when they reconcile? She really doesn't want Olly to suffer Sylvia's long-lasting disdain. Maybe she should just tell it like it is? That she just doesn't fit into his hearing life well enough and that he doesn't approve of her forthcoming TV appearance. Tears well as she realises that for these reasons alone Sylvia sympathies would lie with Olly.

Stepping off the bus, the heavens open and cursing that her raincoat is in the bottom of her case she races the two blocks to her parents' house. Dripping on the doorstep, she presses the bell and ruffles her hair that's sticking in patches to her head.

'Hello darling,' her mother says, ushering her in. 'You look like…' she says looking down.

'Sorry? What?' Greta says, entering the hall.

Her mother turns. 'I said you look like a drowned rat.'

'Oh, right.'

'Leave your wet things there. I'll bring a towel.' She disappears and moments later returns with a thick peachy-pink towel. 'How long are you staying?' she asks, eyeing Greta's bulging case.

My mother, ever the charmer. 'Er, we sort of said a month,' Greta says, rubbing her hair vigorously.

Sylvia nods and fixes a tight smile. 'Tea?'

'Yes please.'

Sylvia gestures for Greta to go through to the lounge whilst she goes to the kitchen. Returning with a tray of fine china teapot, cups and a plate of biscuits, Sylvia sits on the sofa and neatly folds her skirt over her knees.

'Do you want to talk about it, darling?' she asks, passing

Greta a cup.

Greta sighs. 'Not much to tell really, Mum.'

'I see.' Her mother stirs her tea, her mouth twitching.

'It's a mix of things.' Greta hesitates. 'We just haven't been getting along as well as usual, so we thought some time apart might do us good.'

'Mmm.' Her mother sniffs. 'You haven't done one of these dramatic running away things, have you? He does know where you are?'

'Yes, Mum, he knows I'm here. He was the one who suggested I come here.'

'Why are you the one to leave?' Her mother eyes her suspiciously.

Greta's cheeks burn with indignation. 'I know what you're thinking – if I'm the one leaving then I must be in the wrong.'

'Oh darling, don't be so melodramatic. I didn't say anything of the sort. But you're hardly giving me much to go on.' Her mother purses her lips.

'I told you – we're just not getting along so well at the moment. And the reason *I* left is because the lease is in *his* name. Chivalry is alive and well.'

'Well I suppose if he pays the rent -'

Greta's eyes burn at her mother's allegiance to Olly. Hell, why doesn't she just get a t-shirt with 'Team Olly' printed on it? Where is family loyalty? Or is it Sylvia's old chestnut of 'Hearing People Know Best'? It's always been the same; whatever the situation, if it means aligning with a deaf or hearing person, Sylvia will always choose the one who can hear.

'Biscuit?' Her mother offers the plate. Despite the fact that her throat is severely constricted, Greta takes one. 'Oh, darling,' Sylvia says. 'Do you want to go and fetch your father – we bought some bulbs today and he's just putting them in the shed. Ask him if he wants some tea, would you, please?'

'Sure.'

Relieved to escape further conversation, Greta gets up and heads to the back door. As she follows the brick weave path up to the far corner of the garden, past the bare apple and plum trees and the tall pile of leaves, she thinks about her mother. Why does Sylvia have to be so…Sylvia!? Isn't a mother supposed to be soft and caring? Defensive of her children, no matter what? Greta thinks that if she ever has a daughter and that child sought sanctuary from a broken relationship she would welcome her with open arms. She would make her favourite meal, wrap her in a warm blanket – metaphorically and literally - and tend to her broken heart. She would love her unconditionally and offer her space under her roof until she is ready to face the world again. There would be no inquisition of who did what to whom! There would be no questions of how long her daughter needed to stay. She would give her daughter love, peace and understanding – emotions that Sylvia seems incapable of. And, she thinks, as she passes the detritus heaped ready for a bonfire, if she ever has a daughter who can hear she would make sure the child grows up with sign language; there will be no communication problems in *her* house. Her child will be bilingual! With her mind buzzing in righteous indignation, she pulls the handle on the potting shed door and freezes at the sight before her.

'MMMMUUUUUMMMMM!'

Chapter 17

Her mother fails to appear. 'Damn hearing people usually hear everything,' she curses under her breath. Slumped in the corner of the shed, legs akimbo with his head awkwardly leaning on a lower wooden shelf is her father. Random objects, secateurs, string and bulbs are scattered around him on the floor.

Greta bends down and taps his ashen face. 'Dad, Dad!' She places her hand on his chest and feels it's rise and fall. Phew! 'Hold on, Dad. Hold on.' She races back down the garden and flies into the kitchen. Her mother looks up sharply, her face freezing with fear.

'It's Dad. He's collapsed. We need 999.' Greta catches her breath.

Throwing down the sugar bowl, Sylvia races to the telephone in the hall, shakily pushes the buttons and then repeats the questions from the call handler to Greta.

'Is he breathing?' Her mother asks, her eyes wide and scared.

Greta nods emphatically. 'Yes.'

After a while her mother puts her hand over the mouthpiece. 'Greta, go back to your father. They want someone with him.'

Racing back to the shed Greta thinks this is when deafness really sucks; it should be her on the phone whilst her mother tends to her father.

'Dad, Dad,' she says, kneeling down beside him. He opens his eyes wearily and mumbles something that Greta doesn't catch.

'Shhh, shhhh. Ambulance is coming. Just rest,' she soothes.

He closes his eyes and Greta strokes his hair and holds his hand. She feels the tears rising as she wonders how many times he has done the same for her. She wasn't a particularly sickly child, but it was mostly her father who would get up in the night to nurse her, with her mother taking the day shifts. Although in so many ways her parents are like chalk and cheese they are quite the partnership; his light-hearted twinkly-ness balances her mother's uptight controlling nature perfectly. She can't imagine one without the other and, for no other reason than this, he has to pull through.

After a while the potting shed door opens and two young paramedics carrying large panniers of medical supplies enter.

Greta looks up and lip-reads the man. 'Hello there, I'm Tim and this is Mandy.'

'Hi,' Greta says.

Glancing over their shoulders Greta sees her mother's face, fallen and fraught. To give the paramedics more room, she moves to stand next to Sylvia and then tentatively puts an arm around her. Greta feels her mother's stiff body lean into her side. Greta can't remember the last time they shared such genuine nearness; it feels strange, but then, nothing about this situation feels ordinary.

Adrenalin pumps around Greta's body as she holds her mother up whilst watching the paramedics perform tests on her father. Very soon he is equipped with an oxygen mask and is being lifted onto a stretcher.

'OK. Your husband is stable for now,' Mandy addresses Sylvia. 'And we're going to take him to Mercy General so we can find out exactly what happened. Would you like to travel in the ambulance?'

Sylvia nods in bewilderment.

'Mum?' Greta questions, not catching all that Mandy said.

Her mother's chin wobbles. 'They're taking him to hospital.'

'OK, you go with Dad and I'll pack a bag for him and then jump on a bus. Alright?' Greta says.

'Thank you, dear,' Sylvia says, squeezing Greta's hand.

'C'mon, let's get your coat and bag,' Greta says as she starts to steer her mother to the house.

The paramedics stretcher John around the side of the house and into the ambulance and soon Sylvia is being helped up the steep steps to join him. With the slam of the ambulance door, Greta is left standing, shivering in the wind. As she crosses her cardigan around her body, her tears finally fall freely.

This was not the sort of homecoming she had expected.

•••

Hospital waiting rooms with their high-backed chairs, out of date magazines and worried looking people always make Greta want to do something outrageous. As a child in school assembly, where even shuffling in your seat was admonished, she wanted to jump up and dance. She used to worry that in a Tourette's way she would shout out something wholly inappropriate. She surveys the injured souls around her waiting to be seen by the A & E doctors; the predicaments of some are obvious but others, like her, sit with fraught faces awaiting news.

Greta keeps an eye on the receptionist or any medical person who appears for fear that she is going to miss their call. Although she told the kindly woman at the desk that she's deaf, she knows only too well that busy receptionists forget these things. How many times has she waited in the doctors/dentist only to find that when her name was called people looked around, shrugged, and the patient after her was taken in to be seen?

Picking at a loose nail she anxiously wonders what is going on in the rooms behind the security door. This is the place where, on a daily basis, lives are saved or lost and she worries which it'll be for her beloved father. She reminds herself he was stable when he left home, and these medics don't lose patients in transit, do they? Plus her father is a fighter – he's lived with her mother all these years…

She looks up to see the kindly receptionist in front of her. 'You can come through now, love,' she says, patting Greta's arm. 'Come with me.'

Greta is normally adept at reading faces, but this chubby, grey haired woman's expression is imperceptible. She wonders if it's part of the training. She also wonders what kind of news is waiting on the other side of the key coded door.

Greta is led into a side room where she finds her father hooked up to all kinds of flashing and pulsating monitors and her mother seated at his side.

'Mum?'

Sylvia turns, her face drawn and white, and extends her hand to grip her daughter's.

'How is he?' Greta asks.

'The doctor just left. It's a heart attack.' Sylvia's voice shakes. 'Not a bad one though, thankfully. He'll be okay. More of a scare, really.'

'You can say that again.' Greta blows out a long sigh. 'Oh, thank God he'll be okay.'

At that moment her father flutters his eyes open and makes a small noise.

Her mother turns to him and takes his hand. 'John, the doctor says you need to rest, so don't worry about anything. Close your eyes.' She kisses him on his forehead and his lips form a small smile.

'I'm flat on my back – I am resting,' he croaks.

Gentle relief sweeps over the two women at his hint of humour.

'God, Dad, you scared us,' Greta says, moving to the other side of the bed.

'Gretsy.' He tries to take her hand but the multiple wires and gadgets prevent him. 'Sorry. I like to keep you girls on your toes.'

They all gently laugh. Sylvia sets about fussing over his pillows, trying to make him comfortable, and Greta guesses from his washed-out, tired expression that he'd rather she didn't. Her mother talks to him constantly and Greta wishes, as she has throughout her life, that her mother could sign. This is a monumental family moment; her father has suffered a, albeit small, heart attack and the family should be as one, sharing their fears and relief. But as usual Greta finds herself the observer of family life, never on the inside and forever watching from the side-lines. She knows they love her – they're her parents - but she also suspects that if she sidled out of the room right now they wouldn't bat an eye.

Chapter 18

The vibrating alarm clock's plastic pad beneath Mia's pillow shakes her awake. 'Urgh, Monday morning,' she thinks, throwing it onto the floor. She re-closes her eyes and snuggles further under the duvet. Drifting back to sleep, queasiness stabs and rises, causing her stomach to contract. Throwing back the covers she dashes for the bathroom and makes it to the sink just in time. Wiping her face on the towel, Mia perches on the side of the bath contemplating whether her Sunday lunchtime drinking session or the week-old ham in last night's omelette is to blame. Just as she stands up she is forced back over the sink again. Urgh, right, this is a duvet day for sure.

She walks to the kitchen and, grabbing a bowl, makes her way back to bed. Sleep comes quickly and it is only when her phone vibrates on the bed that she's roused again. Picking it up she sees not only a message from Greta but also that it's half way through the morning – this will not look good on her work record. Quickly firing off an apologetic text to her manager she then turns her attention to Greta's message that asks where she is. She replies saying she has some kind of bug and when Greta offers to visit her that evening Mia replies '*yes please*' before punching her pillow into shape, flopping back and surrendering to sleep again.

•

Greta goes up to the first floor of the converted Victorian flats where she finds Mia's door on the latch – prior arrangements are essential if you don't want to spend the whole evening knocking on your deaf friend's door - and entering, she makes her way to the lounge. Aware that just appearing will scare the life out of Mia, she waves her arm around the bedroom door, only to then bob her head around to see Mia fast asleep. Greta surveys the scene; a washing up bowl, alarm clock on the floor and Mia's face pressed against the pillow. Leaving her to sleep she takes to clearing up the tiny flat. Mia may be a wonderful person and a great friend, but domestication isn't her forte. Dirty plates and mugs that look untouched for days litter the surfaces, and the carpet is in need of a good vacuuming.

Taking up the domesticated duties her hands are plunged in hot soapy water when she turns to a tap on her shoulder.

'*Hey,*' Mia signs. '*Thought I felt the floorboards.*'

Wiping her hands, Greta signs, '*Guilty as charged. I'd hug you but…*' she looks Mia up and down, '*God, you look rough.*'

'*Thanks, I've felt better.*'

'*Food poisoning or a bug?*'

'*Dunno. I made myself an omelette last night.*'

'*You cooked?*' Greta smirks. '*That'll be it then.*'

'*Sod off.*' They laugh. '*So*' Mia signs, genuine concern creasing her face. '*What happened with your dad?*'

'*Why don't you go and sit down and I'll make us a cuppa and tell you all about it?*'

Mia raises her thumbs and unsteadily turns to the lounge.

Carrying two mugs of steaming tea, Greta finds Mia wrapped in a blanket on the sofa.

'*So?*' Mia asks.

'*I found him in the potting shed – heart attack.*' Even signing about it makes her wobbly. '*Scared the life out of me. And as for Sylvia, she's really shook up. It was only a minor one but they're keeping him in for observation for a few days.*'

'*He's going to be okay then?*'

'*Yeah. I think he's going to have to take it easy for a while, but he'll be fine.*'

'*What a relief.*' Mia takes a sip of tea. '*Ew.*'

'*Not to your liking?*'

'*It tastes horrid. Sorry – I'm sure it's not your tea - it's my mouth. Uh-oh...*' Mia clamps her hand over her mouth and makes a dash to the bathroom. Greta follows to find her friend, head down the toilet. She rips off some toilet paper and hands it to her.

'*You're in a right ol' state,*' Greta signs.

'*Yep. Can't believe I have anything more to throw up,*' Mia groans. She plonks herself on the floor and leans against the bath. '*You know, thinking about it, I haven't felt right for the last few days. Maybe the omelette's not to blame.*'

Greta studies her friend.

'*What?*' Mia asks.

'*Just a thought, nothing, nothing.*' Greta looks away.

Mia beckons with her hand. '*Come on, spill.*'

'*Have you had a period recently?*'

Mia's brow furrow. '*What?....*' Her eyes grow wide. '*Shit, shit, shit, shit.*' She drags herself upright and heads to the bedroom to her handbag where she steadies herself to pull out a small diary. Greta follows her friend and watches as Mia quickly flicks through the pages, her green-tinged face slowly turning a shade of pale. '*August, September...oh no, oh no, I can't be. I am late!*'

'*OK, let's keep calm.*' Greta signs. '*I'll nip to that chemist on Heath Road and get a tester, OK? We don't have to panic before we know for sure.*'

Mia's eyes bulge. '*Oh my arsing days – supposing I am?*'

'*Let me get the tester kit and then we'll have that conversation, alright?*'

Mia nods, her eyes blank and staring. As Greta races out of the flat Mia sinks back into the sofa and puts her head in her hands. Her stomach swirls with nausea whilst her head spins with thoughts of what might be. It's true she's taken chances in the past, and never been caught, but what if her luck has come to an end? Anxious for Greta to return but petrified of what the test might tell her, she forces herself to breathe deeply. If she is pregnant, her life will alter irrevocably and she is just not ready for that.

After what seems like an eternity Greta appears at the lounge door.

'*Come on then,*' Greta signs, waving the package.

With a wobble Mia rises, takes the box from her friend and disappears to the bathroom. Greta stands by the lounge window looking out at the small park across the road. She watches the children with ruddy faces and skewwhiff clothing playing on the swings and slides and thinks how normally she wouldn't pay this scene any attention, but with her best friend peeing on a stick at this very moment, she wonders whether Mia is ready to bring one of these little people into the world.

Mia suddenly appears holding the white stick. She clears a space on the coffee table and places it down.

'*There's not pee on that is there?*' Greta asks.

Mia scowls. '*Stay focussed. Bigger things to worry about here.*'

Both women fix their eyes on the window of the stick. Will the blue line appear? It occurs to Greta that such a small thing can have such massive implications.

'*You know, Mia, whatever the result, you'll get through. It won't be the end of the world,*' she comforts.

'*It'll be the end of my world as I know it.*'

'*Maybe.*' Greta nods. '*But you'll survive.*'

'*Me, as a mother? Can you imagine?*'

They exchange looks of worry and alarm.

Greta looks at her watch. '*OK, times up.*'

Mia takes a deep breath.

'*You have to look now,*' Greta coaxes.

'*No I don't.*'

'*Yes you do.*'

Mia shakes her head adamantly.

'*OK, want me to look?*' Greta asks.

Mia nods.

Greta reluctantly returns her eyes to the white stick. The blue line could not be any brighter.

Chapter 19

'Almost a week on,' Greta sighs, looking out from the top of the double decker bus at the dusk settling, 'and still no word from Olly.' The first night her father was in the hospital she'd texted him and he'd sent back a brief message asking her to convey his best wishes, but apart from that there'd been no contact. Can he really just shut down so abruptly? She wasn't expecting him to turn up all hearts and flowers, begging her to come back, but she had expected the occasional text. Is he really that hard hearted? Surely she would have noticed if he cared so little? And if he can disengage from their relationship that easily, what on earth have they been playing at these past years?

Stepping off the bus and depositing her chip wrapper in a bin, Greta makes her way to the adult education building. A flutter of excitement fills her belly as she thinks of seeing Jenni and the film crew again…and Connor. In truth, she's hardly given him much thought what with her father's heart attack, Olly's departure and Mia's impending motherhood, but in this moment of knowing she's about to see him again, her heart beats a fraction faster.

Entering the classroom Greta looks at what appears to be a makeover show rather than an arts and disability documentary. Everyone is primped and preened. In place of holey jeans and stretched jumpers there are made up faces, coiffured hair and Sunday best clothes. Wow, this lot scrub up well, she thinks, as she takes in even Malcolm who has shed his usual elbow patch jacket in favour of a smart blue pinstripe one.

'Ah, Greta,' Jenni says, walking over, taking the pencil out of her mouth. 'How are you?'

'Good thanks.'

'I've met most of your fellow students and, oh sorry, hold on, do you want Connor?' She turns over her shoulder. 'Connor!'

He appears from the back of the room, walking towards them

with lowered eyes.

'Right,' Jenni continues with Connor, beside her, interpreting. 'We are going to film some bits and bobs and then we'll do some pieces to camera. Could you lay out your work so we can get some shots of it too, please?' Greta nods.

'So, do you just want us to carry on as normal?' Malcolm asks.

'Yes please,' Jenni replies.

'Us, normal? That's a challenge.' Richard says, smiling.

'Are you going to interview us?' Joan asks, smoothing her hair.

'Yes, we're interested in how a deaf person fits in a class like this,' Jenni answers.

Nigel puffs out his chest. 'Have you noticed we all sign?' he asks.

'Did you all learn for Greta?' Jenni asks. 'Well, that's very impressive.'

As Jenni continues to find out more about the art class participants Greta takes a look at Connor. He's in total professional mode with a fixed glare and polished signing; not a cheeky grin or a knowing look to be had. She wonders if that night when they went for coffee whether he was just being nice; was it all in her mind that there were little sparks between them? Ah well – it doesn't really matter, in fact considering the situation with Olly, her father and Mia, she really doesn't need anything more on her plate.

As Jenni and the cameraman are taking general shots and talking with Joan and Nigel, Richard, her cochlear implant advocate, slides up the bench to her.

'I hope you don't mind,' he half signs and whispers. 'I took the liberty of getting you these.' He lays down a handful of leaflets; the top one entitled, 'Cochlear Implant – Is It For You?' 'I happened to be visiting old pals at the hospital and thought of you.'

'Thank you, Richard, that's very thoughtful. I'll read them.'

'Or bin them – up to you,' he says kindly.

'You know, I have an appointment at audiology on Friday – just getting new ear moulds, I might have a chat then.'

'No harm in finding out, eh?' He smiles and Greta, returning his smile, tucks the leaflets into her handbag. She then opens her portfolio and lays out her charcoal drawings. Connor hovers at the end of the bench, waiting to see when he'll be needed. Greta catches his eye and risks a light smile. His face softens.

'*How are you?*' she signs.

'*I'm okay, thanks. You?*' Just that simple question asked with genuinely kind eyes brings tears to hers. Concern covers his face as he steps towards her. '*You okay?*'

'*Been a tough week. My dad had a heart attack.*'

'*Oh God, I'm so sorry – is he okay?*'

'*Yeah, thankfully it was only a minor one. Still scared the life out of me.*'

'*Not surprising.*'

'*And then there's Olly –*'

Connor's attention averts to Jenni who has started talking. He automatically lifts his hands to interpret. '*Greta, could we get some shots of you working please? And then you could tell us about your piece?*'

'Sure.' Greta's voice wobbles.

Connor nods, his eyes holding hers with nothing but tenderness.

Greta begins work on the charcoal lines of her latest drawing. The characters are separate, isolated, and Greta explains that the broken lines filling the space represent their damaged souls. As she points out the imagery in her work she speaks quickly with her hands naturally gesturing; her passion and enthusiasm enveloping her. This is escapism at its very best; in this moment there is no deaf or hearing, no troubled families or broken hearts – only the art. The pure creative process feeds her soul and gives her the space and peace she needs. Sylvia may dismiss it as 'new age poppycock' – but this is Greta's thing. She continues to describe her inspiration and is only momentarily flustered when she catches a glimpse of admiration in Connor's eyes. She decides that it might be best to avoid his gaze.

An hour and a few re-takes later Jenni announces that they have all they need and gives thanks to everyone for their cooperation.

'Let's take our break now, folks,' Malcolm says as the TV crew are packing up. As Greta packs her work away into the large portfolio folder she looks up to search out Connor. Wanting to steal a quick coffee or brief chat with him, her heart sinks as she sees him throwing his bag on his shoulder, saying goodbye to the crew and heading out.

'You okay there?' Richard asks, appearing beside her.

'Sorry?' she says, tearing her eyes away from the door.

'You look troubled.'

'No, no, I'm fine,' she says, not feeling 'fine' at all. Why would Connor skip out without even saying goodbye? 'Just wanted to catch the interpreter before he left.'

'Oh. You'll see him again, won't you?'

'Yep – one more filming session next week. I'll see him then.'

Saying that, she suddenly realises that amidst everything that's going on in her life the chance of seeing Connor again is a little dot of joy on an otherwise bleak horizon.

Chapter 20

As soon as the council turned their large airy basement into a place to provide stress-busting yoga classes for the workers, Greta and Mia had signed up. The first couple of times they'd positioned themselves at the front to catch the teacher's instructions but soon found that trying to lip-read an upside-down person just doesn't work. These days they roll out their mats at the back and simply follow.

Tonight, with the class already 'settling into their bodies and finding their breath' Mia rushes in, shedding her outer garments and rolling out her mat. Greta opens one eye and smiles at Mia who assumes the position and joins in.

'We're going to chant one 'ohm' altogether to begin our practice,' Beautiful Yoga Teacher says, as usual. 'I'll start and you can all join in.'

'OOOOHHHHHHMMMMM.'

Greta feels the low thrum of communal voices beating through her body. It's a glorious bathing in sound and her nerve endings respond and energise. Having missed a few classes, she realises how much she needs this; to put her energy into something other than thinking and rethinking the sequence of events leading to the 'breather' from Olly. When she'd suggested a month she'd assumed they would keep in touch, but clearly Olly had other ideas and now, as she twists into a seated turn, she asks herself if she misses him. Yes, she does. She misses the two of them together in the flat; cooking, lounging on the sofa, watching TV, sharing a bottle of wine; she misses his winning smile, late night texts and his ability to make her laugh. Okay, so they have their problems, but it's nothing that can't be fixed. She's deaf and he's hearing – that doesn't mean they are doomed to split. Her mind, that is supposed to be calming, wanders back to the first time she watched Children Of A Lesser God and how the deaf/hearing couple in that film wondered if they could find a place to meet 'not in silence and not in sound'. Wistful romance or utter bunkum? With her and Olly she guesses only time will tell…

Having to wake Mia as usual from the final Savasana the two friends roll up their mats in voiceless giggles.

'Can't you ever stay awake?' Greta asks.

'I'm sleeping for two.' Mia half grimaces.

'How you feeling?'

'Still in denial and slightly bilious.'

Greta frowns. *'You contacted Jerry?'*

'Nope.'

'You going to?'

'Nope.'

'Mia!'

'Let me get my head around it first, okay? Haven't you heard of those pregnancy tester things being wrong?' She tucks her mat under her arm. *'And anyway – who's to say it's Jerry's?'*

Greta's eyes shoot wide. *'Mia! Who else?'*

Mia lowers her gaze. *'Kinda depends on dates…'*

'Who's the other likely candidate?'

Mia shuffles her feet. *'Fall Back Finn.'*

Greta rolls her eyes. *'Seriously? He's still hanging around for you?* Mia bites her lip and nods. *'Oh, my friend, I don't think you're on the path to true enlightenment.'*

'Aw shit, really, do you think?' Mia guffaws with a guilty expression. *'OK, I'm outta here!'*

'See ya. I'd say stay out of trouble but…'

Mia turns to walk away and raises two fingers. Greta giggles at her incorrigible friend, throws her mat bag over her shoulder and heads for home.

Entering the Palmer residence with the key her mother had pressed into her hand like money for an ice cream treat, Greta dumps her coat and bag and moves to the lounge doorway where she sees her father, thankfully now with colour back in his cheeks, trying to rest in the armchair. Her mother is fussing all over him.

'Sylvie, I'm fine. It's like a furnace in here,' he complains. Greta can't see her mother's response but by the way she carries on trying to tuck the sides of the blanket around him she guesses that his protest is in vain. 'Gretsy,' he says, looking around her mother.

'Hi Dad, how are you doing?' Greta says, walking in, kissing him on the forehead and taking a seat on the nearby sofa. 'They let you out then?'

Her father smiles, his blue eyes crinkling at the sides. 'Can't keep a good man down.'

'How are you feeling?'

'Warm,' he says, mock wiping his brow.

Her mother, who is still bending over him, looks up. 'John, I don't want you getting pneumonia on top of all this.'

'More like heat exhaustion,' he replies, to which Sylvia reluctantly smiles and raps his arm. He chuckles and squeezes his wife's hand as he holds her gaze. Greta wonders if a child is supposed to feel like a gooseberry in the company of her parents.

'Greta,' her father turns to her. 'How's that filming coming along?' Sylvia moves to sit in the chair next to him.

'Good. It's nearly done. They've filmed at my flat, work and art class. Just one more session in the Broadcasting Hub and it's done.'

'When's it going to be shown?' her father asks.

Greta shrugs. 'Not sure.'

'We're looking forward to it, aren't we Sylv?' He looks to his wife who in return softly smiles.

'Cup of tea?' Sylvia asks.

'I'll make it,' Greta says.

'No, no, dear, you sit with your father.' Her mother pats her father's arm and leaves the room. Greta's never seen her mother displaying such affection for him; it's like she has to keep touching him to make sure he's still here. Greta finds it endearing and rather likes witnessing this caring side to her mother.

'What about that boyfriend of yours?' her father asks after a moment.

'Not heard from him. I think he's taken the idea of a break literally.'

'Don't you worry yourself. You know what I always say? If you love somebody, set them free.' He folds his hands emphatically on his lap.

'Hmm, yes. I've been meaning to say, I used that phrase recently and was told that those words are actually a singer's –

what's his name? Stung?'

Her father chuckles. 'Sting, darling, Sting. Yes, they are his words indeed.'

'All these years, Daddy, and I thought they were yours!' Greta frowns with jokey disapproval.

'See? You can't even trust your old man!' His hearty laugh is quickly followed by a cough and a deep yawn.

Greta raises her eyebrows. 'Dad, how about missing that cuppa and heading to bed?'

'Mmm, you might be right, I am tired. I'll go and tell your mum I'm heading up. Don't want her worrying when she comes back and finds me gone.' He smirks, gets up and kisses Greta on the head. 'Night night.'

'Night, Dad. Sleep well.'

A few moments later her mother appears with a tea tray and slices of coffee cake.

'That looks yummy,' Greta says.

'You and your dad've always loved it.' Sylvia smiles as she sits in the chair he left vacant.

'Dad's gone up, did you see him?'

'Yes, he put his head around the door. I'm glad he's gone to bed. He just needs to rest.' She pauses, her face taking on a sombre expression. 'I can't imagine if it had been worse, you know.' She stares into the middle distance. 'Everything we've made, we've made together; the life we have, we both have to be in it. Why would I want a life without him? What would I do, Greta? Where would I be?' A tear escapes down her cheek. She pulls a tissue from her sleeve and dabs it away.

'Oh Mum.' Greta leans forward and rests her hand on her mother's knee. 'He's fine. It was just a warning – he needs to slow down a little, that's all.'

Her mother nods her head. 'Yes, you're right – we just have to work out what he needs to stop doing.'

'Mmmm,' Greta murmurs, thinking how her father is not going to like that. Sylvia shakes her head,and tucks her tissue back up her sleeve. She pours the tea and passes a cup to Greta.

'How are you anyway, darling?'

'I'm doing okay. I haven't heard from Olly, but I suppose we did say a month.'

'Oh yes about that, darling, I've been thinking…' Greta holds her breath, wondering what's coming next. 'You must stay as long as you like,' her mother continues. 'You do know that, don't you?'

Unable to make contact with her mother's downcast eyes, Greta smiles. Sylvia sniffs and smooths her skirt before picking up the plate.

'Coffee cake, darling?'

Greta gently smiles. 'Thank you, Mum.'

Chapter 21

Friday morning rolls around and Greta finds herself sitting in the stark audiology waiting room. It never ceases to amaze her that, even in this department specifically for people with hearing loss, the nurses stand rooted near the desk and shout for the patients. Greta's eyes burn with the concentration of lip reading. Will she catch her name? Or will she be the one person looking the wrong way only to look back to find an entire waiting room's eyes on her?

'Gre-ta Palmer.' The nurse enunciates each syllable.

Greta raises a finger and then follows her to a side room.

'Hi, I'm Anna. What can we do for you today?' Greta follows the pink lipstick shapes of the pretty nurse's mouth.

'A couple of things. I'd like a new mould please.' Greta points to her aid. 'And I wonder if I could have a chat about a cochlear implant?'

'Okay, I can help you with the mould but I'll have to get my colleague, Lisa, for the implant.' She smiles.

'Great, thanks.'

Anna then sets about filling Greta's ear with the soft playdough type substance that, when removed, will have a tube inserted and then left to set. It will then sit in Greta's ear, holding the hearing aid in place. It's a quick painless procedure that Greta's been through countless times and the two women chat about this and that until the job is done.

'Right, you stay here and I'll get Lisa to run you through the implant, okay?' Anna says and disappears. Greta looks around at the large posters on the wall and just as she's studying what you can and can't deposit in the various bins, the door opens and a short middle-aged woman with bleached curly hair and bright orange lipstick enters.

'Hi,' Greta says.

'Hello. My name.' She points to herself. 'Lisa. I understand you wah al bou inri?' *Oh heavens to Betsy – an audiologist I can't communicate with…* 'It fai long pro by talk you.'

Nope, not getting a thing.

'Do you sign?' Greta asks.

'Sorry,' Lisa says. 'I only know 'please' and 'thank you'.'

Not helpful. 'Sorry,' Greta says. 'I'm finding it hard to follow you. My lip-reading isn't good. Can we write things down?'

'Tell yo wha I yer the,' she says, pulling out the same leaflets that Greta has already read. 'An y oar any questions.'

Greta reverts to the well-known custom used by deaf people since the beginning of time: she nods. She's not getting a word of what this nurse is saying, but she nods. Nodding tells Lisa that she is following her advice to the letter and frees Greta's mind to start planning how she *is* going to get this information. Hmm, maybe another appointment with an interpreter. Now there's an idea! Maybe an interpreter she understands well? An interpreter she is rather fond of? She tries to control the smile tickling her lips. Refocussing on Lisa's tangerine lips forming impossible shapes, she ponders re-booking this through Connor's agency. He certainly wasn't himself last night and it would be an opportunity to check if he's okay and get this info at the same time. Two birds killed.

Just then Lisa leans forward. 'OK?' she says, raising her thumbs.

'Yes.' Greta smiles, trying to gauge whether the appointment is over.

Lisa hands her a card with her contact details. 'Call me,' she says, miming a telephone to her ear.

'Will do,' Greta says. *After I magically inherit the power to hear…*

Leaving the hospital Greta calculates she has a good hour before Rog expects her back at work and so, taking advantage, she nips to a few dress shops to scout out an outfit for her big television appearance.

After a few unsuitable outfits she picks a knee length, slash neck, navy dress that hugs her curves. Perfect. Happy with her purchase, she is heading back along the bustling street when she spots a familiar face on the other side of the road. She stops dead in her tracks. Bobbing her head, she catches sight of the familiar strut and the chin jutted out in determination and her stomach flips at the sight of Olly. She toys with whether to shout out his name, but with the traffic between them would he even hear her? Just then a large lorry slows and blocks her view and by the time it passes Olly has hot footed it into the distance. Is he late for work? Olly was never late for work. Is he falling apart without her? Isn't he even able to get himself to work on time? She wishes she could've seen his face clearer to glimpse whether missing her is written anywhere on it.

As she reaches the large square concrete courtyard outside county hall, she stops and pulls out her phone.

Hiya Olly. Just saw you on the high street. Hope all's well. Love G xxx

Her finger hovers over the 'send' button. Should she break the silence and test the water? Or hold tight and hope that the old adage of absence making the heart grow fonder is going to work in her favour? She puzzles at how she can be so unsure about a man she has spent so many days and nights with. Until a couple of weeks ago they were supposedly a solid couple who would be potentially spending the rest of their lives together. She shivers at the physical and emotional distance now laid out between them. Looking back at her phone something tells her to give it a few more days and with that she hits delete, puts it back in her pocket and enters the building.

Chapter 22

Being newly single Greta considers her options for the evening ahead. Sadly, with Mia still nauseous and tired, she has no one to paint the town red with – not that she fancies that, but a quiet drink and a chat would be nice. No, instead, on this autumnal Friday evening she has little choice except to stay at home with Sylvia and John.

They eat an early dinner, an unexpected trays-on-laps chilli, and then very shortly, John again shows signs of tiredness and takes himself off to bed.

'Fancy TV?' Greta asks her mother.

Sylvia shakes her head. 'Not really. Game of Scrabble?'

'Sure, why not.' Greta gets up and crosses to the large sideboard that dominates the end of the room and fetches the game. The tell-tale scuffed and sellotaped edges show how much it's been played over the years and Greta lays the board on the low glass coffee table and offers the bag of letters to her mother.

'Right, no two letter words and nothing that begins with a capital,' Sylvia says, taking out seven tiles.

'It's not me that tries to cheat,' Greta laughs. 'You want to look at that father of mine.'

Her mother pulls a face and giggles. 'He is a terrible cheat, isn't he?'

'What was that word that time?'

'Mourish – as in wanting more! It didn't matter that even the Oxford Dictionary disagreed - he was adamant.' Sylvia tuts admiringly, shaking her head. 'He's always been strong headed, much like someone else I know.' Her eyes twinkle.

'Me?'

Her mother smiles and then continues to speak, head down, looking at her letters.

'Sorry, what?' Greta asks.

Her mother sighs. 'Nothing dear. It wasn't important.'

Greta bites her tongue. There it is again – 'it's not important'. No, clearly it's not important to Sylvia but it is to her! If she says something now her mother will think she's just making a fuss about nothing, but if she remains silent the pain of indignation and offence will fester.

Sylvia eyes her daughter warily. 'I only said that the apple doesn't fall far from the tree.'

Greta frowns, her green eyes confused and questioning.

'It just means that you are very much like your dad.'

'Oh right, I see. So, he's a tree and I'm an apple?'

Sylvia thinks for a minute and chuckles. 'Yes, I suppose so. We do say some funny things, don't we?'

'It's confusing for a deaf person.'

'Didn't they teach you things like this in school?'

'No, no they didn't.' Greta thinks for a moment. 'In fact, you remember Al?'

'That young man you liked just after you left school?'

Greta nods. 'I remember we were in a café and he looked out of the window and said it was raining cats and dogs. I actually looked up at the sky – I hadn't a clue what he meant!'

'Oh darling.' Sylvia chuckles gently. 'In all honesty though, Greta, you do cope marvellously.'

'I have to.'

Her mother nods. 'Oh yes, how did it go at Audiology?'

'Hah, I got the one nurse I couldn't lip-read! I'm going to have to go back with an interpreter to find out what she said.'

'What a waste of time.' Her mother sniffs.

'I know.' Greta lays a decent five-letter word and smiles. 'Pique.'

'Very good, dear.' Sylvia keeps her eyes on the board. 'Do you think you'll have it done?' she asks with a casual air.

'Er, I'm not sure. There are pros and cons.'

'What are the cons, dear?'

'Complications of surgery, losing the little hearing I've got in that ear, and, from what I've read, coping with people sounding like daleks.'

'Ah I see.' Her mother rearranges her letters on the stand. 'It does seem to work for a lot of people though, doesn't it?'

Greta shrugs. 'I haven't met many people who don't like it.

Except for Mia's friend, Josie, who just doesn't use it, refuses to switch it on.'

'Well, maybe it just wasn't for her. I know if it were me, I'd have it done, but the decision is yours, dear. It's you who has to go through it.' Her mother smiles. 'Oooh, look, seven letters!' She excitedly waves the tiles around before laying them down to spell, 'mistake'.

'Hope that's not an omen,' Greta says.

'Nonsense dear. It just means your mother is getting good at Scrabble!'

The game continues with laughter and playful competition and Greta can't remember the last time she enjoyed spending time with her mother quite so much. Usually the family dynamics are such that, with her father present, it feels very much like two against one, with Greta being the one.

As Sylvia places the final tiles; an astounding four letter word finish, she victoriously reclines back in her seat and grins widely.

'Another game?' she asks.

'Absolutely!' Greta slides the tiles back in the bag. 'A rematch is definitely in order!'

Her mother laughs heartily before becoming serious. 'Darling, would you like me to come with you to the hospital? Your fact-finding appointment?'

Greta gulps and stares at her mother. What should she say? She really doesn't want her mother there. Supposing they get there and her mother talks *for* her as she always does? Memories of being in public and being asked a question only to find her mother jumping in to answer flash before her. She would suffer the frustration of having to remain silent - how could she join in when she doesn't know what has already been said? She can't go through that now – especially not on such an important topic. She looks at her mother's expectant, hopeful eyes. Hmm, to turn down the offer might be perceived as spurning an olive branch. After all the years of friction and not quite connecting, could there be change in the air? Could her father's illness be the catalyst for a new phase in mother daughter relations? Should she give Sylvia another chance?

'Er,' Greta says shakily. 'That would be lovely.'

'Right, that's agreed then.' Her mother purses her lips and

taps her thighs. 'OK, young lady, pass that bag of letters.'

Offering the bag to her mother, Greta half smiles whilst her mind races with some degree of panic at what's just been agreed.

Chapter 23

Connor tries not to be distracted by the phone buzzing in his pocket. The meeting he is interpreting between solicitor and deaf client is not going well with the client refusing to believe that he can't take action against his neighbour for erecting a wall.

'Sorry, Mr Thomson, the wall is not on your land,' the grey-haired solicitor says, over silver half-moon glasses. 'You really can't insist that your neighbour take it down,'

The phone buzzes again, alerting Connor that the person has left a voice message.

'*But it's ugly!*' signs Mr Thomson. '*You wouldn't like it!*' Connor voices over, translating the signs into words.

'Does it block your light?' the solicitor asks.

Mr Thomson's brow knits and he looks to Connor in confusion. Connor holds up a finger to the solicitor and then turning to his client he signs a window with light and then darkness.

Mr Thomson shakes his head emphatically. '*No! Of course not! It's this high!*' he shows the height of a toddler.

The solicitor clears his throat. 'So, may I ask what exactly is your objection?'   '*It's bloody ugly! Us deaf people use our eyes and it hurts mine!*' Connor sees the solicitor resisting a smile.

'Mr Thomson,' the solicitor says. 'Can I ask why it's so ugly?'

Just as Connor raises his hands he feels his phone's vibration again – this time alerting him to a text. A feeling of dread fills his belly – someone definitely wants him.

'*It's like a baby's play pen around his precious fish pond. He's painted it orange.*'

'I see.' The solicitor takes off his glasses. 'It does sound distasteful but legally I'm afraid you have no recourse. Are you on speaking terms?'

'*Hell no,*' Mr Thomson's signs. '*Haven't spoken to the*

miserable sod since June 9ᵗʰ 2010.'

'And what, may I ask,' the solicitor gesticulates with his glasses, 'happened that day?'

'He ran over the wife's cat,' Mr Thomson signs with indignation, punctuating his statement with a righteous nod of his head. *'He then pretended he hadn't, but I know it was him. He couldn't look at me for weeks, practically shut the door in my face when I went round there. My wife cried for weeks...'* Whilst voicing over, Connor looks at the solicitor's bemused expression and bets he wished he'd never asked. *'Years we've lived next to them.'* Mr Thomson continues. *'Used to be good friends at one time. Not easy making friends with hearing people – but they used to be good fun. Not anymore. He does that to us and then won't mix with us and now building this fence -'*

'Mr Thomson,' the solicitor interrupts. 'I am very sorry but there is nothing I can do to help.' Mr Thomson's face drops. 'If I may say,' he continues, 'it sounds like you and your neighbour need to talk; sort it out.' He turns to Connor. 'Can you help with this? Are there any services that could mediate?'

Connor hates it when this happens; he is supposed to be the conduit for language and can't suddenly switch to answering a direct question. He quickly asks Mr Thomson if it's okay for him to answer the question.

'I believe the KDL Deaf Centre can help,' Connor signs and speaks at the same time. 'I will put in a request, if Mr Thomson agrees?'

Mr Thomson nods his agreement and the men stand to shake hands. Not wanting to be trapped in further conversation with Mr Thomson once they are out of the door (there is always something Mr Thomson wants to get off his chest) Connor makes his excuse of another appointment and heads for his car. When he has turned the corner and is out of sight he pulls out his phone. The missed call and text message tell him that he is needed at the nursing home. Filled with panic he runs for his car.

Connor arrives at the red bricked care home in record time and swinging open the door the usual oppressive heat hits him. He quickly walks the short corridor to the reception where he finds the nursing manager.

'Keely?' he asks, his eyes wide.

'Oh, hi Connor, it's okay, don't worry, your mum is comfortable,' she says. 'The doctor was round earlier - she's got pneumonia. He's put her on antibiotics. We just thought we should contact you on the off chance you weren't planning on visiting today.'

'Can I see her?'

'Yes, yes, go on through. She's a bit wiped out.'

'Thanks.'

Connor enters the room. With all the monitors and paraphernalia, the room looks even smaller. The raspberry swirl carpet looks brighter than usual and the smell of disinfectant lingers in the air.

'What's been happening, eh Mum? Can't leave you alone for a day, can I?' he says under his breath.

He pulls up the chair and sits beside her. He hadn't meant to miss his regular visit yesterday, but work had been mad and by the time he'd finished he had a pounding headache and decided that he wanted nothing more than to go to bed. He regrets that decision as he looks at Minnie's ashen appearance with the oxygen mask covering her mouth.

'Oh Mum,' he whispers, and by taking her hand her eyes flicker open. She manages a weak smile.

'Hi Mum. How you feeling?' he signs slowly. *'Had better days, eh?'*

She nods a yes as her eyes gently close again. A few moments pass before she wearily opens them again.

'Have you seen your dad?' Her signs lack their usual distinction and if it wasn't her usual opening question he would have struggled to understand.

Taking her hands Connor gently places them back on the bed. *'It's okay, you rest,'* he signs. *'You need to get better. Sleep. I'll sit here. Don't worry about anything, Mum. I'm here.'*

As his mother drifts back to sleep Connor reaches for his phone and texts his agency to let them know that he is finished for the day. Luckily he doesn't have any further appointments, but even if he did, Maggie is such a good boss, she'd understand. Pneumonia - guess that happens to a lot of old people, he thinks, though he's not sure all of them need oxygen. His mother's face is the colour of the pillow she rests on, only with a tinge of grey. He wonders if she can bounce back. He reaches for her hand again just as she stirs. In a moment her eyes shoot wide open and she wrenches the mask from her face whilst emitting a panicked high shrill. Connor moves to help which only turns her shrill into a shriek as she recoils in fear. The noise is deafening and just as Connor is feeling completely helpless the door flies open and a nurse rushes in.

'It's okay, Minnie, it's ok,' she says, leaning over his mother. Automatically he moves to interpret, to soothe his mother in her natural language, but as he does Minnie screeches again.

'Might be better if you stand over there, love,' the nurse says.

Connor removes himself to the corner of the room and watches as the nurse talks to Minnie, strokes her hand and reassures her that 'everything is okay and how it should be'. His insides shake and his heart plummets at the realisation that this is the first time Minnie hasn't recognised him. Is this the start of the next phase of her demise?

After what seems like an hour, but is probably more like five minutes, Minnie is comfortably settled with her oxygen mask back on.

'You can come back now,' the nurse says over her shoulder. 'She's lucid again.'

Connor gulps hard. 'Thanks.'

'You alright, love?' The nurse rubs his arm and he nods. 'Give me a shout if you need me again, ok?' She turns to Minnie. 'Be round to see you later, love.' Connor pulls up the chair to sit beside his mother as the nurse leaves the room.

Minnie blinks slowly and focuses on Connor. *'Have you seen your dad?'*

'Yes, Mum.' He feels a golf ball trapped in his throat.

Minnie's brow furrows. *'You alright, C?'*

'Yes, Mum.' He forces a smile that sticks his lips to his teeth.

Minnie raises one hand and looks him squarely in the eyes as she signs, *'Whatever it is, love, don't worry. I love you'.*

Tears well in Connor's eyes. *'I love you too, Mum.'*

Chapter 24

'*Thanks for coming with me,*' Greta signs to Mia as they take their seats on the early morning train. '*Supposing they ask me something I can't answer?*'

'*Grets, you'll be fab! It's exciting – it'll just be like the filming you've already done except you'll find out about the others who've been involved. And anyway, you certainly look the part.*'

'*Not too much?*' Greta gestures up and down herself.

'*Not at all.*'

Halving a sachet of sugar, they stir it into their skinny lattes as the train pulls away.

'*How are you doing?*' Greta asks.

'*Er.*' Mia looks out of the window at the blue-grey sky over autumnal trees. '*Coming out of denial slowly. These,*' she says, looking down at her breasts, '*don't lie - they are growing by the day.*'

'*Lucky you.*'

Mia pulls a face. '*Don't be envious. The nausea won't go, I have this taste in my mouth and I can't poop for love nor money!*'

Greta grimaces and takes a sip of her drink. '*Have you been to the doctors yet?*'

Mia nods. '*Yep, had it confirmed. It was nice Dr Cromes. I especially wanted her – I knew she wouldn't make me feel bad, you know?*' Greta nods, knowing how some GPs might have been a little judgemental. '*Anyway, she asked me about my plans and stuff.*'

'*And, what did you tell her?*'

'*That I don't know.*' Mia averts her eyes.

Greta reaches across the table and touches her hand. '*You know it'll be alright, don't you?*'

Mia pulls an exasperated face. '*No, I don't! Come on, Grets, you know me, I can't even look after myself, let alone a baby! I don't shop for food regularly, I get drunk too much, I hate cleaning*' *the flat and I'll be the first to admit that I haven't even grown up yet.'*

Greta taps the side of her cup with the stirrer. *'Are you thinking of an abortion?'*

'I wish it were an option, it would be so easy.' Her eyes lower. *'But it's just not for me; all that Catholic schooling takes its toll.'*

'Right. So, with that out of the way, you can either think about adoption or keeping the baby.'

'That's pretty much where I'm at. Some days I'm sure that adoption is the way to go and then at night, when I imagine this little person growing inside of me, it seems like it's the last thing in the world I want to do.' She sighs deeply.

'You don't have to decide now.'

Mia nods slowly. *'I'm thinking about contacting Jerry too.'*

'He's the father?'

'If the dates the doc said are right, then, yeah.' Mia nods her head slowly.

'If you keep el bambino then a bit of co-parenting might be handy.'

Mia rolls her eyes. *'Not sure about that. I probably won't see him for dust!'*

'Sod him then,' Greta signs, breaking a piece of croissant and popping it in her mouth. *'If he's not interested, I'll be there! Hell, I'll even be your birthing partner!'*

Mia raises her cup. *'You'll never see me in the same light again!'* The sound of the two breaking into laughter makes their fellow passengers turn to look. Greta smiles at Mia, thinking how this sign language lark has its advantages; they can discuss whatever they like (as they just have) in a crowded commuter train and their fellow passengers are none the wiser.

•

Jenni, looking as chic as ever, is waiting at the reception of the Broadcasting Hub to greet the participants.

'Greta!' She smiles and hugs her warmly. 'Lovely to see you again.'

'Hi. I brought Mia, hope it's okay.'

'Yes, yes of course.' Jenni turns to Mia. 'You're more than

110

welcome. We'll find you a seat near the cameras and you can watch.' Mia smiles and raises her thumbs.

'I'll get our intern, Janice, to take you both through to the studio, and when all the participants are here I'll come through and start the briefing, okay?' Jenni smiles.

'Is Connor here?' Greta asks.

'Ah, no.' Jenni frowns. 'The agency let me know that it'll be a different interpreter today. Jane someone. Is that okay?'

Greta forces a smile. 'Yep, that's fine.'

As they follow the young intern through to the studio, disappointment gnaws at Greta's gut; until this moment she hadn't realised just how much she was looking forward to seeing him again. In these days of worrying about her father and what's going on with Olly, the thought of Connor is her one salvation. His laidback nature, the way he looks at her, their communication and the light-hearted flirting are tiny positives in her troubled life. And now she's not even going to have the opportunity to ask him to interpret for her at audiology. Aaargh – she can't just go with her mother! Anyway, she thinks, smoothing her outfit, all this can be thought out later, for now it's show time!

The wide white round stage is set with eight silver and lime chairs placed in a horseshoe. Beside each chair is a small table holding a jug and glass for water. Janice directs Greta to a seat and escorts Mia to a chair off camera.

'Oh My God, Mia, I am shitting myself!' Greta signs. *'These lights are bright.'*

'And you look amazing under them!'

Just then a woman brandishing a large powder pot and a make-up brush appears. Greta smiles and dutifully sits still whilst the woman applies bronze powder over her face. When she's finished the woman squeezes Greta's arm.

'We've gone for Greek goddess,' she says kindly, smiling.

'Just alive would be good,' Greta jokes.

Just then Jenni appears with the other five candidates. There's one young dark haired handsome man in a wheelchair, a support worker with a wispy blonde blind woman on her arm, a slightly older fellow with Downs Syndrome, a hippy looking woman with one arm and a man whose disability isn't obvious. Beside Jenni is a neatly presented middle aged woman who waves to Greta.

'Hi, my name's Jane,' she signs. 'I'm the interpreter.' Greta raises her thumb. 'How do you like to work?'

'I'll use my voice but will look at you for the rest.'

'Great, no problem.'

'OK,' Jenni begins. 'First of all, I'd like to thank you all for coming and for your continued commitment to this documentary.' Greta watches Jane's interpretation and as clear and as understandable as it is, a part of her pines for the comfort blanket of Connor. 'You've all been filmed individually and you'll each have your own episode, the order of which hasn't been decided yet, but we'll let you know. For the final programme, we want an 'around the table' discussion. We're just going to fit you all with microphones.'

As a scruffy man with low hanging jeans starts to fit microphones and battery packs on each participant, Jenni continues.

'Let's do some introductions, OK?' Everyone nods. 'I'll start – you all know me, Jenni Fields, and I am responsible for The Art of Being Disabled. It's a project close to my heart and I'm so excited that soon I'll be sharing it with hopefully millions of viewers.' She turns and gestures to the man in the wheelchair.

'Hi, I'm Sam and I'm a sculptor. Looking forward to seeing the end result of all this.'

'Jo,' the blind young woman says. 'And this is my support worker, Mandy. I'm an admin clerk by day and a musician by night.'

'I'm Griff,' the fellow with Downs says. 'I dance.'

'What kind?' asks Jo.

'Any kind you want,' Griff replies to light laughter.

'I'm Donna and I'm an actress.'

'Been in anything we'd know?' asks Griff.

'A few minor roles in a couple of films – but it's more community films.' She flashes him a winning smile.

'My name's Matt. I'm your local Banksy.' Everyone giggles and, as he doesn't offer any insight into his disability, heads turn to Greta.

'Hi, my name is Greta.' They all smile encouragingly. 'I specialise in charcoal drawings with a depressive theme.'

They all give small chuckles.

'I'm sure your work is charming,' Donna says, smiling.

'Right,' Jenni says, addressing the group. 'Now you're all fitted with microphones we need to do a sound check.' As each participant's level is monitored Jenni passes a pile of papers to Sam. 'Please take one and pass them on. And I'll give you time to read through so you can get an idea of what we're going to be talking about, OK?'

As each participant receives their papers, light chatter breaks out. Greta looks out to Mia and they exchange grins. Greta reads through the list of questions that cover topics such as whether there's a need for more disabled artists, how disability influences art, and what future aspirations they all hold.

'OK,' Jenni says after a few minutes. 'Can we put the crib sheets out of camera please.' Everyone hands their paper to the intern. 'OK, so I'll throw out a question for discussion and you all join in as and when. Just be yourselves, you've all got something of value to contribute so please don't be shy. We can stop filming if anyone needs to, so please just say. Right, any questions before we start?' Looking around everyone shakes their head. 'If we're all ready then? Let's roll the cameras.'

Chapter 25

'Good evening.' Jenni smiles to the camera. 'My name is Jenni Fields and welcome to the final episode of The Art of Being Disabled. Over the past six weeks you've been introduced to our artists.' The camera pans to each participant. 'Sam, Jo, Griff, Donna, Matt and Greta, and tonight we are going to talk to the artists to find out a little more about their thoughts on disability and how disabled people are represented in the arts.'

Greta's stomach performs a little somersault.

'Firstly,' Jenni continues, turning to the panel, 'Welcome and thank you for joining me.' Everyone nods, smiles and makes small responses. ''I'd like to start with how you feel your art is influenced by your disability? Any thoughts on that?'

Griff jumps in. 'Nobody thinks that a person with Downs Syndrome can dance. We're seen as incapable, but dancing is something we can do. I have flexible joints,' He throws his arms over his head and everyone gasps at how far back they go. 'So that makes me perfect for dancing.'

'Thank you, Griff.' Jenni looks at the others.

'Being blind,' Jo starts. 'I find that I have an acute sense of sound – it's like my ears are compensating for my eyes. It makes my music sharper.' She shrugs. 'I think so anyway.'

Everyone gives a small laugh.

'Being a disabled actress,' Donna says. 'I find that I can empathise with the struggles facing the characters I play – it gives me a greater insight.

Greta takes a deep breath. 'I think that with any art the artist's experiences have to be a part of it – it's about expressing yourself. For example, I don't set out to do it, but I find that a lot of my drawings represent isolation. As a deaf person, this is my experience.'

Donna frowns. 'You feel isolated all the time?'

Greta looks away from the interpreter to Donna. 'No, not all the time, only in some situations.' Not wanting to repeat her earlier interview and the tears that followed, Greta takes a steadying breath. 'Imagine a room full of, say, Spanish people and you're the only one who can't speak the language – how do you feel?'

'So, having an interpreter solves the problem?' asks Banksy Matt.

'To some extent, yes. Maybe I need to start drawing an extra figure in my work – a person who bridges the gap,' Greta says with a light-hearted shrug.

'It's an interesting concept that disabled artists could incorporate whatever they need into their work. For you, Greta, it would be an interpreter,' Jenni says.

'For me, it's my support worker or a dog,' adds Jo, the night musician.

'I reject a prosthetic,' Donna says. 'This is me, and I accept me as I am. If people are offended by my lack of arm then it really is their problem.'

'Mine is obviously my chair,' says Sculptor Sam.

'And for me, it's people's understanding,' Banksy Matt says. 'With bi-polar disorder I need the people around me to know and understand what happens to me. It's an interesting thought but I don't think your audience needs to have an insight into your disability – the work of art should stand on its own. A performance or a painting should be judged on its merit and not on whether it was created by a disabled person.'

From there the conversation twists and turns with very little input from Jenni. Actress Donna declares the label, 'disabled', shouldn't even exist, 'we are all disabled in one way or another – who draws that line?' she argues, and Sculptor Sam controversially claims that non-disabled artists are boring in comparison. Dancer Griff becomes choked when he recounts his relationship with his family and how it prompted him to start dancing and Musician Jo raises the issue of whether her music is genuinely appreciated or whether it's a sympathy vote. As the time flies by Greta loses herself in the discussions, completely forgetting that it is all being filmed.

'What about the future then?' Jenni asks, rounding up the session. 'How about the one wish question?' She turns to her left. 'Sam?'

'I wish there was no difference between disabled and non-disabled artists.'

'Totally disagree,' Actress Donna says. 'We need to celebrate our differences! People need to be all encompassing – embracing art from all sectors!' She waggles her to-the-elbow arm, accentuating her point.

'That's kind of what I meant,' says Sculptor Sam.

'I think there should be a difference.' Banksy Matt says. 'We aren't like non-disabled people – we are different. But if I had one wish it would be to focus on the art and not on the artist.'

'Kind of wouldn't be here then,' Musician Jo says quietly.

'What about you, Jo?' Jenni asks.

'I just want my music to reach as many people as possible, and if that means using disability as a platform then that's what I'll do.' She shrugs lightly.

'Fair enough,' Jenni responds. 'Griff?'

'I want to dance at Sadler's Wells.'

'Wonderful. Greta?'

'Er, well, I'm considering a cochlear implant so I'd like to see if, when I can hear more, whether this will impact on the topics of my drawings. I like to think it might bring a fresh perspective.'

Actress Donna turns in her seat. 'Love, if you don't mind me saying, you're going down the wrong alley. You're not going to find what you're looking for through trying to mainstream yourself.'

The room is silent as Greta follows the slight delay in translation. 'What do you mean?'

'You're trying to fix your deafness,' Donna says. 'Trying to make yourself more like people who can hear. It's not going to work, it's who you are that counts, it's self-acceptance - that's what's important. Whether your ears work or not doesn't matter.'

Greta bites her lip. The cameras, lights and all eyes on her are overwhelming. Her eyes dart and her cheeks burn with humiliation and indignation. How dare this disability rights hippy talk to her like this?

'So, Donna, what's your wish for the future?' Jenni intercedes.

Turning back to Jenni she says, 'I want to be a role model for amputees. Just because we lack a limb it doesn't mean we can't reach for the stars.' She waggles her arm again.

'And on that note, let me thank you all for being a part of The Art of Being Disabled.' Jenni then turns to the camera. 'Well, that's all for now. I hope you've enjoyed this fascinating look at disabled artists, their views and their work. Thank you for watching. Good night.'

Relieved sighs and chatter break out as the cameras stop rolling. Greta grimaces at Mia.

'Oh My God, that was painful!' she signs.

'Urgh,' Mia signs back with her eye on Donna. 'Bet she's a vegan. And what is wrong with wearing a bra?'

'That was horrible, what she said. Hope they edit it. I didn't get the chance to respond. I feel totally patronised!'

'Don't worry – she'll just come across as a bully. Why do these right-on types think they know everything?'

Jane, the interpreter, approaches Greta. 'Was that okay?'

'Oh yes, fine. Thanks.'

'I know you've worked with Connor – hope swapping didn't throw you.'

'Oh, is that what happened?' Greta's stomach bubbles with nerves. 'You had to swap?'

'Yeah, I don't know why. I think he put in a request – though with the job I was doing he definitely got the short straw.' Jane laughs. 'Been lovely to meet you.'

'You too,' As Jane walks away Greta's chest heaves and her heart sinks wondering why he asked to swap; did he not want to see her? Just then she feels her phone buzz in her pocket. Pulling it out her heart leaps as she reads the message on the screen.

Hi Switch. Can we meet? I miss you. xx

Chapter 26

With ten minutes to spare before she has to get up, Greta stretches out her legs and sinks into the soft mattress. There's something about her teenage bed that induces sleep – it's probably all those lie-ins until noon that used to drive her mother mad. Pulling the duvet up to her chin she reflects on the filming at the Broadcasting Hub that mostly went well; shame about the ending and that awful woman. Guess she'll just have to wait and see how it all comes out in the edit.

Her mind flicks to Olly's message. She hadn't answered it immediately as she had to attend to handshakes and goodbyes, but ten minutes into the train journey when Mia's eyes could no longer stay open, Greta pulled the phone out of her pocket.

She wondered what to say. For him to text that he missed her is quite a big deal – maybe this trial separation has been just what they needed. She'd twirled a lock of hair round her finger and then composed a response, deleted it, typed it again, amended it and eventually sent it.

Hi Olly, yes would love to see you. Miss you too x

By the time they were half way home a message pinged back and before long they had fixed plans to meet on Saturday night at their old haunt, The Pigs' Trotters. His texts were warm and friendly, and so now, staring up at the artexed ceiling, she feels a small tug of excitement in her belly that maybe this is the start of the new and improved Greta and Olly. Through having loved and almost lost he'll be a changed man and will communicate his feelings more, think about himself a little less and maybe even learn a few signs?

Her mother's head appears around the door. 'Morning Greta,' she says. 'Just wanted to make sure you're not oversleeping.' A smile plays on her lips.

'Morning Mum. What's funny?'

'I have been standing there knocking for ages. Silly me!' She rolls her eyes. 'I think me and your father are out of touch with having you here.'

'Well, it might not be for much longer – Olly texted me yesterday.'

Sylvia moves to the bed and sits. 'Did he? What did he say?'

'He misses me. Wants to see me. So, we're going out on Saturday night.'

'That's marvellous, dear.' Her mother claps her hands together. 'Be good to talk about things, won't it? See a path forward.'

'Blimey Mum, are you that keen to get rid of me?'

'Don't be ridiculous, darling, of course not. I just want you to be settled and happy. Olly is good for you – you two can put this blip behind you and get on with your lives.'

Sylvia swings out of the room and Greta swears that if she could hear it would be the sound of her mother humming a jaunty tune.

Her phone buzzes on her bedside table. Picking it up Mia's name flashing tells her that it's a video call. Sitting up and propping the phone up on the side she hits 'receive' and waves 'hello'.

'Morning, gorgeous!' Mia signs. The way her dark curls are shooting in a hundred directions and the tiny flowered wallpaper behind her indicates that she isn't out of bed either. *'I'm not going in today – feeling pukey but wanted to catch you. You going to The Jolly Sailor tonight?'*

'Hang on, hang on,' Greta signs, holding her palms out. *'You're feeling pukey and yet you're going to the pub tonight?'*

Mia pulls a face. *'It's called morning sickness for a reason! Around six o'clock I tend to feel much better – it's just the way it goes.'* She puffs hair out of her eyes.

Greta laughs. *'Right, yeah, OK, I'm game. Why not? Could do me good.'*

Mia's brow furrows. *'You okay?'*

'Olly texted me. Says he misses me.'

'Ah. So, are you seeing him?' Mia asks.

'Going out Saturday night. I don't really know what to think – but it's good that he misses me, isn't it?'

'Yeah, mate, of course. Go. See what he wants to say. Maybe he's a reformed character.'

Greta purses her lips. *'He doesn't need that much reforming – just a little brush up maybe.'*

'Bet Sylvia's chuffed.' Mia picks at a thread on her night t-shirt.

'Clucking like a mother hen. She's pretty intent on me and him staying together. It's always amazed me that he puts in little effort with her but she worships the ground he walks on.'

'I think he just has the right look, right job, right aspirations, you know?' Mia replies.

'Hmmm.' Greta shrugs. *'Anyway, what time we meeting tonight?'*

'How about coming to me straight from work and then we can get ready together and head out?'

'Haven't done that for a long time!' Greta giggles at the memory of the regular monthly preparation sessions, usually at Mia's flat, when they would open a cheap bottle of white and then doll themselves up to the nines. It was the calendar highlight of the month; the one event every deaf person in the area would flock to. *'Let's do it, Mia!'*

The corners of Mia's mouth downturn. *'I'll get a bottle of lemonade...'* she signs.

'How times change, my friend!'

Mia pats her belly. *'I know.'*

'How you feeling?'

'You know? Okay, apart from the sickness. I mean, I've been thinking a lot and I really think I can do this. I'm definitely going to contact Jerry too.'

'Haven't you done that yet?' Mia shakes her head. *'Cluck cluck chicken!'*

Mia smiles. *'I know. Normally I'd have a couple of drinks and go for it.'*

'Aw, my poor little tee-total luvvie.'

Mia salutes her friend with two fingers. *'It's very hard having to face life sober! Anyway, he might be there tonight.'*

'Oooh yeah, hadn't thought of that! Is that why you're off today? Time to preen?'

Mia sticks out her tongue *'Hanging up now!'*

'See you tonight!'

Greta smiles and is happily snuggling back down in bed

when the door swings open to reveal her mother standing with her hands on her hips.

'Greta Elise!'

'OK, OK - I'm up!'

Chapter 27

A red and black patterned carpet that has soaked up a thousand spilt drinks, dog-eared menus on sticky tables and riotous happy hours are the main attractions of The Jolly Sailor. It's a multi-level modern pub housed in a beamed building and has been the once-a-month haunt ever since the deaf youth decided that the deaf club was the domain of the oldies. Greta always felt that somewhere a little up-market might be preferable, but this place is kind of fit for purpose; many of the chic places with low intimate lighting just aren't conducive to people who need to see to communicate.

'What you having?' Greta asks Mia.

'Er, soda and lime, ta. I'll come with you.'

The two head for the long curved oak bar, waving and smiling at familiar faces along the way. Greta watches the young bar staff going through their monthly ritual of trying to understand the array of deaf people asking for drinks. A while back they placed little pencils and pads along the bar for the really tricky customers which Greta considered quite astute. Although, as the vibrations thump in her chest she thinks that turning down the music might be the first step...

The barman pulls back his long-hair and thrusts his ear towards Greta. 'Eh?'

'Soda and lime.' Greta automatically finger-spells the 'S' and 'L' as if it could help. 'And a white wine.' He frowns at her sign. Looking around for a pad and pencil she feels someone push in behind her and grab her server's attention. Abruptly turning she finds herself face to face with Connor.

'Soda and lime and a white wine please, mate.' he shouts.

The barman smiles with relief and raises his thumb - *oh, now he can sign!* - and goes off to make the drinks.

'Hi.' Connor faces Greta, his lip slightly twitching. *'Hope you didn't mind?'* He gestures to the bar.

'Er, I could've done it on my own.'

'No, I know you could – I just thought I'd help. Sorry.' He blushes wondering why he always stuffs things up with this girl - of course he shouldn't have placed her order - she's not a child!

She gives him a small smile. *'No worries.'*

'How are you?' He fixes her with a stare.

'Good thanks. Finished filming for the programme – just waiting to hear when it'll be shown.'

The barman returns with the drinks.

'Please, let me,' Connor signs, reaching for his wallet.

'Thank you.' Greta smiles. *'You want to join us? We're just going to find a table.'*

'Oh thanks, but no, I'm meeting a few old friends and hoping to bump into my brother. Good to see you again though.' He passes the two drinks and with a nod and a smile then turns back to the bar to pay. Signing goodbye and walking away Greta yet again has the feeling that she's done something to upset him; he's just not the same man she went to the coffee shop with. Did he just feel sorry for her that night after the way Olly behaved? They'd seemed so close - had she imagined it? Shrugging her shoulders, she turns back to Mia and nods for her to follow to the other side of the pub, where they sit at a long trestle table.

The evening jogs along nicely. Not having been here for so long Greta is welcomed back to the bosom of the Deaf Community with gusto. People ask where she's been, what she's been doing and where she's been hiding. No sooner has she caught up with one group of friends than others appear. She feels a little like royalty in a whirl of hugs and laughter. She inwardly vows to never leave it so long again.

'So,' Lucy, a fellow old school friend starts. *'Look what I did.'* She pulls back her shiny brown hair to reveal the round disk shaped cochlear implant processor magnetised to just above her ear.

'Oh wow! I didn't know,' Greta signs. *'When did you have it done?'*

'About six months ago.'

'And? Do you like it?'

'Honestly, I was so sceptical,' Lucy signs. *'I heard all these stories about bionic ears and all that, but wondered if it was over hyped. But then I kept getting ear infections and the doctor said it*

was my hearing aids that were causing them so I decided to look into a CI. Honestly Greta, I am so glad I did. It wasn't easy at first – everything sounds very robotic – but you get used to it and they tune you in and then retune you and now, well, I know I don't hear like they do - honestly, it's different - but I hear some things so well. Wish I'd had it done ages ago!'

Greta smiles. *'I'm so pleased for you. No negatives at all?'*

'It's a pain in the arse at airport security but apart from that, no.'

'I could live with that! Don't fly much anyway.' Just then Greta's eye just catches Jerry leaning on the nook bar, a pint in his hand, surveying the scene. She can see what attracted Mia to him with his strong chin, chiselled features and golden-brown dreadlocks that lightly brush the bar. Hurriedly making her apologies to Lucy, Greta scurries off to find Mia, who she finds still seated at the table. She waves for her attention.

'Twelve o'clock, Jerry,' she surreptitiously signs.

Mia gulps. *'I feel sick.'*

'You feel sick all the time. Get over there.'

'Where?' She leans forward to see him and then shoots back in her seat. *'Aargh.'*

'Come on, Mia, you have to talk to him.'

'Talking is easy – it's signing that's difficult!'

'Very funny. Go!' Greta points to the bar.

Mia rises and makes her way along the line of seated deaf people, apologising and thanking them for letting her out. Jerry is looking the opposite direction as Mia approaches and taps him on the arm.

'Hey there, stranger!' she signs.

'Mia! How great to see you!' His baby blue eyes light up with a wide grin. *'How are you?'*

'Not bad.' She lowers her eyes and feels the heat rising in her neck. *'How about you?'*

'Good, all good.' He leans forward, beaming. *'You managed to finish that cake then?'*

'Ha ha, very funny. It took a while.'

'Did you get your NDO joining pack?' He pushes a stray dreadlock back over his shoulder.

'Yeah yeah. No problem. I'm a fully paid up card carrying

deaf person.' She makes a solidarity fist.

'Pleased to hear it. You know, I think they should sell cheaper drinks to those in the organisation. Talking of which,' he eyes her empty glass. *'What you having? I'd suggest avoiding the vodka this time.'* His eyebrows bounce up and down suggestively.

'Er, er, I'm okay thanks.' She looks at her glass. *'In fact, there's something I need to tell you -'*

'Jerry!' A rather squat brunette in a clinging emerald green dress drunkenly stumbles between them. *'I was wondering where you are. I've been looking for you.'*

Jerry smiles. *'Mia, this is Lucinda. Lucinda, Mia.'*

Lucinda looks at Mia before turning back to Jerry.

'I emailed you this week. You didn't get back to me.' She pouts her full scarlet lips.

'I haven't forgotten, I'm still working on it. I'll get back soon.' He crosses his heart. *'I promise.'*

'Anyway, that's business, let's not mix it with pleasure.' Lucinda runs a finger down his arm and then strokes his torso.

'You never change, Luce.' He smirks.

'And what does that mean?' Lucinda laughingly hits him (Mia didn't think that people over the age of sixteen still did that.) *'You are a cheeky devil; a very bad influence.'*

'Am I now?'

Mia doesn't know if it's pregnancy hormones or this sickening flirty conversation but she feels bilious. She can clearly see that these two have history, (and a future if Lucinda gets her way) and so, feeling totally surplus to requirements Mia wonders if they'd notice if she slipped away. She would honestly try to join in but Lucinda employs the age-old trick of half turning her back to her. Hmm, Lucinda may be drunk, but stupid she isn't.

'I'm just going to..' Mia signals to re-join her friends.

'Oh no, wait,' Jerry signs. *'You wanted to talk about something?'*

Mia waves dismissively. *'No, no worries. Nothing important. See you.'* She nods to Lucinda and makes her way back to the safety of her friends.

Greta pounces. *'And?'*

'Didn't you see? Lucinda Lush wouldn't leave us alone.'

'You going to catch him later?'

'No, I'm not. Not so sure I'm that enamoured with a man who's impressed with a woman like that.' Her eyes drift back to Lucinda who is now almost on top of a twinkly-eyed smiling Jerry.

'Aw, mate,' Greta puts her arm around her friend. *'I didn't think it was about wanting him, I thought it was about shared parenting?'*

'It is, I suppose.' She sighs deeply. *'Anyway, what about your interpreter fella, eh?'*

Greta feels her cheeks heat up. *'Don't know what you mean.'*

'Gre-ta?' She raises her eyebrows.

'Nothing happening there either. And neither should it! I'm going out with Olly on Saturday – that's where my head's at.'

Mia nods. *'Yeah, course, sure. Another drink?'*

'Yeah, why not.'

Greta watches Mia make her way through the room of a hundred flying hands. As the crowd parts, Greta just catches sight of Connor laughing and heading for the door with a group of friends. Her smile slowly slips from her lips as she looks down at her empty glass. It really isn't a case of Connor vs Olly; she hasn't got two suitors, it's not some love triangle that needs sorting. So why does she feel downhearted? Connor is nothing more than a crush. Olly is the man she has chosen to share her life with and her carefully planned future with him will soon be back on track. They will learn from this hiccup and be happier and more in love than ever.

So, what is this unease in her belly? Watching the saloon style doors swing shut she tries to dismiss the idea that it could have anything at all to do with the man who's just left.

Chapter 28

With a towel wrapped around her, Greta takes skinny jeans and the red top with the soft falling neckline, that Olly loves her to wear, from the wardrobe and places them on the bed. She crosses to her underwear drawer and wonders if it's presumptuous to pick the black and pink bra and knickers that he bought her last Christmas? Is that jinxing the evening? Will they end up in bed? Or will they do that 'take thing slowly and just date' thing? Knowing Olly, she guesses it'll be the former, but not wishing to appear expectant she chooses the subtler duck egg blue matching set.

Dressed and ready with perfect make up and a liberal application of perfume she skips downstairs to the lounge where her parents are watching a wildlife documentary.

'Oooh dressed to kill, Gretsy,' her father says, looking up with a big smile.

'Tuck your top in, dear,' her mother says, gesturing as such.

'No, Mum, I like it like this.'

'Where's he taking you?' her father asks.

'Pigs' Trotters.'

Her father chuckles. 'Oh, that's romantic.'

'It kind of is - it was 'our' place.'

'Fair enough.' Her father says as both he and Sylvia look to the door. 'That'll be him.'

'Don't wait up,' Greta says.

'Wait a minute,' Sylvia says, getting up. 'Where are your manners? Bring him in. Let him say hello.'

Greta inwardly groans. She doesn't need this now; her mother fawning all over Olly and them engaging in a conversation she can't fully be a part of. But before she has time to argue her mother has raced past her to the door, leaving her helpless but to watch the pair greet each other.

'Hi Greta,' Olly says in passing as her mother practically

drags him by the arm to the lounge. Greta stands half in the doorway, smiling benignly, watching the three of them chat and laugh. Finally, after a pause Olly turns to Greta.

'Right, you ready?'

She nods. Her parents bid their farewells and offer jokes about the time they expect him to 'bring their daughter back home'. Olly gives them his cheekiest grin, kisses her mother's cheek and then, taking Greta's arm, guides her out of the house.

'Ol' Sylvia doesn't change, does she?' he says, as his foot hits the throttle. As Greta's head hits the headrest she can't help thinking how his reckless driving is somehow familiarly comforting. How does a bad habit in your partner become something endearing?

'Sylvia is Sylvia,' she says.

'I on't na I mid ee re.'

'What?' Greta says, finding his forgetting to face her not such an adorable trait.

He looks to her and smiles. 'Tell you later, Switch.'

She smiles back. As he returns his eyes to the road she takes the opportunity to look him over. His hair has grown and he's using more gel to keep it in place. He's wearing the blue shirt that she loves and the scent of Issey Miyake overpowers the pungent leather upholstery. She knows all of this is for her and a warm feeling rises at the possibilities of the evening ahead.

Entering the pub with its quaint beams and brass rubbings Olly heads for the bar.

'The usual?' he asks Greta as he jumps up onto a bar stool.

'Er, red wine please. Shall I get a table?'

'Don't fancy the bar stools?' he teases.

She pulls a face. 'Somewhere quieter would be good.'

He raises his thumb, gives a dazzling smile and leans over to peck her cheek. 'Sure.'

Greta smiles as she turns to find somewhere to sit. Making her way through the early evening crowd, she spots Jerry seated at a table with a fellow she's seen around the deaf scene. As they seem deep in conversation she decides against saying hello. Instead she parks herself on a low stool at a small round table near the back of the pub. She quickly whips out her compact mirror to check her face and hair, adjusts her top and waits patiently for Olly. Very soon she sees him making his way with a drink in each hand and three bags of crisps hanging out of his mouth. She knows they'll all be salt and vinegar.

'Here you go,' he says, placing the drinks and blowing the crisps from his mouth.

'What're you like?' She laughs. 'Ooh all salt and vinegar - what a surprise!'

He straddles the stool. 'You love them too! Well, you used to…' He looks up at her with those dark lashed eyes.

'Olly, we've only been apart a few weeks - I haven't changed that much.'

'Good, Switch, cos I liked you the way you were.'

'Liked?'

He looks down at his pint and back up. 'Okay, loved.' They exchange silent smiles and Olly reaches for her hand. 'How've you been?'

'Okay, I suppose. Not easy with Dad. Gave us all a scare.'

'Yeah, I'm sure. Bad timing with us being apart and all that too.' She bites her tongue from saying how he should've stepped up to support her despite their agreement to take a break. 'Still,' he continues. 'He looks like he's doing okay.'

'Yes he is. Mum's been on good form too.'

Olly chokes on his gulp of beer. 'Wow! Sylvia not driving you mad?'

'No. In fact she's quite different since Dad's heart attack. Like I said, I think it scared us all. Anyway, how've you been? Out every night drinking?'

Olly looks suitably chagrined. 'Something like that.' He stares into his drink for a moment. 'It's given me time to think though.'

'Yeah?'

'I've missed you,' he says.

She smiles and squeezes his hand. 'I've missed you too.'

He exhales. 'Are we good then?'

'Olly, just cos we've missed each other it doesn't really solve our problems.'

'What are our problems? That I wasn't keen on you going on that television show? Well, that's over now, isn't it? And I will try harder to include you when we're with my friends. We've always known it's not easy.'

'True.' She chews her lip. 'Would you learn a bit of sign language for me?'

He leans his head provocatively to one side. 'Why don't you teach me?'

'OK deal.' She grins. 'A sign a day.'

He cups his hand under her chin and kisses her softly. As she feels his warm lips over hers she realises just how much she's missed him. His sweet masculine smell envelops her and as he releases her, his face is filled with longing. That's her Olly. This is where she belongs. This is the man she loves.

'Drink up,' he says, his breath coming unevenly. He reaches in his pocket for his car keys.

Taking the last sip of her wine she says, 'Oh - what was it you said in the car?'

'When?'

'Earlier, when you were driving. You said you'd tell me later.'

He furrows his brow. 'Dunno. Can't remember.' He shrugs. 'Probably wasn't important.'

Hmmm.

They grab their coats and are heading for the door when she sees Jerry heading towards them.

'Hey, Greta, right?' he signs.

'Hi Jerry. How you doing?' she signs and then realises Olly won't understand. 'Sorry,' she signs and speaks at the same time. 'Jerry, this is Olly. Olly, Jerry.' Jerry extends his hand and Olly reluctantly takes it. Greta turns to Olly. 'Jerry is Mia's friend.'

'Oh,' Olly says, exhaling with evident relief. 'Nice to meet you,' he says slightly too loudly with over emphasised lips.

Jerry nods. *'Yeeaaah, okay.. Nice to meet you too. Have a great evening.'* He smiles and walks away.

'Is that her latest squeeze?' Olly asks as they make their way to the car.

'Kind of.'

'Tell me more.'

'It was a one night stand that has consequences.'

The realisation hits his face. 'Mia's up the duff? Oh, that's priceless!' He throws his head back laughing, tosses his keys in the air and cockily catches them. 'Does the poor sucker know?'

'Olly it's not funny and no, he doesn't.'

Howling with laughter Olly unlocks the car and slides in.

'Olly,' Greta continues with a warning tone. 'It's *not* public knowledge.'

He zips his lips with his fingers and pulls an angelic face. 'Right, where to?'

She shrugs. 'I don't mind.'

'Back to where we left off, Switch? I've missed you.'

'Me too, you too.'

'That doesn't even make sense.' He laughs and lurches towards her, pulling her body towards his. As he passionately covers her lips with his she responds eagerly and they slide further into the bucket seat. Their kisses are full of longing and a mutual desire to revisit a place they've been to a thousand times. Their limbs tangle and their hearts beat in loud throbs and very soon the Audi's windows are mistily steamed.

'Home, Switch,' he says in a low growl. Scrabbling back into the driver's seat he starts the engine and sets off racing the roads.

Chapter 29

'Come along, Greta, what time's your appointment?' Sylvia says, slipping her feet into her shoes.

'Not until 10.30 - plenty of time,' Greta says, slowly buttoning her coat.

'We've got to get parked, don't forget.'

Greta sighs. Why did she agree to her mother accompanying her to the CI appointment? The weight of the impending decision sits onto her shoulders heavily enough without her mother adding to the pressure.

'OK, OK I'm ready.' Greta says, heaving her bag on her shoulder.

They climb into her mother's small Peugeot and make their way to the hospital. Sylvia talks incessantly about something and nothing and Greta makes small noises in agreement. Greta does realise that, at times, her mother is the sole person she doesn't mind not following.

Seated in the waiting room Greta is at least pleased that she has her mother's ears to rely on for when they announce her turn; 'hearing people do have their uses', she thinks, half smiling. To avoid having to pretend to be interested in her mother's small talk Greta picks up a ragged copy of Take A Break and immerses herself in similar nothingness.

'Come on, darling,' her mother says, tapping her arm.

Both rise and follow a waiting nurse into a side room. Her mother leads the way and when Greta steps into the room she's momentarily thrown by the sight of Connor. She had wanted him for this assignment but when she put in her request to the hospital they informed her that she would get 'whoever was available on that day'. He smiles and gestures to the seat opposite the audiologist.

'Hello Greta, my name is Barbara Hewson and I'm a senior audiologist.'

'Hello,' her mother jumps in. 'Sylvia Palmer, Greta's mother, lovely to meet you.' She smiles widely and extends her hand. Barbara takes it and shakes it firmly. As the two exchange pleasantries Greta looks to Connor who interprets. He's wearing grey trousers and a dark grey shirt that accentuates the green in his eyes. His hair is messy but rather endearingly it looks like he's tried to control the curls with some product. She inwardly chuckles that he could never be labelled a fashionista.

'Right,' Barbara says, turning to Greta. 'I hear you're considering a cochlear implant?'

'Yep. I'm not totally sure though.'

'That's fine. What we could do is test you to see if you're eligible and then discuss it further. You don't have to make an immediate decision but there is a long waiting list, so the sooner you decide, the sooner you'll go on the list.' She smiles kindly.

'What are the tests?'

'Firstly, we'll do an up to date audiogram and then some lip-reading perception tests.'

'She's very good at lip-reading, aren't you, Greta?' her mother adds.

A silence passes as Greta waits for Connor to interpret. 'Yes, I am,' Greta says, thinking how the irony is lost on half the participants in the room.

'Right,' Barbara continues. 'If you'd like to wait in the seating area just across from here.' She points to the door. 'And someone will call you for the audiogram. OK? Any questions so far?'

Greta and Sylvia shake their heads, give their thanks and leave the room. They sit on the low plastic chairs, Greta and Sylvia, side by side and Connor opposite.

Sylvia looks at Connor. 'Sorry, I don't think I caught your name?'

'Connor Walsh,' he says, flashing his badge.

'Have you two met before?' her mother continues.

'Yes, Mum. Connor was the interpreter on the TV programme,' Greta says.

'Ah, I see.' Sylvia's nose wriggles like a bad smell has permeated the room. 'When are they broadcasting that?' she asks Connor directly.

'Oh, I don't know,' he says and turns to Greta, *'Do you know?'*

'Know what?'

'When they're broadcasting The Art of Being Disabled?'

'Oh,' Greta says, switching her voice on for her mother. 'No, I don't know. I presume they'll let me know.'

Silence falls. Simultaneously Greta pretends to read the poster on the wall to avoid conversing with Sylvia and Connor pulls out his phone to avoid the awkwardness of translating for family. Sylvia reaches for Homes & Garden.

A few minutes later a door opens and a squat Chinese nurse appears. The three rise.

'Just Miss Palmer, please,' Connor interprets the nurse's words.

'I'll need the interpreter for instructions, if that's ok?' Greta says.

'Of course,' the nurse says. *'Interpreter can be with you at the start - that's fine.'*

'See you in a bit, Mum.'

Sylvia nods as Greta and Connor go through to a soundproofed booth with studded walls. Greta sits and places the large headphones over her ears and watches Connor relay what she has to do. As a child with mildly fluctuating hearing she went through this test many times, but in recent years her hearing, or lack of, having levelled has meant she hasn't needed testing. Understanding that she has to 'press a certain button when she hears a sound', 'not to worry if it's quiet for a while' and not to 'guess-press', Connor gives her the thumbs up and leaves her in the booth.

The test begins and Greta strains to hear low and high beeps and conscientiously presses the yellow button at the slightest sound. As she finishes, the nurse attends to the machine and the ensuing print-out. It suddenly dawns on Greta that her desire to *pass* this test is nonsensical. How can she? It's not like she can study for it! Or develop skills to improve her performance. What a strange thing that deaf people have to go through: a test that they have no chance of 'passing'. If you are born deaf, the first test you receive in life you are bound to fail, and then you continue to fail it every time – someone needs to do a study on what *that* does to self-esteem!

'Come, come now.' The nurse beckons her back out into the

waiting room where Connor immediately stands to interpret. *'The audiologist will do the other tests soon.'*

'Thank you,' Greta says and takes her seat once again.

'How did that go, darling?' her mother asks.

'Same as always, Mum, I can't hear.'

'Well, a cochlear implant could change all that.' Sylvia quickly replies.

'Hmm,' Greta says, catching Connor's subtly raised eyebrows.

Very soon Greta and Connor are taken back into the audiologist's room where Greta is subjected to lip-reading/guessing what Barbara is saying from behind a sheet of A4 paper. Greta throws out, 'dog', 'philandering', 'bamboozle' and 'chutney', safe in the knowledge that she doesn't have a chance in hell of getting any of them right. Barbara diligently records the results and then excuses herself as she swivels her chair around to study the spiky graph of the audiogram test and calculate the scores of the lip-reading.

Greta looks at Connor who gently breaks into a smile.

'Bamboozle?' he finger-spells. *'Chutney? What the ?'* He giggles quietly.

'Never understood daft medics who put paper over their mouths!'

'Fair point.' He laughs. *'I should've slyly interpreted them for you. Her face would've been a picture.'*

They both break into laughter which elicits a comment of, 'glad you're having fun,' from Barbara. Exchanging naughty schoolchildren expressions Connor and Greta repress further giggles.

'Right,' Barbara swings round in her chair. 'I'll just get your mother in.' And before Greta can desist Barbara is out the door and signalling to Sylvia to join them. Greta sighs.

'So, the good news,' Barbara starts with Connor interpreting, *'is that you are eligible for a unilateral cochlear implant. This is your audiogram.'* She holds up the paper with the chart. *'As you can see with the decibels above ninety you are categorised as profoundly deaf. This coupled with a score of four on the lip-reading assessment...'* Connor's face flickers a faint smile. *'Means you're an eligible candidate.'*

'Well that's wonderful news,' Sylvia enthuses. 'So, you really think a cochlear implant can help her?'

'Absolutely. In fact, Greta, you're an ideal candidate.' Barbara smiles.

'Well, dear?' She can feel her mother's metaphorical fingers on her back. Pushing, pushing.

'Which ear would you implant?' Greta asks.

'Your left,' Barbara answers, checking the chart.

'That's my best one.'

'Yes, we like to implant the better ear - greater chance of a success.'

'But if it goes wrong…'

'Of course there are risks,' Barbara continues. 'But there are risks associated with all operations. I can give you all the information to read. But I have to say, this is a tried and tested operation with superb results. People who have your level of deafness have had their hearing boosted to the point of being able to talk on the phone.'

Sylvia's eyes light up the room. 'Gosh.'

'Ok, right. I need time to think about this,' Greta says, feeling a strong urge to put on the brakes.

'Absolutely,' Barbara says. 'You can take all the time you want. We keep these test results on your file for a year - so you can resume the process at any time. OK?'

'Thank you.'

Barbara hands Greta a few information sheets and with goodbyes dispensed they leave the consultation room.

'I'm going to pay for the parking and then I need to nip to the ladies,' her mother says. 'Meet you at the car in five minutes?'

Greta nods and registers a sigh of relief as Sylvia disappears down the corridor.

'How you doing there?' Connor asks, his emerald eyes glinting with concern.

'Honestly?' She frowns. *'I don't know. It's a lot to take in. It's not just an operation, is it? It's like a statement that you think you can be cured, isn't it? That the doctors have been right all along and your pride in your identity and your language has all been a bit fake.'*

'Wow - you have thought about this,' he signs, clearly quite surprised. *'What about on a functional level though? Surely the biggest plus is that you might hear your nearest and dearest*

clearer.'

Greta looks in the direction her mother took. *'Hmm, and that's a good thing?'*

They both laugh.

'It's not just your mum though, is it?' Connor signs. Greta's frown deepens. *'While you were having the hearing test your mum was telling me all about your reunion with Olly.'*

'Ah, was she. And what exactly was she saying?'

'Just that you'd split because of the programme but you'd both seen the errors of your ways and had recently got back together. Says you're moving back to the flat and how she's never seen you so happy.'

Hmm, Greta thinks, Sylvia sure knows how to spin a story…

'Something like that, yeah,' she signs.

'I'm happy for you, Greta,' She looks at his smile that doesn't quite reach his eyes and in return gives him a weak smile. *'Anyway,'* he signs, glancing at his watch. *'I'd better head - got another appointment over the other side of town.'*

'Thanks, Connor.'

'See you. And good luck, Greta.'

'Thanks. Bye.'

He turns on his heels and walks away and Greta feels that sinking feeling once again.

Chapter 30

It's a huge decision. Monumental. And for times of deep contemplation Greta does what she always does; heads for the railway station and jumps on a train to the sea for some fresh clean-thinking air. Arriving at Sudsea Station she takes the long winding road lined with the pretty wooden chalets to the dunes. The bright winter sun shines down and wearing her thick padded coat, woolly hat and gloves, she is appropriately kitted out to stroll the sands.

What is it about the sea that calms and clarifies? Greta stares out at the tumbling dark waves that lick the shore and wonders if she really wants to undergo the surgeon's knife? Someone cutting into her head and implanting a receptor that will be there for the rest of her life? What if it goes wrong and she loses the little amount of hearing she has? What if some of her deaf friends treat her differently? What if they think she's shunned the deaf culture that forms a part of who she is? What if she ends up a hybrid; somewhere between deaf and hearing? Will she be a broken deaf person who has tried to be fixed? And if that is the case, is getting fixed such a sin?

Her phone buzzes in her pocket and pulling it out she sees that Mia is a step ahead in the decision stakes.

Hi mate, lived my life never seeing babies but now they are ALL AROUND ME - can't get away from them. I think the universe is telling me something so in true yogic style I'm 'listening' and...I'm definitely keeping Sprogly.:-) How you doing back with Olly? How's it working out? Love xx

Greta types a quick reply, enthusing at her friend's decision and informing her that all is well. She hits send and tucking her phone back in her pocket reflects on the first few days of being back with Olly. In truth, it's kind of a mad sex-a-thon. He is attentive beyond belief - both between the sheets and out. He's cooking her favourite food and actually asking what she wants to watch on the TV - she can do no wrong. Admittedly the 'learn one sign a day' goal has already slipped but he's using the language of love - and in that he's approaching fluency. Yes, it was the right decision to reunite. They can make it - if a relationship is worth having it's worth working at.

As she wanders towards the long ornamental pier with its gift shops and benches she sees a couple throwing bread to the seagulls. The man's protective arm is around the woman and with their heads back laughing he reminds her of Connor. Of course it's not him, but the reaction in Greta pulls her up short. Hmmm, time to forget him, she thinks. He was a mild flirtation, flattering in his attention, but now she must commit wholly to Olly – there was certainly no point going back to him if she doesn't. All thoughts of Connor must be shelved now. It's time to stop flights of fancy. Olly is The One.

Commitment. That's the word of the day…and it's a big word. Committing to Olly, committing to a cochlear implant. So - why *would* she want an implant? Well, some of her friends have them and are happy enough…and it would be nice to hear music. She remembers a drunken evening with some hearing friends when they were singing along to various songs and, realising Greta was left out, decided to tell her the words. Greta was astounded at the drivel of the lyrics - they were neither deep nor meaningful! 'You're the one that I want. Ooh ooh ooh honey.' Hardly life changing, is it? So, from that evening Greta decided it *must* be the music itself that is evocative; the actual melodies that make people go 'awwwwww' and misty eyed. She'd like to experience that.

As she strolls the pier she thinks of how Olly is putting his heart into their relationship and maybe she can help take their relationship to the next level by having the cochlear implant. When do they suffer most rows? When does she feel distant from him? When does he become most frustrated? It's in situations where she can't hear. Yes, he loves her for who she is - deafness and all, but if she had more hearing, could join in with his friends, not miss conversations, surely that would improve the quality of their lives together? She wouldn't be doing it for him - that would be wrong, but she would be doing it for her future and maybe for her art? What was it Richard said? If she had an implant she might have a different world perspective? Give her a fresh take on her drawing? It could be the start of a new life chapter for her with all the hopes and possibilities that that would bring. (The only sticking block would be

Sylvia's smugly happy face, but a life changing decision shouldn't be denied just because it would please your mother.)

Feeling tingly warm Greta takes off her bobble hat and shakes her hair in the wind. Gosh, that feels good. Liberating even. It's the end of one era and the advent of the rest of her life and it's time to seriously look at her future.

Her decision is made.

Chapter 31

TWO MONTHS LATER...

'For goodness sake, Mia,' Greta signs as they dust off the snow from the fronts of their coats. *'Who has a scan this close to Christmas?'*

'Me!' Mia signs, heaving her coat off. *'Flipping hot in here,'* she moans, fanning herself with her appointment letter. *'And I'd kill my grandmother to pee.'* Shuffling to the hospital reception desk she punches her details onto the touch screen and takes a numbered ticket. The two women take seats in the waiting area.

'How you feeling then?' Greta asks.

'Great actually. Stopped puking which is good. Don't even mind this expanding.' She rubs her swollen belly affectionately. *'Can eat anything I please and I won't worry about shedding it until after I've dropped Sprogly.'*

'Not literally.'

Mia pulls a face. *'Haven't bumped into Jerry either, so all's good. This really is about me, you know. Me and Sprogly. I'm going to be one of those mums who is at one with her child.'*

'Blimey, Mia. Next you're going to tell me that you're going to give birth cross legged on a beanbag with incense burning!'

'Sod off.' They both laugh and then look to the number board. *'We're up next, thank goodness. My bladder's going to burst.'* She chews her lip.

'Soon be over. This is just a routine scan, right?'

'Yeah, yeah. But there's something about pregnancy that makes you paranoid. You get some dark thoughts like what if your baby doesn't have a brain, or is missing a vital organ, or has three hands?'

'Good for signing and drinking!' Greta jokes.

'Don't make me laugh, I'll wet myself.' Mia winces.

'Sorry.' Greta curbs her smile.

Mia puts her hand on Greta's arm. *'Thanks, mate. Not just for this, but for the whole birth partnering thing.'*

'Mia, you're my best mate, I love you. I'm honoured to be the person you're going to hurl abuse at and whose hand you're going to squeeze the life out of.'

'Aw, you sign the sweetest things.' Mia chuckles.

At that moment they see people looking around expectantly. Looking up at the number board they see Mia's number. Greta squeezes her friend's arm.

'Come on, you're up!'

The radiologist welcomes Mia into the small room and gestures for her to sit on the bed. Greta takes a seat in the corner.

'Mia Gregory? Hello, I'm Rita,' the kindly woman with tired eyes speaks clearly. 'Now, there was a request for an interpreter but so far, one hasn't turned up.'

A light bulb pings over Greta's head. Oh no - supposing, just supposing it's him! Since the appointment with the audiologist Greta hasn't seen hide nor hair of him. In fact, when he does spring to mind she purposefully pushes the thought of him away. It's been time to make up ground with Olly - with no distractions.

Mia raises her thumb to Rita. *'S'ok.'*

'Did you want to wait?' Mia shakes her head. 'OK. If you lie down and just wriggle down the front of your trousers.' Mia reclines and smiles nervously at Greta. 'OK, here comes the cold gel.' Rita fake shivers, smiles and then sloshes the gel over Mia's bump. Turning on the monitor she then places the probe onto her belly. 'Do you have any hearing?'

Mia puts her thumb and finger a small distance apart to show the 'little' hearing she has.

'Ah, that's a shame - what about if I turn it up as loud as it can go?' Rita smiles brightly.

Mia shrugs her shoulders in a 'give it a go' type fashion. Rita turns the dial and Mia hears the muted rhythmical thumping. Her eyes tear up as she narrows them in concentration; she wants to hear this more than she's wanted to hear anything in her whole life. Greta moves to Mia's side.

'*Can you hear that?*' Mia signs, a tear trickling into her ear.

'*Faintly,*' Greta signs.

'Here you go, ladies,' Rita says, swinging the monitor round on its axel. 'Here is Baby Gregory.' Mia and Greta stare at the black and white grainy image of a peanut on the screen. 'Here's Baby's head, here are legs and arms,' she says pointing to each part. 'And here's the little beating heart.'

Mia's tears dissolve into wracking sobs of joy and wonder.

'My love, you gotta keep still if you want a photo,' Rita says to Mia who squeezes Greta's hand and takes a steadying breath.

'Is it a boy or girl?' Mia asks Rita.

'Do you really want to know?'

Mia stops to think. 'Yes, yes I do.'

Rita turns back to the monitor and peers at the screen.

'Hmm difficult to be exact, Baby is in the wrong position, but I'm rarely wrong on these things and I'd say you're having a girl.' Rita turns to a sound at the door. 'Come in.'

With a bright red face, Jane, the interpreter, steps into the room.

'*I am so sorry,*' she signs to Mia. '*I got stuck in traffic.*' She then repeats it verbally to Rita.

'*Don't worry,*' Mia signs and Rita says at pretty much the same time.

'We're pretty much done, anyway,' Rita says to which Jane apologises again.

As Mia wipes the gel from her belly and readjusts her clothing, Rita attends to form filling and Jane hovers. Reaching for her handbag and coat Greta berates herself for thinking that Connor might have appeared today - as if they would send a man! Probably better this way - she doesn't need to see him again...

'*Hi again, how are you?*' Jane says, catching Greta's eye.

'*I'm good thanks. You?*'

'*Yeah, apart from the traffic!*'

'*How's Connor?*' The signs bypass her brain completely - what an indiscreet sign-blurt! Her cheeks redden. Luckily for her, Jane is still preoccupied by the traffic and doesn't pick up on it.

'*Aw, he's having a bit of a rough time at the moment. His mother died. Did you know her?*'

Greta's heart immediately hurts for this man she hardly

knows. *'No, no I didn't.'*

'Yeah, she was ill for a while. He was very close to her, poor guy. He's been off work.'

Greta's instinct is to go to him, find him and comfort him. She exhales a small sigh knowing that can't happen.

'Will you give him my love, please.'

'Sure,' Jane signs.

With farewells and future appointment dates arranged, Mia and Greta are making their way out when Mia, now on cloud nine, suggests a celebratory decaffeinated coffee. They both head straight to the hospital cafe. Taking seats near the huge yucca plant that stretches up to the glass ceiling. Mia stirs her drink and looks up at Greta.

'So, how's Olly?' she asks.

Greta stops for a moment. Reuniting with Olly has placed a larger wedge than before between her and Mia. She knows it. Her best friend doesn't approve and believes that Greta could do better for herself. She senses it as clearly as if Mia actually told her. But what can she do? For Greta, love conquers all, and not even best friends can cast a shadow on that. Choosing her signs carefully, Greta starts,

'It's good. He's different. Kinder. He'd do anything for me. We wanted to see the new Star Wars film, well he did, and he checked it was subtitled first. He's definitely thinking about my needs.'

'Oh good, I'm glad.' Mia musters an encouraging smile. *'As long as you're happy.'*

'I am, Mia. Really. And I do think that the cochlear implant will do both of us good too, if you know what I mean.'

'Any news on when that'll be?' Mia asks.

'Got a few more tests to be done. Should be the next few months though.'

'Cool.' Mia signs. *'So, is it still just you and him for Christmas?'*

'Well, we're now popping over to Mum and Dad's in the morning. My brother's there. But yeah, after that it's just me and him at the flat.' Greta pauses. *'How about you? Still heading off to your family?'*

'Yep. Tomorrow. Deidre has finally accepted that I'm a

harlot so it should be okay.'

They both laugh at the one thing they have most in common: their mothers.

'Happy Christmas, Mia. 2018 is going to be a roller coaster ride and it's gonna be fantastic.' Greta raises her coffee cup.

'Happy Christmas, Grets. I hope so.'

Chapter 32

'Come on Olly,' Greta says over her shoulder as he lags behind her on the walk up her parents' drive.

'Shhh, not so loud, Switch,' he says, his eyes like mirrors to the number of drinks he consumed the night before. 'Just a quick one or two,' he'd said as he coaxed her from their cosy lounge out to The King's Head at the end of their road. Once there, they'd found the usual suspects, those whose second home is the pub, lining the bar. It's not Greta's cup of tea: it's a drinking hole that Olly likes to sometimes pop into for a quick pint, but being the season of goodwill and time to be jolly, Greta had dutifully agreed to tag along.

And being Christmas Eve everyone was in lively spirits. Drinks were flowing freely and conversations were loud and fast. Lip-reading sober people is tiring but lip-reading drunken revellers turned out to be near impossible, but, aware of being labelled a party pooping killjoy, Greta had stuck it out. Well, until a 'conversation' with Stubsy where she was having to guess the majority of what he was saying (you'd have to be equally drunk to enjoy that monologue!) made her finally throw in the towel.

'Olly,' she shouted in his ear. 'I'm going to head off, okay?'

'Switch!' he said, pouring himself over her and holding her so tightly she feared she'd stop breathing. 'Don't leave me.'

'I'm not *leaving* you - I'm just going home to bed. You stay - enjoy yourself.'

'I bloody love you,' he slobbered.

'Love you too.' She'd kissed him full on the lips and left him to celebrate until well past the dawn of Christmas Day. Looking at him now, standing on Sylvia and John's doorstep with his head hanging, arms full of bags, and the whiff of alcohol emanating from his pores, she questions whether she should've frog marched him home.

'Happy Christmas, you two!' Sylvia says, flinging open the door. In time honoured tradition Sylvia is immaculate in a Jaeger dress, cream pearls, pink lipstick and drop earrings. Greta has never understood the need to be impeccably presented on Christmas Day and has always wondered if Sylvia thinks that the Queen somehow inspects her subjects whilst delivering the speech. 'Darling,' her mother says, embracing her before turning to Olly. 'Uh-oh looks like someone had a good time last night,' she teases him.

Olly smiles sheepishly and hugs Sylvia. 'Should've spent the evening here with you, Sylvia - I'd feel much better.' He flashes his illuminating smile and Sylvia dissolves into girlish giggles.

'Come on, your father's just opened the champagne. Bucks Fizz?'

'Come on, tough guy.' Greta says, digging Olly in the ribs and chuckling at his pale green pallor. 'Hair of the dog.'

They walk through to the lounge to find John, resplendent in a snowman jumper, pouring the drinks. Greta is pleased to see that not only are his cheeks tinged pink but there's also a sparkle back in his eyes.

'Ah, there's my girl,' her father says, kissing her and handing her a flute of champagne.

Olly and Greta are just greeting Mikey and Elizabeth who are seated on the sofa, when Sylvia wafts in with a plate of canapés and offers them around.

'Well, this is lovely,' she says, sitting on the armchair, crossing her legs and smoothing her dress over her knees. 'All the family together.' She turns to Mikey and Elizabeth. 'So, what did you two do last night?'

'We had a quiet night at home,' Elizabeth says.

John replies, Olly chips in, Mikey adds something and they all laugh. Greta's eyes dart from one to the other. It's hopeless - already she's completely lost. She fakes a smile thinking how it really shouldn't be feasible to feel alone with loved ones…but it is. Here is where the isolation strikes. Here is where she smiles and nods the most. Sinking her nose into her Bucks Fizz, she vaguely watches the laughter and conversation until her brother catches her eye.

'OK, Fartface, you gonna be Santa this year?' he asks, grinning.

Greta nods and with a general hubbub of consent moves to the tree and distributes the gifts. Trying to influence a modicum of order to give her at least a chance of following what is being said, she makes a suggestion.

'Can we do one at a time? Watch each other?'

With nods of agreement, Sylvia is the first to open her gift from Greta and Olly. Carefully slicing bright red shiny paper Sylvia looks suitably pleased with a Nespresso machine.

'Thought you might like that, Mum,' Greta says.

'Oh I do, darling. Thank you. Have you had a coffee from one of these?'

'I tried it when I went to…' She trails off as Sylvia nods past her to Olly. Turning, Greta sees Olly explaining the ins and outs of his and Greta's experience of drinking Nespresso coffee. Sylvia doesn't look back to her daughter. Not once.

As the last present is opened Greta realises she's had nothing from Olly. Catching his eye she pulls a wide-eyed 'and where's my gift?' expression. He taps his nose, gives a wicked grin and mouths, 'la-ter.' He then moves near to her, sweeps her hair from her face and kisses her softly on the lips. He pulls away and turns to Mikey who is clearly taunting them not to 'do that in public'. Laughter fills the lounge until Sylvia stands and announces that everyone should wash their hands as dinner will be five minutes.

Her mother has decorated the table beautifully; golden crackers, table confetti and two tall candelabras sit on a vibrant red tablecloth. The best cutlery, crockery and napkins are in use - it truly is Christmas Day. As the rest take their seats Greta goes to the kitchen to offer help. There, her mother issues her with dishes of sprouts, roast potatoes, carrots, pigs in blankets and stuffing; all to be placed in the hostess trolley. Greta likes this job - it's brief respite from conversation…

Her father produces a fine Bordeaux and fills the glasses. He then stands at the head of the table and carves the bird. As is usual with dinners, the conversation flits from person to person and Greta keeps up as much as she can. However, when Elizabeth starts asking her directly about the cochlear implant, Greta is extremely grateful.

'So, when's it going to happen?' Elizabeth asks, cutting up a potato.

'Well, I have a few more tests to go through. I tell you some of them are horrid! They poured water in my ears - ugh. They need to test the inner workings of your ear - it's a lot about balance. I'll be glad when it's over. I think the operation will be sometime around Easter.'

'Are you nervous?' Elizabeth asks before turning to Sylvia who has chipped in.

Greta leans forward. 'Sorry, Mum, what did you say?'

'I said you've got nerves of steel, darling.' She dabs the napkin at the corners of her mouth. 'Isn't that right?'

'It is *a bit* daunting,' Greta says. 'Someone cutting into your head.'

Olly places his hand on her arm. 'Whoa Grets - we're eating here!'

Everyone laughs.

'Will you hear normally?' Elizabeth continues.

'Er...well, hard to know what's normal. I think at first it'll sound a bit robotic, but after a lot of training it gets better.'

'Wow, it's amazing, isn't it!' Elizabeth takes another sip of her wine. 'What exactly will you be able to hear?'

Greta suppresses a sigh. Who knows? 'Er, I don't know. A friend of mine heard the water running down the sink for the first time, but I'm hoping for music. I'd like to hear more than a pounding beat.'

'I think you're jolly brave, Greta. Not sure I could go through it,' Elizabeth says.

'My sis, the hero,' Mikey says to which Greta sticks her tongue out at him.

'It's gonna be great,' Olly says, putting his hand over hers. 'When I'm in bed and I need a cup of tea I'll be able to yell.' His eyes twinkle as he laughs.

'I can switch it off, you know!' Greta bats back.

'I wish they'd had this operation when you were young,' her mother laments. 'Would've given you a better chance.'

Greta swallows hard, feeling the pain of a raw nerve being hit. A better chance? Of what? Talking? Listening? Of success in life? Her mother's words tap into the idea that somehow there could've been a better version of herself; that she isn't 'enough'. As Greta well knows, the sentiment is well intentioned - it always is -

who wouldn't want the best for their child? But still...it hurts. Sighing, she thinks how it's Christmas Day and despite the fact that half the families in the land are probably arguing, it's not going to happen here. She zips her hands and buttons her lip.

As plates are cleared and Christmas pudding is served Olly leans over to Greta and whispers,

'Hey Switch, I want to give you your present. What time can we get out of here?' He smirks and his eyebrows do a little dance.

Greta gestures to her mouth. 'After this last mouthful of Christmas pudding.'

Chapter 33

'*Pull it?*' Connor holds out a cheap green and red cracker.

'*Go on then*,' his brother half smiles. '*I still don't see the point though - don't hear the bang and it's always a crappy gift.*' Sure enough the cracker falls apart to reveal a red plastic fish that 'magically' curls when placed on your palm. '*Useful.*'

'*Oh come on, Gerald, we've got to make the most of today…*' Connor signs.

'*Don't say it.*'

They lock gazes and both tentatively sign, '*It's what Mum would've wanted.*'

Gerald sighs and his eyes mist over. '*She loved Christmas, didn't she? In the kitchen all morning, lunch at one on the dot, a glass of sherry and a sniff of wine and then cleared away for the Queen's speech.*'

'*I remember Dad standing and saluting Her Maj*' Connor smiles fondly.

'*I think he'd been at the whisky macs that year.*'

They both laugh and then turn to their turkey with minimal trimmings lunch.

It was always going to be a difficult one. Minnie had succumbed to the pneumonia and slipped away peacefully ten days earlier. Unfortunately, with the Christmas 'backlog' her funeral can't take place until the first week of January and the brothers have found themselves in a no man's limbo land of grief. They'd agreed to a 'non-Christmas' with lunch at Connor's flat and then just kicking back and watching television. This year isn't one for celebration.

'*It was for the best though, wasn't it? She was suffering, wasn't she?*' Gerald says, trying hard to swallow his food.

Connor looks fondly at his younger brother. '*Yeah. There was no way she was going back to who she was. She would've deteriorated before our eyes. It's kinder to us, I suppose.*'

'I just feel like an orphan.'

Connor nods, sips from his beer bottle and takes a moment before signing, *'Hey, do you remember that time we had the genius idea to go out on the streets to acquire money?'*

Gerald smiles. *'Orphaned deaf and dumb boys.'* He exaggerates the old fashioned and rarely used sign of 'deaf and dumb'.

'Would've worked if our neighbour hadn't spotted us and told Mum,' Connor signs.

'Oh God - did she go mad at us!'

'Told us to give back the fifty pence we'd got!' Connor laughs.

'And when we asked her how, she said, 'not my problem!'' Gerald impersonates his mother's emphatic hand movements and sniggers at the memory.

'Back on the streets trying to find the kind gullible people who'd donated to our cause.' Connor continues to reminisce. *'I seem to recall most of them were women too - you always did have a way!'*

'What can I say, brother dear,' Gerald touches an eyebrow mockingly. *'When you've got it, you've got it!'*

Both men gently chuckle.

So many childhood memories - such an unusual upbringing, especially for Connor being the only hearing member of the family. To be fair, his parents didn't ask him to interpret for them - they were far too proud for that - but Connor's home experience was vastly different to that of his friends'. For example, his mates' parents could shout to each other from differing rooms, do chores and talk at the same time, jig to the radio and most importantly didn't drag their offspring to the deaf club religiously every Thursday evening.

Minnie and George Walsh were popular members of the deaf club and throughout the years they were voted onto the management committee. This meant they would be attending to 'official' matters whilst their two young sons were left to roam amongst groups of signing deaf people sitting at tables or standing at the bar. It would be unfair to say the lads were unsupervised, as the deaf club members, who were basically one large family, took it upon themselves to watch over and, on occasion, chastise any child present. Many a time Connor and Gerald were reported to their parents for making mischief.

Standing to clear the plates Connor taps the table to get Gerald's attention. *'Pudding?'*

'Later?' his brother signs. *'Shall we?'* He nods to the sofa and television at the other end of the large studio flat.

'Sure. You switch it on and I'll be with you in a moment. Want more drinks and nibbles?' Gerald nods. Connor, having no intention of washing up, stacks the few plates, dishes and pans in the kitchenette area and returns to be with his brother. Placing a couple of beers and a bowl of nuts on the coffee table, Connor sits and turns to his brother.

'So, how's the love life? Any lucky girl on the scene?'

'Not really. I met one girl, deaf. She was in the deaf pub that night when I missed you.' He stops to think. *'Hmm, she was nice, very good fun.'* He breaks into a mischievous grin.

'I'm noting your normal level of commitment...'

'Hey! I've got the rest of my life to meet Miss Right and settle down.' Gerald takes a swig of his beer. *'How about you?'* He narrows his eyes at his brother who inhales deeply. *'Oh no,'* Gerald signs. *'Not heartbroken again!'*

'No!' Connor shifts in his seat. *'I met someone - really really liked her, but she's already attached.'*

Gerald sucks in his cheeks. *'Kick her to the curb. Don't go there.'*

The colour rises in Connor's face. *'I have and I haven't. I'm not stupid.'* He looks down and sees the un-pulled cracker he'd brought over from the table. Happy for a diversion he holds it out. *'We didn't pull yours.'*

His brother rolls his eyes and reluctantly takes hold of the cracker end. As it splits open, a small plastic comb falls to the floor. Picking it up, Connor waves it at his brother.

'Hey Gerald - just what you need with those dreadlocks!'

'Very funny,' his brother signs, fingering his long brown locks. *'And jeez, Connor, can't you be like the rest of the world and just call me Jerry?'*

Chapter 34

'Come on, Mia,' Solange, her older sister, half-signing and speaking, frowns. 'It's me you're talking to.'

'Solly, I can do this on my own - I don't need a man.' Mia pulls her battered half-stuffed Tigger to her chest.

Slouched in the bedroom they used to share, awaiting the cry for lunch, the sisters are indulging in a much missed catch-up. With Solange living the other end of the country after landing an executive role in an up and coming renewable energy company, the times to meet are few. Skype helps a lot, but there's nothing like lounging on their old twin beds, just being together, like they did all through their early school days. Plus, the converted attic bedroom acts as a perfect hiding place from Deidre and her constant demands. Surely peeling vegetables last night means their work is done?

'So, what's he like? The daddy?'

Mia shrugs. *'Tall, muscly, high cheekbones, golden dreadlocks...'*

'Hahahaha, you don't half pick 'em! He sounds like a nightmare!'

'Well,' Mia's hands falter. *'Er, it's either him or Fall Back Finn...'*

Solange's eyes almost pop out of their sockets. 'Oh you are priceless!' She falls back onto the crocheted blanket bedspread laughing wildly to which Mia picks up a nearby gonk and hurls it at her.

'OK Miss Prim,' Mia retorts. *'Just cos you've only slept with two men...'*

Solange controls her laughter. 'You've always had an appetite in that department. How many did we count to?'

'Er, this time last year it was thirty-eight - but as I told you at the time, eight don't count as I didn't enjoy them,' she signs

indignantly.

'Oh Mia, I love you. You don't do anything by the rules, do you?'

Mia chews her lip. *'Did Mum say anything?'*

'She asked me to talk some sense into you and coax you to get the fella on board - not to do it on your own as you 'won't cope'.'

'Is that 'cos these,' Mia waggles her ears, *'don't work?'*

'C'mon Mee, I think if you were a picture of hearing-ness she'd worry about you being a single mum. She's been through it, remember?'

'Hmmm. Well I did try to tell him - Jerry - but he was too infatuated with some bimbo who was pouring herself all over him. She was like a dog peeing, marking her territory...'

'Nice image...'

'And I'm guessing by the way he was enjoying it, he's a player. I don't know though. To be honest I don't remember a lot of our night of lust - how shameful is that?' Mia pauses to think. *'And if by some long shot it is Finn's, then my child was conceived out of Wednesday evening boredom,'* she adds glumly.

'You have got a TV, right?' Solange says to which another miniature toy is lobbed at her head. 'Seriously though, Mee,' she continues, catching the toy. 'Do you like this Jerry?'

'It doesn't really matter - he's not gonna want to settle down with his one night shag. Maybe I'm just supposed to do this on my own...'

'Physically maybe - but a bit of financial assistance wouldn't go amiss.' Gazing at the peeling poster of the Jonas Brothers, Mia nods. Solange suddenly looks at the door. 'There's the call. Gird your loins, it's Dinner with Deidre!'

Mia signs the cross over herself. *'Let battle commence.'*

***

Instead of an afternoon playing charades where Sylvia would again accuse Greta of 'cheating by using sign language' (God forbid that a deaf person should have the upper hand,) Olly and Greta bid their farewells and climb into the Audi. With the pedal to the floor, bombing along the lanes, he leans over to run his fingers seductively up her thigh and at every given opportunity steals kisses. She responds by stroking his hair and neck and before long their pulses are racing faster than the car engine. Arriving at the flat, trembling with passion, they fall in the front door and Olly pushes her up against the wall. They kiss ardently, still frantically making up for the weeks apart, tearing clothes from each other until only pieces of underwear remain. As Olly pulls away to remove the last of her clothing, Greta suddenly remembers this is how it used to be - this is their lust and love. Perfect.   'Not here,' she says, holding his face in her hands, trying to catch her breath.

He gives out a low groan. 'Where then?'

She takes his hand and they walk naked to the lounge where she pulls the large sofa cushions onto the floor just beneath the Christmas tree. She lies down.

'Just here please.'

He looks down at her with nothing but lust in his eyes. 'You're the best present a boy could have...'

Pulling the sofa throw over them, Olly snuggles against her. She breathes in his familiar smell and sighs. How could they have been apart? They are so good together! Lying with his head on her chest she softly strokes his hair and thinks about the high-quality sex they've enjoyed since reuniting. Not that she'd put it like that to him – she giggles at the thought of making herself sound like some kind of sex quality assurance inspector!

'Wh ee Wch?' Olly says.

She lifts his head to face her. 'What was that?'

'Sorry. What you giggling at?' He kisses the tip of her nose.

'Nothing - just happy.'

He smiles, his handsome features still capable of making her melt - what is it about a man after sex? His normally sleek hair is ruffled, his skin glistens, and his smile is soft and languid. He returns his head to rest on her breasts. She gently strokes his hair and is just thinking how this is possibly her best Christmas to date when her body feels a gentle rhythmic vibration. Lifting her head, she sees Olly snoring like a small baby pig. Trapped beneath him, but not wishing to be anywhere else, she surrenders and blinks her eyes closed.

'Switch, Switch.' He leans over her and gently jogs her shoulder. 'Wake up - we need to eat.'

She rubs her eyes, a little disorientated. 'Huh?'

'It's five o'clock - come on - I'm hungry.'

'Get yourself something then.' She was having such a good dream involving George Lamb and a hot summer's beach...

'I did.' He pulls her arm to sit her up and only then does she see the coffee table crammed with an array of meats, cheeses, grapes, crackers, olives, pate, vine leaves, crisps, a bottle of wine and two goblets.

She rubs her eyes. 'Oh Olly, this looks wonderful!'

Lovingly wrapping his old checked shirt around her, he smiles. 'I love you, Switch.' He kisses her lightly.

She puts her arms around him and holds him tightly. She doesn't want to think about these past weeks when they've been apart - supposing they hadn't made it back together again? She would have lost the love of her life. Her throat constricts as she whispers,

'I love you too.'

They move the cushions to sit across from each other at the coffee table. He has brought out the flowery plates she keeps for special occasions, spotted napkins and her favourite pewter goblets. They pile their plates, fill their wine and chatter away. There's no mention of putting the television on, or of going to the pub - they are locked in their own bubble - happy to just be together.

'Oh, this cheese is good,' Greta says, cutting another chunk and putting it on a cracker. 'You spoil me.'

Olly smiles. 'You're worth it.' They clink glasses again. 'So, what do you think about new year?'

'Sorry?' she says, still focussing on the cheese.

'I said, what do you want to do on new year?'

'Ah. I hadn't thought really. What do you fancy?'

'Nice and simple - anything with you,' he says, looking lovingly into her eyes.

'No wild night out? Wow, Olly Emerson, you've changed!' she laughs.

His face crumples a little. 'Hey!'

Greta puts her hand on his. 'Sorry, yes - new years with you would be rather splendid.'

''Rather splendid'? You sound like Hugh Grant in that film!'
He chuckles.

'And since when have you watched a Hugh Grant film?'

With a small blush in his cheeks, he turns his attention to the paté on his knife. 'Oh, you know Stubsy and his girly side - loves a Hugh Grant film. He made us all watch it. Want some of this?' He holds out the knife.

'No thanks.' Her stomach forms a small tight knot. 'So, what other weird and wonderful things did you get up to in the weeks we were apart?'

He eyes her seriously. 'Aw c'mon Switch...'

'No, no, I'm not accusing - just asking.'

Olly leans across the table and takes her face in his hands. 'I went out and got drunk a lot. I hung out with the boys. I missed you. End of story. No skeletons to find here, OK? Most of the time I just wanted to be back here with you. Fact.'

'Really?' she asks wide-eyed.

'Absolutely.'

With that he moves around to her side of the table, kisses her gently, eases her back onto the floor and their bodies become one again.

Gazing up in a post-coital glow at the silver tinsel and red baubles hanging above them, Greta exhales deeply and smiles. She turns to look at Olly, sleeping peacefully, his hair a tangled mess and a vague smile on his slightly parted lips. She loves him. A lot. So, that Hugh Grant comment sparked an ember of fear - Olly would never watch a romantic film from choice - but if he says it's one of his mates' guilty secrets then that is the truth. It really doesn't matter anyhow as they are back together, happily devouring each other, and utterly in love.

Opening one eye, Olly breaks into a slow wide smile.

'Evening,' Greta says, beaming.

'Blimey Switch, I think we're in danger of breaking Little Olly,' he says, peering under the throw.

'Hahaha - no chance.'

'Well I hope not as I wouldn't want to deny you your pleasure. We've got a long way to go...' Half sitting up, he leans over to the tree and plucks a small box from a branch. 'I've been meaning to give you this.'

Greta sits up and takes the small blue crushed velvet box as tears well in her eyes. Is this what she thinks it is? Cross legged on the cushions she slowly opens it to see a simple diamond solitaire ring. Her eyes shoot wide and her mouth drops open. Half crying and half laughing, her shoulders shake.

He looks her deeply in the eyes. 'So, will you, Switch?'

Chapter 35

With life returning to normal after the festive season, Mia sits at her dining room table with a bowl of soup and a chunk of bread, pondering the year ahead. Greta is coming over in a while for a much-needed evening of gossip and for this Mia has left the front door ajar. She's just thinking how she can't wait to hear the exact events leading up to the great proposal when the floorboards vibrate. Looking up, she's taken aback to see not Greta but a middle-aged woman with fluffy ginger hair and a caring smile, wearing a navy-blue nurses uniform.

'Sorry?' Mia says, getting up.

'Mia Gregory?' the woman says.

'Yes.' Mia's heart beats in her chest.

'Hello, my name is Roo mm or ee community mif.'

'Sorry,' Mia says again. 'I'm deaf.' She emphasises her words by placing her index and middle fingers to her ear; the sign for 'deaf'.

'Oh, oh.' The woman flusters, shaking her head and rooting in her large bag. Mia can only assume that she didn't know.

'Please sit down,' Mia says, gesturing to the sofa.

'Thank you,' the woman says, her tongue extending out of her mouth on the 'th'. She then reaches for her name badge and shows Mia that her name is Ruth and she is a Community Midwife. 'Right, how can we do this?' she mouths.

'Have you got an interpreter?'

Ruth puzzles.

Mia grabs a piece of paper and a pen and writes the question. Ruth shakes her head and then writes. 'Are you okay without one?' Mia nods.

As Ruth forages in her bag again Mia's heart beats wildly; why is this woman here in her flat? Didn't they say something at that blood test appointment like 'you won't hear anything unless there's a problem'? Feeling the dryness of her mouth, she swallows hard.

Ruth looks up, gives another motherly smile and passes a leaflet to Mia entitled 'All You Need To Know About Amniocentesis'. The leaflet shakes in Mia's hand.

'It isn't certain your baby has a defect,' Ruth starts. 'But ee ah oh…'

'Please,' Mia interrupts and holds up the pen. Ruth takes it and lowering her head she begins to write. Mia gazes at her whilst her heart pounds out of her chest. Finally Ruth passes her the paper.

YOU HAD A BLOOD TEST.

RESULT IS THAT YOU HAVE A 200 TO 1 CHANCE YOUR BABY IS DOWNS SYNDROME.

IT COULD BE A WRONG READING.

YOU CAN HAVE AMNIO TO FIND OUT FOR SURE.

WHAT IS AMNIO? IT IS A LONG NEEDLE THAT GOES IN YOUR BELLY AND SOME OF THE AMNIOTIC FLUID IS TAKEN. FROM THAT WE CAN TELL FOR SURE.

200 TO 1 MEANS YOU MIGHT NOT HAVE A DOWNS BABY BUT WE HAVE TO HAVE A CUT OFF POINT AND YOUR RESULT IS BORDER LINE.

Mia trembles. The room seems to spin as she focusses on the words and tries to come to terms with what they mean. How can she be having a child with Downs? She thought that was something that happened to older women - not a first-time pregnancy. But supposing she is carrying a Downs child? Supposing she is the one in how ever many? Does she want to know for sure? To be prepared? Damn that blood test - she hates needles and only had it done because the nice doctor had recommended it.

She takes the pen from Ruth.

I'M IN BIG SHOCK. NOT SURE I WANT AMNIO. HOW BIG IS THE NEEDLE?

Ruth holds her index fingers about three inches apart.

Mia swallows hard and writes again.

NO, I CAN'T!

Ruth gestures for Mia to pass the pen and paper.

I CAN'T INFLUENCE YOUR DECISION - BUT IT SAYS IN THE LEAFLET THAT THIS PROCEDURE CARRIES THE RISK OF MISCARRIAGE.

Reading the words Mia looks up and shrugs in a 'there you

go, then' manner. Ruth continues to write.

WHAT WE CAN DO IS A FULL STRUCTURAL SCAN THOUGH. IT'S NOT AS THOROUGH AS AMNIO BUT WE CAN LOOK AT WHAT WE CALL SOFT MARKERS. YOU'D STILL KNOW IF YOUR BABY IS DOWNS.

Mia finds solace in this alternative to the needle.

YES PLEASE, she writes.

'I'll arrange it for you,' Ruth gestures and moves her lips widely. 'Quickly as I can.'

'Thank you.'

Ruth tilts her head to one side. 'You be OK, my love?'

Mia nods. 'My friend is coming over.'

Knowing that her voice isn't always understood, and seeing Ruth's frown, Mia raises her thumbs in reassurance.

'I'll leave you to it then,' Ruth says. 'You'll get a letter soon.'

Mia nods again and thanks Ruth who gathers her bag and leaves.

Mia sits in a stunned silence, her thoughts racing. There was a girl at her school, Tracey, she remembers, she had Downs - but she must have had it quite mildly. Tracey was extremely competent - especially at gymnastics as she could extend her limbs like no other, which apparently was specific to Downs Syndrome. They'd always got on well mainly due to Tracey's wicked sense of humour; Tracey may have looked like the innocent little 'victim' of her disability but she could pull a prank better than all the boarders. But what if Mia's baby has worse Downs? Is there a term for that? Extreme Downs? What if she gives birth to a child who has little to no quality of life? What would become of her own life too? Day after day caring for a seriously disabled child would mean that Mia's existence would become narrower too.

Just then the floorboards rattle and Mia looks up to see Greta.

'Mia?' Greta signs, concern written all over her face.

Bursting into tears Mia lurches herself towards Greta. Throwing her arms around her, she howls like a frightened animal, never more relieved than now to see her best friend.

Chapter 36

Greta arrives at her desk. With Dodgy Rog and Joanie having taken extensive leave into the new year, only Joy is present - and without her nattering partner in crime even she tends to keep her head down. After dissembling the few Christmas decorations and putting them in the large cardboard box, Greta browses the small collection of emails that have accumulated over the holiday. She highlights the ones that need attention and deletes the ones that talk about staff removing their food from the fridge to avoid a new year bad smell and where to find the collection for so and so's retirement. Dealing with the relevant emails she then turns her attention to Facebook and it's while she is viewing a video of cats doing the craziest things that an email pops up.

Dear Greta,

Firstly, Happy New Year to you!

I am writing to let you know that The Art of Being Disabled is scheduled to be broadcast on Thursday evenings at 8pm starting on 13ᵗʰ January. Your particular episode will be the first to be shown.

Many thanks again for your involvement and wishing you all the best in your future.

Kind regards,

Jenni.

How exciting! Quickly she taps out a group email to her nearest and dearest informing them of the date. Not a few minutes have passed before her father, who received a tablet for Christmas and is seemingly now glued to it, responds asking if she and Olly would like to go to theirs to watch it all together. He would also invite Mikey and Elizabeth if she liked. Pre-split she would have first checked with Olly before replying, but now it seems that she pretty much has carte blanche to make decisions for the pair of them. Letting her dad know that they would love to watch it with them, she then wanders down to the coffee machine for her fourth cup of the day.

Back at her desk, her mind wanders to Mia and she checks to see if she has replied. She hasn't. The night before, arriving at Mia's flat to find her friend so distressed, had been harrowing. Greta had quickly made two cups of strong tea and then joined her friend on the sofa to hear all about the midwife's visit. Understandably Mia was in shock and their conversation was peppered with Mia putting her head in her hands and crying.

'You remember Annie? My mum's friend's daughter?' Greta had tried to comfort. *'She had the same thing. Midwife turned up on her doorstep - I think her odds were the same as yours too. Anyway - I think you are making exactly the right choice as she had it done and then she miscarried. So sad.'*

'Oh Grets, until recently I didn't want this baby at all. But now.' She'd looked down and rubbed her hand over her belly. *'Sprogly is a part of me - I felt a movement yesterday. Would she be moving if she's Downs?'* Her eyes were bleary and desperate.

Greta had pulled a noncommittal expression.

'Mia, you have to take this one step at a time. Do you want me to come with you to the scan?'

'Would you?'

'Of course.' Greta had given a small smile. *'Have you thought any more about telling Jerry?'*

'Urgh,' Mia had run her fingers through her unruly afro. *'That's what Deidre wants. She thinks even if he won't stand by me he needs to step up and financially support his child.'*

'I can imagine Deidre saying that.' Greta signs, nodding.

'Didn't like to tell her that he might not be the only one in the running for father.'

Despite the serious nature of it all, the two had giggled. For Greta, it had felt like a much-needed release of energy.; a small shard of light in the darkness.

Disrupting her train of thought Joy bobs up over the two-foot high desk divider.

'I'm go-ing to lunch,' she says slowly, gesturing to the door.

'O-kay.' Greta raises her thumbs.

As Joy grabs her bag and heads for the lift Greta suddenly remembers the post that had plopped through the letterbox that morning. Due to their now ritual of early morning sex Greta was finding herself leaving the flat later and later. Olly's arms were so warm and comfortable that she struggled to tear herself away from them. As she was leaving, the letters had fallen at her feet, and not wanting to be even later, she'd scooped them up and stuffed them into her bag.

Pulling them out now she sees a couple of bills and a letter from the hospital. With a tremor in her belly she opens it and finds the details and date for her next appointment. So far she has undergone the balance tests and the next step is for a CT Scan and an ECG. Wow - they really do want to check that she is firing on all cylinders. She marks the box asking her if she has special requirements and writes that she needs a sign language interpreter. Fleetingly it crosses her mind whether it might be Connor. He hasn't featured too highly in her thoughts recently - she's been far too busy with Olly - but now she wonders how he's coping since his mother's death. Feeling stronger and resolute in her feelings for Olly she's confident that if Connor did turn out to be the interpreter it wouldn't cause her heart to flutter. In fact, it would just be nice to catch up with him. She puts the form in the prepaid envelope and nips to the post tray. Done.

Returning to her desk she puts the hospital appointment in her diary, makes a mental note to ask Rog for the time off and then, deciding she's done enough work for one morning, flicks off her monitor, grabs her bag and heads out for lunch.

Chapter 37

Connor sits in the small interview room at the back of the office with his notebook and coffee waiting for Maggie who appears to be running late. She had insisted that he took as much compassionate leave as he needed and so today is the day that he's finally returned to work.

In this windowless, carpeted room there's only a small round wood topped table and two chairs. He stares at the clock on the wall. Time has been strange recently - moving at a different speed to normal everyday life. When his mother died, even though it felt like the earth was spinning in slow motion, he struggled to make sense of everything around him. People offered platitudes, 'she's at peace now', 'at least she's not in pain any more', 'she died a peaceful death', but none of it eased the sheer hollowness he felt within. Nothing could fill that gap. Nothing and nobody could give him what he needed most: his mother.

'Sorry, Connor. Traffic was a nightmare,' Maggie says, rushing in, throwing off her red silk scarf and mustard-yellow duffel coat.

'Mags, sit, I'll get you a coffee,' he says, rising.

'Don't worry.' She waves him to sit down. 'I've got another meeting after this, so we need to crack on, if that's ok?'

'Sure.'

She sits, exhales and gathers herself. 'Right. How are you? How you doing?'

Connor shrugs. 'Oh, you know, good days and bad days.'

'Of course. How's Gerald?'

'Same really,' he says with a small shrug.

'Well, I've booked Chris to interpret the funeral tomorrow, okay?' She gives a small kind smile.

'Aw thanks, Mags, he's great. He can get prep from Father

McInty at St Faiths.'

'We're already on it.' She pulls out her notepad. 'Now, what about you? Do you want a phased return as I offered?'

'No, honestly, I think I need to escape to work. I'll come back in full time after tomorrow is over.'

'As long as you're sure.' She makes a note. 'Oh, I received an email from that TV programme you worked on...' His heartbeat quickens. 'It's being shown next Thursday, the thirteenth. Just thought you might like to watch it.' She gives him a knowing look.

He raises one eyebrow and sighs. 'Thanks, Mags. The last job I did with that particular client was at the hospital and I got left in the waiting room with her mum who told me all about how she had reunited with her fella. Happy as pigs in muck apparently. Didn't even know they'd split.' He sniffs.

Maggie pulls a sympathetic face. 'I see.'

'You know, with my mum dying I don't know that I care so much now anyway. Death puts everything into perspective, doesn't it? I don't want to be wasting my life hanging around for someone who's not available, do I? Best to put a lid on that one and just forget it. New year, new whatever.'

'Okay.' She takes off her glasses to look at him. 'So, are you lifting the self-imposed ban on working with her? The hospital has asked us for a couple of appointments and I noticed they're for her.'

It's a moment of decision...the thought of seeing Greta again warms his belly; it could lift his spirits. But what's the point if it can only be short-lived? One interpreting assignment and she'd be going home to that controlling idiot she lives with. Is the pleasure of seeing her worth the pain that will inevitably follow?

'Yes, that's fine,' he says, before actually considering if it is.

'You sure?'

'Yep. Let's face it, the Deaf Community is so small I'm going to run into her at some point. I'm not asking you to specifically put me with her, but I'm dropping the ban.' He tries to smile.

Maggie narrows her eyes at him. 'OK, Connor, I'll bear that in mind.' They exchange smiles. 'I'll sort out your work appointments and email them across to you, OK?'

'Thanks, Mags.'

'Anything else you want to talk about? I'm aware there's

nothing interpreting-wise as you haven't been here.'

'Just wanted to thank you for being so understanding. Not many bosses would let someone take this much time off.'

'You're no good to me if you're distracted.' She closes her notepad with a thud. 'Right, if there's nothing else?'

'You that keen to get to the next meeting?' His eyes tease her.

'No, I need coffee!'

'OK, I'll get out of your way,' he says, laughing and getting up.

'Connor, if I don't see you before, I'll see you at the funeral. I'll be the one beside you, just a few rows behind. I've got your back, kiddo.'

For the thousandth time in the past few weeks his eyes fill with tears. 'Thanks, Mags.'

Chapter 38

Greta flies out of work and heads straight for her parents' house. Buoyed with the excitement of tonight's screening of *her* episode of The Art of Being Disabled she skips along the pavement.

'What time do you want me there then?' Olly had asked that morning whilst they shared the bathroom mirror; him shaving and her applying mascara.

'Mum said tea at six and then we'll be ready to sit down and watch it at eight,' she replied, her head tilted back, sweeping the brush through her lashes.

'Not like it can't be recorded,' he'd mumbled.

'I CAN read your lips, you know, even when you don't want me to.'

'Ha!' He wiped his face on the towel, pinched Greta's bottom which jolted her mascara wand to smudge her eyelid.

'Olly!'

'OK, I'm out of here,' he said, laughing. 'See you at the folks'.'

'Don't be late!' she'd shouted after him.

Now, as Greta waltzes up the path, Sylvia, impeccably dressed in her Christmas Jaeger, is standing at the door.

'Hi, Mum,' Greta says, kissing her on the cheek. 'You look nice.'

'Thank you, darling. Come on in.' Depositing her coat and shoes Greta is making her way through to the lounge when her mother turns and signals that the phone is ringing. 'You go on through.'

Greta takes a seat on the large armchair and is casually browsing a magazine when her mother comes flying in.

'Oh darling,' she says, clasping her hands together. 'That was the hospital. They'd tried your flat and couldn't get hold of you so they called here.'

'What? Why didn't they try my mobile?' Greta says, fishing it out of her pocket and finding no missed calls or texts.

'Don't be silly, dear, they know you can't use the phone. Anyway - they have a cancellation for the next set of tests you need doing, the CT and ECG - and it's tomorrow.' She beams.

'Oh no!' Greta says, panic rising, 'What time?'

'Eleven thirty.'

'Argh, I can't do that - I'm working. And I doubt they'd get an interpreter at such short notice.'

Sylvia's face twitches. 'But I told them you'd be there.'

'Mum!' Greta stares at her, open mouthed. 'You had no right to! Why didn't you come and ask me?'

'Oh Greta, what's more important, your work or your hearing?' Her mother bristles.

'Mum! It's not about that! That call was for me!'

'Oh, yes, 'mum' is wrong again!' She throws her hands up in the air. 'Silly Sylvia, only wanting what's best for her daughter, has spoilt things again!' Her mother's bottom lip threatens to quiver.

Greta fixes her gaze on her mother. 'So you told them I'd definitely be there?'

Her mother shrugs her shoulders helplessly, sighs and nods.

Greta stops for a moment. It is beyond infuriating that her mother didn't consult her, but in all fairness, she would like to speed up this process. Perhaps a text to Rog, begging and apologising for the short notice might swing it for her. And as for whether an interpreter will be there or not - she'll just have to pack a pad and pen.

'Then I guess I'll have to go,' she says quietly.

Maintaining a wounded expression, Sylvia replies, 'That's settled then.'

'Ah, what's going on here then?' her father chirpily asks as he enters the room.

'Nothing, darling,' Sylvia says, unnecessarily plumping a cushion.

'Gretsy.' Her father moves to kiss her. 'All ready for the big night?'

'Yep - can't wait.'

As Sylvia bustles off to the kitchen Greta shelves her anger and irritation. Her mother speaking on her behalf isn't a new thing.

On so many occasions Greta has had her opinion formed, her answer on the tip of her tongue, only to find her mother waxing lyrical for her. If Greta were to challenge her, it would just cause a scene, and one thing Greta has learnt over the years is that some 'hearing' people are highly prone to extreme embarrassment. Greta's theory is that they feel inadequate and worry that not only will they not understand the deaf person but that they'll also offend. To be fair, for most people it comes from the right place - good intentions - but it still makes life awkward.

Greta and her father chat about this and that until her mother returns.

'Greta, is Oliver joining us for tea?' Sylvia asks, glancing at her watch.

'Er, yes, I think so. But he might be caught up at work. Let me text him.' Just as she reaches for her phone a message pops up.

Sorry, Switch, got held up. Eat and I'll be there asap. X

'He's gonna be late - he says to go ahead,' she says, hoping that he will be there in time for the programme. Suddenly the memory of *that night* filming at the flat pops into her mind - his drunkenness, her embarrassment - and she really hopes that their present state of bliss is swaying him to support her in her moment in the spotlight.

With the arrival of Mikey and Elizabeth the only other person absent at the dining room table is Mia. She had given her profuse apologies citing the worry of the imminent scan rendering her 'just not up to it'. Greta told her she was wise as it's been proved that a night in with Sylvia generally tends to heighten anxieties anyway.

'So,' Elizabeth says across the table. 'Have you seen the programme already?'

'No, that's why I'm nervous - don't know what it's going to come out like!' Greta says, passing the tureen of potatoes down the table. 'You never know with these things, do you?'

'Oooh very dodgy, Fartface,' her brother chips in. 'You should always check and approve something like this before it airs. They might have made you out to be a complete moron.'

'Michael!' her mother interjects. 'Don't tease your sister. I'm sure that's not the case.'

Sylvia's tight lips and worried eyes belie her words and Greta suspects that her mother totally shares her brother's view. Greta throws him a scowl and in return he winks, grins widely and shovels a forkful of pork loin into his mouth. Families....

With teas and coffees dispensed and minutes to go before show time, Sylvia disappears from the lounge and returns with Olly in tow. He greets everyone in turn, leaving Greta until last.

'Switch,' he says, as he plonks himself down on the sofa and leans in to kiss her. As he pulls away the vague smell of beer hits her nostrils. *Hmmm, got held up, eh...*

'OK, shh everyone, here we go,' John says, smiling and turning up the volume.

The programme starts with a colourful montage of images of disabled people and then Jenni appears, introducing the ideas behind the show and what to expect over the coming weeks.

'But first up tonight,' she says to camera, her blonde hair: glossier than ever, her face: a make-up artist's perfection. 'We are starting with a young deaf woman. Council worker by day and artist by night, Greta Palmer started drawing from a young age and wishes to pursue a career expressing herself through her art. But does she feel the odds are stacked against her? And how does her disability influence her art?'

Not a bad start, Greta thinks, surveying the lounge for reactions. Her father, Mikey and Elizabeth are all smiling at the screen, but her mother is visibly twitching like she's suffering the after taste of a lemon. Wow, Greta thinks, if she doesn't like the introduction she's not going to like the rest of it! Taking a sip of tea, she turns back to the screen to watch clips of herself in County Hall and at the flat. She nervously eyes Olly whose expression is imperceptible. Is he also scared that they won't represent her well? Is he harbouring hidden nerves for her? Or is he just glazed over from alcohol?

Mikey, who is sitting nearer the television, turns in his chair to face Greta.

'Not so shabby, Grets,' he says, giving her the thumbs up.

Quite a compliment indeed from her brother who is usually more at home with throwing out insults. She smiles and returns her eyes to the screen in time to see the part of the interview at County Hall where she'd choked. Oh no... The camera had zoomed in on her vulnerable expression, clearly showing her chin wobbling when she verbalised the areas of her life - mainly her social life - where she experiences isolation. Immediately she senses a change of atmosphere in the room - a communal metaphorical shifting in seats. This is starting to feel like some bizarre dream where she's stripped naked, reading her diary out loud. Luckily the documentary's focus shifts to a more light-hearted theme and then the ad break cuts in.

'Well,' her father says smiling. 'You look wonderful on there, Greta, darling. Very brave of you to do this.' No one replies and Greta actually wishes the earth would open. She looks to Olly.

'Yeah, nice job.' He kisses her cheek briefly before getting up. 'Just need the loo.'

'More tea, anyone?' her mother asks.

As the British answer to any predicament is tea, everyone leaps into action to collect cups and make more of it. Greta sighs. Why did she think this was going to be a good idea? With her phone buzzing she looks at a message from Mia.

Well done, Greta - you're my hero. Loving the show xxx

Aw, at least she can count on Mia.

As the family return with a fresh pot and more biscuits they settle to watch the second half. Thankfully there are no further heart-stopping moments, moreover, there are interviews with a deaf organisation, a brief look at past deaf artists and Greta explaining her art work and what it means to her. It is in the third and final part that footage of Greta in the flat is shown. It is when they pan around her small kitchen that she sees him - Connor. He is interpreting a question and she has her eyes fixed on him. Although the clip is only a few seconds she feels Olly, as if receiving an electric shock, come alive beside her. She tentatively reaches for his hand but he moves it out of her reach. Out of the corner of her eye she can see his jaw, square and tense; clearly he hasn't softened to the happenings of that particular evening.

Greta isn't imagining Olly and Sylvia's collective exhale as the titles roll; their faces show nothing but pure relief.

'Well done, Greta,' her father says, rising and crossing the room to her. He puts his hands on her shoulders and looks down into her face. 'I'm so proud of you.'

'Thanks, Dad.' She rises to hug him, grateful for one parent who champions her efforts.

'I thought it was wonderful.' Elizabeth smiles encouragingly. 'I think you came across really well.'

'Yeah, Fartface - nice one,' Mikey joins in.

Greta looks to her mother who is busying herself collecting teacups and placing them on a tray. Greta inwardly sighs and turns to Olly who also has a face like a slapped derriere.

'Shall we?' he says, nodding his head towards the door.

'Sure.'

As they are putting on coats and shoes John and Elizabeth continue to discuss the merits of the show, Sylvia smiles politely and Olly mutters his goodbyes.

Once strapped in the Audi, Greta looks across to him and exhales deeply.

'Go on then, what did you think?'

He shoves the gearstick back into neutral.

'Why ask me now when I'm about to drive? You always say you can't understand me when I'm driving.'

Not wanting a row and not even wanting to consider if those pints he drank earlier have put him over the limit, they drive the rest of the way home in silence.

Chapter 39

Olly strides ahead, opens the front door and heads straight for the fridge. Grabbing a stubby beer, he cracks it open and, taking a swig, shuffles his feet. Greta positions herself across the kitchen to face him. She shrugs and gives him a wide-eyed look of 'so?'

'What?' he says, taking another mouthful of lager.

'What's got you so worked up?'

He shakes his head. 'Nothing.'

'Well, what did you think of the programme? You've hardly said anything.'

'Thought it was okay. Not really my kind of thing, you know.' He checks out his bottle.

Determined to remain positive, Greta says, 'I was pleasantly surprised. I was worried I'd come across badly, but I think they captured me well. I'm glad it's done, I can stop worrying now.' She sighs and shifts uncomfortably under his gaze. 'Olly,' she pleads. 'Just say it - whatever it is you want to say.'

He stops to think for a moment. 'Did you see him when we split up?'

She feels the heat flood to her cheeks. 'What?'

'Him, that interpreter bloke. Did you see him after we split?'

Isn't it funny, she thinks, when you know that your answer to the question isn't going to end the conversation? 'Yes' and they'll have a flaming row; 'no' and he won't believe her and they'll have a flaming row.

'He's interpreted for me.'

Olly's face pinches. 'Has he now? And what else has he *done for you?*'

'Okay, back up a minute.' She raises her hands. 'I have seen him in a professional capacity, that's all. But IF I had seen him personally I would've been free to do that - we took a breather, remember?'

Greta's heart is beating so hard she's sure it's visible. Olly looks away, takes a swig of his beer and then slowly returns his eyes to hers.

'Do you know what happened when you saw him on the screen tonight?' he asks, his eyes boring into hers. 'You went rigid and had to catch your breath. Now I'm no Sherlock but you can't tell me you don't have feelings for him.'

No, she can't tell him that. But what can she tell him? That she has, or rather had, a ridiculous crush on Connor but her love for Olly is stronger? That she has made her choice? Knowing Olly this is not the route to take…

She moves across the room and takes his hands.

'Olly, I'm with you. I love you. I don't want anyone else.'

He leans back slightly and narrows his eyes. 'You didn't answer the question.'

'Oh for Christ sakes Olly, what do you want me to say?'

'Oh I don't know, the truth'd be good.' His face contorts.

'Haven't the past few weeks been magical? Just you and me back on track? Wouldn't you have sensed if I had someone else? Or if I was holding back? For God's sake, I agreed to marry you, Olly! I wouldn't be doing that if I wanted someone else, would I?'

'How would I know?' He knocks back the rest of his beer and opens the fridge door for another.

She puts her hand on his arm. 'Please don't.'

'Oh sod off, Greta,' he says, knocking her hand away. 'You're not my mother.' He opens another and leans back on the counter. They stand inches apart, his angry stance to her hunched shoulders.

'I don't know how we resolve this,' she says. 'What can I say to prove that I don't want him?' Her eyes implore him. 'And can we just note that I haven't even asked you if you saw anyone else whilst we were apart.'

His eyes flicker. 'Would it worry you if I did?'

'I wouldn't be best pleased.'

'Well I didn't, OK.' She stares at him, his comment about Hugh Grant flashing through her mind. He leans in, touches her face and softens. 'I swear.'

She eyes him in earnest. 'And I swear I didn't either.' She puts her hands on his chest. 'Guess we are going to have to believe and trust on this, eh?'

'Uh-huh. Come here.' He sighs again and pulls her in by her waist. 'I hate to think of losing you to some poncy interpreter…' She opens and closes her mouth. 'But in truth I don't think he's your type anyway. You like your men to be men, don'tcha?' His lips curl into a smile as he leans forward and kisses her with so much force that her neck cranes back. She knows it's the kiss of a few beers and one that will lead to make-up sex but she's not quite at that point yet; this whole matter doesn't quite feel resolved. But how can she cure Olly's bout of jealousy? Like she said, they are just going to have to take it on trust.

He spins her around so her back is against the worktop and begins fumbling with her clothes. Entwined, Greta goes through the motions but all the while she has a sense that he is seeking revenge rather than romance. She feels the pain in her lower back at being shoved against the counter and the crook in her neck from the pressure of his kisses. It's a brief, harsh, frantic lovemaking that is one person led and leaves only one person satisfied. Two minutes tops and he's tucking his shirt back into his trousers.

He kisses her firmly on the lips and pulls away. 'Wanna watch TV?' he asks.

'Sure.' She smooths her hair and rearranges her clothes. 'I'm just going to get changed.'

He grabs her hand to pull her back. 'We okay, Switch?'

'I am if you are.'

'I kind of am.' He flicks his fringe from his eyes.

'What do you mean?'

He breathes out. 'I am as long as you don't see him again.' He tilts his head. 'You do understand, don't you?'

'What? How?' she asks, exasperation rising. 'Supposing he is booked for me? What do I do? Ask the agency for another interpreter?'

'Yep, exactly that,' he says, and walks out of the room.

Chapter 40

Mia is standing in the clothing department of Tesco. She needs jeans. For the past few weeks she has walked around with her jeans' button undone, but this morning, finding that the zip won't even move a centimetre, she decided it was time for the dreaded elasticated waist. They should have a system of hiring pregnancy clothes, she thinks grumpily as she holds up the unfashionable item, because after she's dropped this baby there's no way she's wearing these again. Ever. Just as she's tossing up between the lesser of two evils: black or blue, she feels a tap on her shoulder. Spinning around, she's brought up short by the sight of Jerry.

'Hi, thought that was you!' He grins from ear to ear. Looking up into his swimming pool blue eyes she quickly adjusts her large winter coat to cover her body. *'How are you?'* he signs.

'Good, I'm good,' she signs. *'Just doing a spot of shopping.'*

'Me too, but not for clothes,' he signs, waving his arm around over the rows of maternity clothes. She pauses for a moment, waiting for the penny to drop - for him to suddenly realise which section they're standing in...*'They've got a cafe in here, haven't they - fancy a coffee?'* he asks.

'Absolutely,' she signs quickly and then places the elasticated wonders back on the rail.

Finding a table near the window in the crowded cafe she tells him to take a seat and that it's on her. Despite his chivalrous attempt to dissuade her, she persists and is soon at the counter buying drinks and sweet stuff.

Returning to the table Jerry smiles at the mini cakes she's chosen.

'Deja vu?' He laughs.

'Yeah, don't worry, I'm not gonna make you do anything daft to get them. Dig in.'

They tuck into the marshmallow delights, mini cheesecakes

and strawberry swirls whilst catching up on each other's lives. It's a little one sided but Mia is more than happy to sit and watch him sign animatedly about the comings and goings at the NDO and all the other things that have been happening in his life. As she relates Christmas stories of being at home with Deidre he tells her of his own sad Christmas and of Minnie's death.

'Jerry, I'm so sorry,' she signs.

He shrugs. *'What can you do, eh? Gonna miss her - she was a great mum.'*

'I think I met her once, back in the deaf club days.'

'Yeah, she was always there. Me and my brother used to be running amok while Ma and Pa were dealing with the next deaf outing or committee meeting. They were busy.'

'Popular too.'

He smiles, tilting his head to one side. *'Thanks. Yeah, they were.'*

Is Sprogly moving or has her tummy just flipped? It wouldn't be a big surprise as Jerry has never looked so gorgeous; his pinned up golden dreadlocks only managing to define his square jaw with its smattering of stubble further. She becomes aware that her mouth has dropped open.

'You okay?' he asks.

'Yeah, yeah. Just a bit hot in here, that's all,' she signs, pushing stray curls from her forehead.

'Not surprised,' He surveys her oversized heavy coat. *'It's really warm in here. Take that off.'*

She looks at him, her eyes unsure. It's either remove the coat and reveal her bump or pass out from heat exhaustion. (And then someone would remove her coat and he'd see it anyway...) OK, fight or flight, sink or swim. She slowly pulls the coat from her shoulders and watches as his eyes travel from hers down to her extended belly. She looks down and places her hands on it and rubs gently. She looks up at him with questioning eyes...

Studying his shell-shocked expression, she thinks that 'speechless' would be the word to describe him. Well it would be if they were using speech. Signless, yes that's it, she thinks, he's signless. Actually, he looks paralysed. His body has ceased to move but she can see that behind those icy blue eyes his brain is working like the clappers. The moments tick by until she sees panic starting to replace paralysis.

'*Breathe,*' she signs, coaxing him by moving her hand in and out from her chest.

His eyes are dazed with a hint of desperation. '*Is it mine?*' His Adams apple protrudes as he gulps.

Again, fight or flight, sink or swim...

'*Do you want Sprogly to be?*'

He lifts his shoulders helplessly. '*Sprogly? Oh Christ.*' He puts his head in his hands.

Mia looks at the tables around them and wonders whether, regardless of their ignorance of sign language, people are following their little drama. She touches his arm and he lifts his head.

'*The dates seem likely it's yours,*' she signs gently.

'*Jeez Mia. This is a lot to take in. I only nipped out for a loaf of bread and I'm going home a father?*' he signs, wincing with disbelief.

'*Yeah, it's a lot to take in...*'

'*How far?*'

'*To?*'

'*You know.*' He points to her stomach. '*How near to having it?*'

'*Oh, due late May.*'

'*Right, I see.*' He looks down at his coffee cup and the plate of finished cakes. His breathing is visible, in and out, whilst his eyes dart around. Mia's had the best part of three months to get used to the idea but it's frighteningly new and alarming to him. She sits back, eyeing him carefully, giving him time to digest. She considers her brief encounters with this man and how she certainly wouldn't expect him to want to play mummies and daddies any time soon. Players usually want to keep on playing. And anyway, the two of them, virtual strangers, cramped in her flat, with smelly nappies and not having two pennies to rub together - is that what *she* wants?

'*Jerry?*' She gently taps his arm.

He looks up. '*Sorry. Look, this is a big shock...*'

'*I know.*'

'*But I don't think I can do it. You know, change my life and all that,*' he signs, his piercing eyes holding a sadness she's never seen before. '*I'll help you where I can. If you know what I mean.*' He trails off, his fingers lingering in mid-air.

She swallows hard. *'Yes, of course. I didn't expect anything more. That's fine. Absolutely fine.'*

'I'm sorry.' He lets out a long sigh. *'You going to keep it?'*

She stops and takes a deep breath. *'Yes. And just so you know the radiologist thinks she's a girl.'*

'A girl, huh?' His face softens and flickers of light return to his eyes. *'You've had a scan then?'*

Mia shifts in her seat and takes another deep breath. *'Er. The midwife turned up the other day. I had this blood test that looks for whether there are any problems with the baby and they want me to have another scan.'*

His eyes are wide. *'Is she deaf?'*

'Oh, no. She might be Downs Syndrome.'

His chest falls. *'What?'*

'I just have to have another scan to see.'

'You're going to take on a kid with Downs?'

That's the exact same question she's been asking herself. *'Well,'* she starts. *'You and I are disabled, right?'* He nods. *'So why should a different disability be any...er..different? Would you ask me that question if she was deaf?'*

He thinks for a few moments. *'When's the scan?'*

'I'm still waiting to find out.'

He scrabbles in his jacket pockets and eventually pulls out a scrappy piece of paper and a pen. He writes and hands it to her.

'Here's my mobile number. When you get the date, let me know.'

'Why?' she asks, taking the piece of paper.

'I'm coming with you.'

'But you said...?'

'I can't promise anything. I need to think about all of this, but I can't let you go to that scan alone - I'm not that much of a bastard. It's okay if I come, isn't it?'

She nods. *'Sure.'*

He drains the dregs of his coffee, places his cup on the table and looks at her with what she deciphers as something approaching sympathy. Or could it be regret?

'I'd better get going.' He stands. *'I'll wait to hear from you, okay?'*

She nods and looks down again at the piece of paper.

By the time she looks up again, he's gone.

Chapter 41

As Greta enters the art class all her fellow students raise their hands and, in the sign language equivalent of clapping, wave and shake them, much like jazz hands. Greta has always loved this visual applause; she also loves when people stomp on the floor, the vibrations of which resonate throughout her body. She takes in their beaming faces. Richard stands prompting the others to join in, and taking small bows, Greta blushes and gestures for them to stop.

'You,' Nigel says, pointing to her. 'Were mar-vel-lous!' The sign for 'marvellous', that he's obviously found on the internet, is signed backwards but this in itself touches her heart - it's the *want* to communicate that's far more important than the skill.

'Thank you,' she speaks and signs. 'Did you like seeing yourselves?'

'I thought it was done very nicely,' Joan says, smiling. 'I'd say we looked quite the professionals.'

'Adult Ed tell me they've had quite a few enquiries about this class since it aired,' Malcolm adds.

'Oh, not sure we want lots of clingers-on!' Joan replies with a small snort.

'Don't worry, they'll probably just join for a term then we'll never see them again!' Malcolm says. ''Were you pleased with it?' he turns to Greta.

'I was, yes. I feel quite the star.' She giggles, feeling slightly ridiculous.

'Well, I hope it inspires you to keep going with your art - I think it did rather a lovely job of showing no matter the barriers a person may be facing there is always an outlet for art.' Malcolm gestures around him to the walls covered with huge etched drawings and bold paintings; the work of many students who have passed through the doors. 'Right, tonight I would like you all to carry on with your individual pieces and I'll be around to talk with each of you individually. OK?'

Everyone nods and smiles as they set up for their work. Light chatter breaks out and a happy buzz sits in the atmosphere. Clearly The Art of Being Disabled has given everyone a little boost.

Richard taps the long trestle table. 'How's that other plan coming along?' he asks.

'The cochlear?' Greta says to which he nods. 'Yep, I had another appointment yesterday. I'm getting through the tests and then I meet with the consultant for the results. Then, I guess, if he says that we're good to go, it really is up to me.'

'How do you feel?'

'It depends what day of the week it is.' Her lips turn down as she shrugs. 'Some days I think it's definitely what I should do and that I just need to man-up and do it.' She pauses. 'And then at other times I wonder why I'm doing it. Like, what do I really want? Yes, of course, I'd love to hear music, and the voices of the people I love but…'

Richard frowns. 'That 'but' is what you need to sort out.'

'Hmmm. I don't know how.'

'How about an old-fashioned list of pros and cons?'

She looks kindly at her friend. 'You know, Richard, that is a simple yet brilliant idea. Thank you.'

He smiles. 'When you do the list don't think about it too hard. Just write what comes to mind - your gut feelings.' He coughs lightly. 'Tell me, what do your parents think? And that young man of yours? Are they for it?'

Greta's eyes open with surprise as she wonders if Richard has some kind of CCTV on her.

'Well,' she starts. 'My boyfriend thinks if it gives me more chance of fitting into conversations then I'd be mad not to do it. And my mother - well, she wants what's best for me.' Greta exhales lightly. 'To be honest I think she carries a lot of guilt about me being deaf, so anything that could lessen it would be good for her. As for my dear Dad - he wants whatever I want and will support me in whatever I do. If I went home tonight and told him I was going to the moon he'd smile and ask what time I'm off.'

Richard chuckles softly. 'Sounds like a good chap.'

'They all mean well, you know.'

Richard's eyes soften. 'You'll get there, Greta. Don't fret.'

'Thank you,' she half says and half mouths as they both return to focus on their drawings.

*

With only the hall light on in the flat Greta knows that Olly isn't home. She guesses he's in the pub so she makes herself a cup of tea, chooses the comfortable armchair, pulls a blanket over her lap and reaches for her pad and pen. What did Richard say? Don't think about it too hard…just write what comes. Ten minutes later she is staring at her list:

PROS
Hear music
Join in more
Make Sylvia happy
Gain Respect
Make Olly happy

CONS
Someone cutting into my head
Lose my deaf identity
Possible dizziness/side effects
Someone cutting into my head
If goes wrong = complete deafness
Anaesthetic
Someone cutting into my head…

She sighs. OK, she thinks, running her finger down the page, there are more cons than pros but most of them are focussed around the actual operation. And the pros - if the op is a success - of being able to 'join in more', 'hear music' and 'gain respect' really are immense! So, is it just about taking a leap of faith? Take a chance that things will turn out well? She wouldn't think twice about an operation on, say, a broken leg - so why question this one? Hmmm, this one isn't vital. She is already a functioning human being. So, is this about being an enhanced functioning human being? One who isn't on the side-lines? An equal in society? Yes it is, she sighs. But it also means someone cutting into her head, and then a whole bucket load of possible nasty side effects, not to mention the big question mark over her identity.

She neatly folds the piece of paper and silently thanks Richard for this brilliant, yet sadly ineffective, idea. She remains without clarity. Feeling the floorboards rumble she looks to see Olly standing at the door watching her.

'You alright?' he asks.

'Yeah, yeah, just trying to decide about the cochlear implant.'

'Thought you were gonna wait until all the test results came in? See if you're eligible first?' She nods and looks down at her piece of paper. 'What you got there?' he asks.

She holds it out to him and watches as he peruses the list. He gives a short laugh before looking back up.

'I don't think you're worried about how you'll be after the op, I think it's just the op itself that's scaring you.' He crosses the room and sits beside her. 'I think you know it's the right thing to do,' he says, jiggling her leg.

'Do I?'

'Yeah. And you do know that when they cut into your head you'll be knocked out, don't you?'

She pulls a face. 'Duh!'

'Go for it, Switch. What if you don't have it done - won't you always wonder what life could've been like? You've had twenty-six years of not hearing everything, why not try the rest of your life hearing lots of things?'

She half smiles as he puts his arms around her and pulls her in for a deep embrace. Feeling his voice vibrating on her shoulder, she knows that he is saying something. And, not for the first time, she can't help but wonder if he does it on purpose…

Chapter 42

In the small Italian restaurant with its white tablecloths and not too dim lighting, Greta, without her voice, signs the traditional 'Happy Birthday' song.

'Happy Birthday dear Mi-a,' she signs, using her best friend's sign-name that depicts wild crazy afro hair. *'Happy Birthday to you!'*

Mia grins from ear to ear and leans over to blow out the solitary candle sticking out of their tiramisu to share. Greta waves her hands in applause.

'Did you make a wish? Last word?'

'Friday.' Mia signs, her lips twitching.

'That doesn't take a genius,' Greta signs, her eyes soft with sympathy. *'The scan, huh?'*

'To be honest, Grets, I just want it over and done with. Fed up with thinking about it.' Mia takes the candle out of the pudding and places it on the table.

'Jerry still going?' Greta asks before taking a mouthful of pudding.

'Yep. He's gonna meet me there. We've been texting a bit. He's obviously been thinking about it a lot and he wants to stand by me, which is good.' She gives a wary look. *'But he wants a DNA test once Sprogly is born.'*

'Really?' Greta's eyes shoot open. *'Does he know about Fall Back Finn?'*

Mia shakes her head. *'I told him that she is his from the dates, but his brother has been talking to him, saying that he needs to make sure. I think his brother thinks he's being hoodwinked into taking responsibility for a kid that's not his.'* She shrugs.

'I bet he's hearing, his brother. They always know best.' Greta signs with a roll of her eyes.

Mia nods. *'Seems like a right know-it-all. I understand he's only being protective - he's the older brother - but he's really planted the seed that I'm some sort of tart.'* She takes a mouthful of tiramisu indignantly. *'Jerry is asking me all kinds of questions. It's rich isn't it, considering I didn't ask for anything from him in the first place?'*

Mia offers the last mouthful to Greta.

'It's your birthday.' Greta smiles.

Mia shovels it in and scrapes her bowl. *'Anyway - we still going together?'*

'Yep,' Greta wipes her hands on her napkin. *'My final CI appointment is around the same time. D Day for me too.'*

'How are you feeling?' Mia's brow furrows.

'Same as you. I'm fed up with thinking about it. My heart tells me one thing, Olly tells me another. I hope that talking it through with the consultant I'll reach a decision - but, let's face it, he's going to want me to have it, isn't he?' Glumly they both stare at their empty bowl. *'You know, if it wasn't for Sprogly,'* Greta continues, giving a quick nod to her friend's belly. *'I'd be suggesting a night cap. Remember those limoncello days?'*

'Strangely, no,' Mia signs. *'And neither do you.'*

***

Greta kisses her friend goodbye and heads to her parents' house. A few days earlier Olly had announced that his boss needed him for a trip up north for the night and as Greta doesn't like being alone in the flat, ('deaf-fear' is the term Mia coined for when you can't hear the things that go bump in the night,) she decided to stay with Sylvia and John.

'Hello Gretsy,' her father says, as she arrives home and plonks herself on the sofa. 'You're home early.'

'Pregnancy makes Mia tired. Great evening though,' Greta says.

Her mother looks up from her magazine. 'Ooh Greta darling, I'm glad you're here. We need to talk about the wedding.'

Greta should've seen this coming. On Christmas Day after she accepted Olly's proposal he had tried to place the solitaire ring on her finger but it was too small. Not wanting to break the news to her parents without a ring (Sylvia would not have been impressed) they had waited. Finally, last weekend they had made their announcement and Sylvia had been beside herself. In fact, the last time Greta can remember seeing her mother that excited was when the Mayor accepted Sylvia's invitation to make a speech at her charity gala ball.

'Oh, this is marvellous! Wonderful! Oh darlings!' Sylvia had gushed at the news. She'd quivered with questions and even bypassed the fizzy wine for the real stuff. After a customary glass of bubbly Olly had made an excuse for them to leave and had inadvertently left Sylvia hanging without a formal plan to follow.

'Have you and Oliver set a date?' her mother asks eagerly.

'Not exactly. We were thinking of next year, autumn maybe.'

Her mother looks aghast. 'Autumn? What happened to summer?'

'We were thinking it would be cheaper off peak.' Greta says, trying not to grin at her father's sly wink.

'Darling,' her mother says, placing her hands together. 'Your father and I will pay for the wedding. You don't need to worry about that.'

'Oh no, Mum, no. We couldn't ask you to do that,' Greta says.

'Greta, how many times will our little girl get married? We insist, don't we John?' Her father shrugs and smiles.

'That's really kind of you,' Greta says seeing the way this is heading: Sylvia gets to pay, Sylvia gets her way. 'But,' Greta hesitates. 'Maybe we can divvy it up? You pay for part of it?'

'Let's talk about money when we have to pay for it, hmm?' Sylvia says. 'Anyway, we don't even know how much we're talking about; the Country Club put their prices up every year.' Sylvia purses her lips in a smile.

Olly and Greta haven't even considered the country club, home of the suburban social climbers, let alone decided on it. In fact, in the brief conversation they'd had about the wedding, Olly had suggested that the two of them do it on a beach in the Maldives to which Greta had laughed and said she wanted a small English country hotel.

'Mum,' Greta says, gathering every diplomatic bone in her body. 'Olly and I weren't thinking of the country club. It's lovely there and everything, but just not really our scene.'

Sylvia's eyes are worryingly wide. 'Well where were you thinking of?'

'I want a small pretty country hotel, like The Boat Inn.

'The Boat Inn?' Her mother responds as if her daughter has told her she wants a novelty wedding in a bowling alley. 'But it's so small!' she wails.

Greta smiles jollily. 'Yes. I want a small wedding; intimate.'

'How many people?'

'Just immediate family and close friends.'

'But darling, what about your godparents? Philip and Janice? And Marjory who's known you since you were in the cot - you have to invite her. And Felicity and Brian?' Sylvia is nearing apoplexy.

'Mum,' Greta swallows hard. 'They're your friends…'

'Who have been very good to you over the years. They would be devastated to miss your wedding.' Greta suspects it's her mother who'd be devastated. 'You're only going to get married once, Greta, you've got to do this properly.'

And that means her mother's way. As with so many things in her life, her mother is once again taking control; asserting her own will over her daughter's. The big posh country club wedding is not for Greta; it's all for Sylvia. It's the ultimate opportunity to peacock their family's standing in life, show Sylvia's friends how refined and classy The Palmer Family are. For Sylvia, it has to be the wedding of weddings. Greta knows this isn't a battle that can be won in the here and now; this one will rumble on back and forth with Greta compromising and biting her tongue along the way.

'Look, Mum, it's not all up to me,' Greta placates. 'I'll talk to Olly.'

The air sizzles with tension as Sylvia, with burning cheeks, knows she's been snookered.

Amidst the uncomfortable silence that settles, John stands. 'Cup of tea anyone?'

Chapter 43

As Greta pulls back the flowery duvet and climbs into bed, she wonders if staying at her parents' house was such a wise decision. She props herself up with pillows and reaches for her laptop, deciding that checking emails in her room is infinitely preferable to enduring Sylvia's perpetually pursed lips.

'You have fifty-two emails,' her inbox informs her. That's a lot! Even taking into consideration all the companies who regularly inform her of products she has no inclination to buy, she rarely gets more than fifteen a day.

As she clicks on each email she sees they have been forwarded from Jenni Fields. They seem to be from people who have emailed The Art of Being Disabled. Wanting to start at the beginning she scrolls down to see Jenni's original email.

Hi Greta,

Hope all is well. Just wanted to let you know that we've had a phenomenal response to your appearance in The Art of Being Disabled. You've struck a chord with people. I'm going to forward all the emails to you and if we receive any more I will send them on.

Best wishes,

Jenni.

Greta begins clicking each of the thirty odd emails. Most are congratulating her on her appearance with some remarking how 'brave' she is. She thinks that it's an odd concept. What is brave about being deaf? It's not like it's a choice; a decision to be made. And why is it brave to go on the television? Is the thinking behind it that disabled people should hide away and therefore she is displaying courage by putting herself out there? She shrugs and considers that maybe it's just an outdated term. She moves to the next email which is from a man who thinks she is 'top totty' and enquires if she's single.

Giggling, she sifts through the rest until she comes upon one from Archways Art Gallery.

Dear Ms. Palmer,

We are writing in connection with your appearance on The Art of Being Disabled.

We were very impressed with the quality of your work and would be interested to meet you to discuss displaying, with a view to selling, some of your pieces.

If you are interested please contact me on the above email/telephone number.

Yours sincerely,

Marcus Allbright.

Her heart pumps wildly as she reads it four times over. An art gallery? Want to display my work? They like my work? Wow! Wonder what kind of art gallery they are...Assuming they are probably a little back street place with uninspiring works of art, she pulls up Google. With shaking hands, she types in the name and sees that this particular gallery is situated in east London, sells only twenty first century work and is frequented by the likes of Jude Law and Gwyneth Paltrow. Oh My Word! Trendy! This is amazing!

Knowing her response needs to be calm and measured - a quick response wouldn't come across as professional - she passes time by sipping her hot chocolate (wishing it was something stronger) and reading all the other emails.

When she has read the last missive from a kindly well-wisher, she leans back on her pillows. With joy and excitement gurgling in her belly she takes a moment to smile. OK, she thinks, this could be the start of something big...or it could be nothing at all. She needs to talk with them and see what kind of an arrangement they are thinking. Will they take a huge percentage if they sell one of her pieces? And if they do, and it gets her noticed, does it matter? As with many things it's getting your name known that is key. The television programme certainly seems to have become a springboard for her and for that she is beyond grateful.

Dear Marcus,

Thank you for your email.

I would be most interested in meeting you to discuss the possibility of you displaying and selling my work. Please let me know a convenient time and I will be happy to attend.

Best wishes,
Greta Palmer.

She hits send and then writes another, this time to Jenni to thank her for all she's done.

She then closes her laptop, places it on the side table and snuggles under the covers. Too wired to sleep, Greta sinks into the comfort of the bed. She watches the moon's reflection, peeping through the gap in the curtains, casting light and shade around the room, and starts to realise that her cheeks ache from the mile-wide smile plastered across her face. Being quite the perfectionist and having someone from an establishment such as Archways validate her work is so very flattering; such an encouraging recognition of her work!

She puffs her pillow and turns on her side. She glows with joy remembering the set of circumstances that led her to this - if she and Mia hadn't got drunk that night they would never have filled in the application for the show and none of this would be happening. Sighing happily, she considers that this is true serendipity.

As sleep beckons, she remembers Olly and her mother's reticence about her taking part in the show. Ha! A warm satisfaction engulfs her as she wonders if maybe now they'll eat their words…

Chapter 44

The following evening, as soon as Olly returns from his trip, they hurriedly get ready to go on what is to be a double date with Stubsy and his new woman. It's puzzling that any rational female would find Stubsy's beer belly, lank hair and stubbly chin attractive - but some such person exists and her name is Stacey. Around seven the pair pull up in Stubsy's battered Nissan to transport them all to a new local bistro for dinner.

'Alright mate,' Olly says, as they slide into the back. 'Nice to meet you, Stace,' he continues, touching her shoulder and flashing her a wide smile. Turning in her seat, she returns the greeting and blushes.

Stubsy drives in typical Stubsy style; throttle to the floor and swerving to miss someone on a zebra crossing and Greta lets out a small sigh of relief when they arrive. She is pleasantly surprised to find Le Garriquet, the town's latest bistro, is rather sophisticated with padded booth seating and brown glass table tops. Not so pleasing are the tea lights for illumination. Lip-reading in the dark never gets any easier...

'Olly,' she says in a low voice as they take their seats opposite Stubsy and Stacey. 'Do you think I could ask for a few more tea lights? I'm never going to see lips.'

He quickly covers a look of mild irritation with a smile. 'It's not that dark, Switch,' he whispers. 'Can't you try?' When her face drops he adds, 'I'll help you. Promise.'

'So, Stubsy, my old friend,' he says, turning back to his friend. 'How did you manage to get yourself the lovely Stacey?' Greta thinks how her fiancé is ever the charmer as Stacey blushes behind her freckles and plays with her frizzy hair.

'Ah, you know, mate, when you've got it, you've got it!' Stubsy says, making them all laugh as he touches his eyebrow in a James Bond style. 'I actually met the very lovely Stacey at the pictures. You know, she was queuing, I was queuing, our eyes met…'

'Well, truth be told,' she says, revealing gapped teeth. 'I was waiting to buy popcorn and he came over. I thought he was just trying to queue jump.' They exchange adoring looks and move forward to kiss.

Olly pretends to put his fingers down his throat and makes a retching sound.

'I think it's lovely,' Greta says, digging him in the ribs. 'Doesn't matter where you meet - it's just that you met that's important. What were you seeing anyway? The new Hugh Grant film?'

Stubsy's brow furrow and Stacey giggles.

'Him?' she says, pointing to her boyfriend. 'A Hugh Grant film? Pah! It was that Transformers one.'

'Hasn't he told you he's a fan of Hugh Grant?' Greta says, her eyes teasingly twinkling.

'Eh?' Stubsy says, his face completely filled with confusion.

'Oh Stubsy, don't be shy, your secret's out. Olly told me how you love a Hughie film!' Greta says with a giggle.

They look at Greta questioningly.

'Uh-oh,' Olly interjects. 'We've got a case of 'Greta Didn't Get It' again.' He laughs and Stubsy joins in whilst Stacey pulls a sympathetic face. Indignation forces colour and heat to Greta's cheeks.

How dare he!

Despite feeling utterly humiliated, she attempts a smile. Whilst the others continue to laugh and move on to another topic she wants the ground to swallow her up. How could he put her down like that? It's always so easy to blame the deaf person as, let's face it, nine times out of ten they are the ones who get it wrong. But not this time.

Just then the waiter approaches and asks what they'd like to drink. As Stubsy and Stacey place their order, Olly turns to face Greta.

'Switch,' he says through barely readable lips. 'Don't make him look an arse when he's trying to impress his new bird. Have a heart.'

'I was only joking!' she whispers, her heart still pumping

rapidly. 'And don't put me down in front of people.'

'Sorry, I didn't mean to. My bad,' he says and kisses her gently on the lips. They turn back to find the others watching them.

'Get a room!' Stubsy derides with delight. 'But before that, order a bloody drink!'

•

The evening progresses with a tapas style meal washed down with wine for the women, pints of beer for Olly and coca cola for Stubsy. The men chat about football and video games whilst the women discuss, or rather Stacey discusses her burgeoning hairdressing self-employment.

'I'm building quite a reputation,' she says. 'I used to work for a shop, HeadLong on Smith Street, d'you know it?' Greta shakes her head. 'But the manager was a right pain in the arse. Decided I'd be better on my own. My mum always says you should follow your dreams. She wanted to be a dancer but her dad, that's my grandad, wouldn't let her. Said she'd come to no good, so she gave up and got an office job. She was never happy. So, I told myself 'Stace, you're not going to end up like your mum. You're going to follow your dreams.' So that's when I bought the mobile hairdressing tray, which I must say is quite expensive. But once I've set myself up it'll pay for itself. Advertising, now that's a problem. You don't want to know about that…'

And so it goes. Initially Greta peers over the tea lights, trying desperately to catch every word, but very soon comes to realise that she's not essential to this conversation. Instead she nods and smiles at various points, realising once again that there are times when it really is fine not to understand.

Pudding arrives and Stubsy turns his attention to Greta.

'I forgot we have a star in our midst,' he says. Stacey frowns. 'Yes, young Greta here was on television. She's an art-iste!' he adds jokingly, to which Greta pokes her tongue out at him.

'And not a piss art-iste,' Olly says for laughs.

'What was it about?' asks Stacey.

'It was a documentary about disabled people and the arts. They selected six people with different disabilities and devoted a show to each one every week.' Greta smiles. 'Apparently the viewing ratings were really high.'

Stacey nods, suitably impressed.

'Don't over-egg it, Grets. It wasn't like it was X Factor,' Olly says.

'Maybe not, but yesterday I got an email. An art gallery in East London want to have a chat with me about my work. How about that?' she says gleefully. Clearly taken aback, Olly's face flickers with varying emotions - surprise and disdain being the most obvious.

'Aren't you pleased for me?' she adds.

'Why didn't you tell me?' he asks, forcing a smile.

'Well, I've not seen you,' she says, sensing the change in atmosphere. 'You were away last night and this evening we were both rushing to get ready. I wanted to tell you properly.'

Realising that all eyes are on him, Olly breaks into a smile. 'Yeah, course I'm pleased for you, Switch. Well done.' He kisses her on the cheek and returns to his pudding.

Stacey gives a quizzical look and Stubsy lowers his eyes back to his food. Greta stabs at her chocolate brownie and raises it to her mouth. Suddenly having lost her appetite she replaces it in the bowl and wipes her mouth on her napkin.

'How about those Hammers, eh?' Olly says to Stubsy, restarting their laddie conversations.

Stacey leans forward to Greta.

'I'm doing a woman's hair near to where you live so if you ever want your hair doing in your own home, give me a call.' She slides her pink business card across the table. 'You've got good hair. Natural curls, aren't they? I can tell. A perm can't get curls like that. Not that my profession like perms anymore - too many chemicals. And too many curling tongs available that are easy to use…'

Like turning the volume down on a stereo Greta zones out. Whilst Stacey continues with her hairdressing monologue Greta wonders why the man who is supposed to love her isn't her biggest supporter? Why doesn't he share her dreams? When he got a promotion at work she'd cooked his favourite meal and bought a bottle of fizzy plonk - why doesn't *he* want to celebrate *her* achievements?

As if reading her thoughts, whilst still enthusing about the latest West Ham signing, Olly slips his hand in hers and gives it a little squeeze. And only through force of habit she squeezes it back.

Chapter 45

Olly whistles as he kicks off his shoes and heads for his end of the sofa in the lounge. Greta hangs up her coat and eyes him switching on the television, waiting for the soccer to start. Deciding that she can't wait any longer, she strides into the room and boldly turns the television off.

'Oi!' he says, looking up at her.

'We need to talk.'

He rolls his eyes. 'Look Switch, don't get your knickers in a twist. You just sprung it on me, OK? I was a bit hurt that you hadn't told me in private rather than announcing it like that.'

'What difference does it make?'

'Because that's what couples do - we share things. Alone and together. Not with the world and his brother.'

'I'd hardly call Stubsy and Stacey the world and his brother!' She stops as Olly gives her his best hard-done-by look. 'OK, OK, I'm sorry,' she says. 'Maybe I should've told you first.'

'Come here.' He pulls her to him onto the sofa. 'I am pleased for you, Switch.' He gives her a peck on the lips,and follows it up with a long languid kiss that leaves her smiling. 'OK?'

She nods. 'Mmmm. Oh - while I've got you, Sylvia is asking questions about the wedding. When, where etc. She wants the country club and wants to pay for it. I told her I'd talk to you.'

'Pfft, no way. Let's do Bahamas and ask her to pay for that.' He grins mischievously.

'Seriously, Olly.'

'Let's go with the Boat Inn, like you wanted.'

'Really?' Her eyes light up. 'Do you mean it?'

'Yeah, anything for my girl.' He squeezes her and then hits the remote control, switching on the television.

'One more thing, Olly. I'd like a theme for the wedding too.'

He keeps his eyes on the screen. 'Hmm? Yeah sure. Argh, I've missed the start.'

'An elephant theme.'

'Sure, sure, whatever you want, Switch,' he says, not taking his eyes from the television. 'Oh, oh, oh, yes! Get in!' He punches the air. 'You beauty!'

Greta silently wonders if their relationship will be different, better even, after they are married. Is this how it is meant to be with men? They like their footie and aren't troubled by such trivia as wedding preparations? He wants to marry her - isn't that enough? Committing his life to hers is huge. Shouldn't she just be happy about that? Won't the rest sort itself out? When they have their settled, secure life together they will be totally happy. Their marriage will be the icing on their cake. Oooh, that's another thing she needs to talk to him about. She sees him fully focussed on that white ball bouncing around the pitch and quickly decides not to ask. At this moment there's no point as he would not give two hoots whether they have two tiers or three.

•••

Mia sits in front of her laptop. Her latest obsession is researching anything and everything connected with Downs Syndrome. There are websites galore heralding success stories: the gourmet style cafe in America that people flock to where all the workers have Downs, the athletes who compete in the Special Olympics and the successful make-up artist who works in Hollywood. Taking a sip of tea, she knows that she has to be positively prepared for the scan tomorrow. There'll be no tears, no grieving for the child she was expecting to have. No, instead she will expect to have a round, chubby baby with Downs Syndrome, and that way she can't be disappointed.

Just then a text pops up on her phone. Seeing it's from Jerry she wonders if he's going to bail on her. Opening it up, he is merely checking that the appointment is still on. He says he will meet her there and asks how she is feeling.

I'm ok, she writes back. *Whatever the outcome is, it'll be fine. I'll see you there.*

He responds with a simple *'see you there'.* As she puts her phone down she thinks about the one night with him, not that she can recall much of it. She does remember waking in the night and looking across at him and thinking how beautiful his strong tanned face was and how vulnerable he looked when he was sleeping. She didn't know him from Adam and yet intuitively she knew she really liked him; not just the sexual athletic side of him either, but the person himself. She didn't harbour great hopes of a relationship, but it could have been fun to get to know him. Who knows what might have blossomed if she hadn't have fallen pregnant?

But like it or not, the shadow of this (originally) unwanted pregnancy has sullied any chance of being together. It's not the way to start a relationship, is it? Young couples who have gone through courtship and then married for love even struggle when the baby comes along. What chance would she and Jerry have? They hardly know each other and apart from both being deaf the only thing they have in common is that they both had sex on the same night, at the same time. Together.

So, she thinks, twisting a frizzed curl around her fingers, will the scan show her what she needs to know? Will her unborn child definitely be disabled? And assuming Jerry does turn up, what will his reaction be? All these questions will be answered tomorrow, but for tonight she returns to surfing the web. With so much feeling out of her control, all she can do is arm herself with the facts and information and wait for the sun to come up.

Chapter 46

John sits at the dining room table whilst Sylvia serves the lamb chops, boiled potatoes and green vegetables onto their plates.

'Wine darling?' he asks, offering up the opened Merlot.

'Please,' she says. She passes him his plate and takes her seat. She looks at her husband. 'You're looking tired, dear.'

'And you're looking lovely too.' He smiles.

'John,' she says with a short frown and a warning tone.

'Sylvia, I'm fine. Stop worrying,' he responds with kind firmness. He cuts into his food. 'Anyway.' He coughs gently. 'As I have so miraculously cheated death I've been doing some thinking.'

'Hmm?' She looks up.

'I thought maybe we could take a trip?'

'What a lovely idea - the Broads or the Cotswolds? Either are lovely this time of year.' She smiles, putting a forkful of lamb into her mouth.

'I was thinking a little further afield...er...like around the world?' John sees his wife visibly swallow. 'You know,' he continues. 'Trip of a lifetime, that sort of thing.'

Sylvia's cutlery hovers over her plate. 'Around the world?'

He nods with a small grin. 'Why not? Take a year off.'

'A year off?' Her eyeballs almost pop out of her head. 'Have you lost your senses?'

John's smile fades. 'No, in fact I don't think I've ever been more lucid. I had a near death experience and now I've recovered. I want to grab life - I want to live!'

'What do you think we're doing?' Her exasperated voice rises to a pitch that only dogs can hear.

'Calm down, Sylvie. Don't you want to see foreign countries? It's not like we can't afford it.'

'But, what about the children?'

He takes a breath. 'Sylvie, they're not children anymore.'

'But what about Greta...' she trails off, her face a mix of puzzlement and concern. 'What would she do without us?'

John eyes her with tenderness. 'Sylvia, have you seen her recently? Our little girl's all grown up.'

'But -'

'Darling, she has her own life; she has a job, lives away, she's been on television - she's even getting married for goodness sake.' He looks closely at his wife - is it fear accumulated from years of raising a deaf daughter that he sees etched on her face? Greta being born deaf had dealt a considerable blow to both of them; they just weren't expecting it and had spent their daughter's formative years in a continual whirl of bewilderment. The 'experts' advised the right way to raise their child and in between hospital visits and speech therapy sessions they grieved for the child they were meant to have. Disability wasn't a part of their family - they knew no other deaf people and it felt like they had entered a frighteningly alien world. Would their daughter ever talk? With hearing aids would she hear? Would she gain qualifications at school? Would she work? And what kind of work? In a factory or some other menial job? What would the future hold for their beloved yet heartbreakingly flawed daughter? Would they always have to support her more than their friends supported their children? What on earth did the future hold? The problem was that they just didn't know.

Somewhere through the years as John watched his daughter grow he began to see that her deafness wasn't the sum of her but merely a part of who she was. He stopped focussing on her not being able to hear and instead appreciated what she could do. She was beautiful, bright and caring and the way she handled being deaf was quite extraordinary. She didn't let it get her down; she accepted who she was and he admired her for that. He remembers at the end of each school year the children were given a line drawing of bubble men on a tree. Some were standing, some sitting, some happy, some sad and some were clinging on by their fingertips. The children had to mark which one they identified with and without fail, every year, Greta marked herself as the one standing on the top of the tree, arms open, every inch the champion. And she was. She studied hard, attained decent grades and even attempted the challenges of learning French and the flute. The only person who didn't perceive deafness as a barrier was Greta.

Sitting here, looking at his wife's tortured expression, he knows that his attitude has evolved over the years whilst hers hasn't. Quite simply his wife stopped somewhere around Greta's schooldays, and in plain terms, she is stuck.

'Sylvia?' he coaxes.

'Hmm?'

John rises, moves around the table and pulls up a chair next to her and rests his hands on her knees.

'Sylvia, of course she'll always need us, so will Mikey, but not like before. Time's moved on. Look at us, we're not spring chickens anymore.'

'I know,' she says, nodding her head, her pink lips quivering through a tight smile.

'Think about it - you and me on a big boat seeing the world together. Don't you fancy that?' Tears fill his wife's eyes. He takes her hand and kisses it. 'If there are any emergencies, Greta, or Mikey come to that, can contact us and we can fly home - we'll only be a flight away.'

'I'm just not sure, John,' she says, her voice hoarse with emotion. 'What about Greta's operation?'

'We'll be here for that, of course. We'll stay until she's healed. In fact, I was thinking that maybe she could move in here with Olly; look after the house for us.' The lines at the corners of his eyes crease as he exhales deeply. 'Sylve, our job is done, these are our days now. It's time to let go.'

Tears fall from Sylvia's eyes, running in rivulets over her cheekbones. He wraps her in a warm embrace and strokes her hair as her shoulders shake. When she pulls away he reaches for a napkin and lovingly dabs the corners of her eyes.

'I know you're right, John,' she says. 'Greta is ready to let go – it's just me who's not.'

Chapter 47

Greta and Mia stand in the hospital corridor facing the audiology sign pointing to the left and the one for radiology to the right.

'Right, this is it then,' Greta signs. *'Whoever finishes first comes to find the other, OK?'*

Mia nods. For all her bravado on the train about accepting the outcome of the scan and the joys of having a child who wouldn't be 'normal and boring' her taut face tells a different tale. Greta hugs her and then signs.

'Wish I could come with you.'

'I got a text from Jerry - he's here already, so I'm not alone.' Her smile doesn't reach her eyes. *'Better get there.'*

'See you soon.' Greta watches Mia disappear along the grey corridor, and then making her way to audiology she checks in at the reception.

'Greta Palmer,' the receptionist says, reading her screen. 'Right, your interpreter is already here.' She looks up and nods to the waiting room. Greta turns and her stomach somersaults to see Connor's familiar face. Involuntarily she breaks into a wide smile. Damn, it's good to see him.

'Hello there, stranger,' she signs, walking towards him.

He rises and his arms reflexively reach out. Quickly reining them in, he awkwardly signs, *'Good to see you. How are you?'*

'I'm good, thanks. How about you? I heard about your mum, sorry.'

He looks down. *'Yeah, it's not been easy, but I'm getting there, thanks.'*

They exchange soft smiles. She takes in his casual dark jeans, checked shirt and shorter hair, and feels herself relax under his green-eyed gaze.

'Anyway,' he eventually signs. *'Are you ready for today? It's the final appointment, right? Make your mind up time!'* He smiles.

'Yep.'

'And have you? Made your mind up?'

'Nope.'

They both laugh.

'You've done the old pros and cons?' he asks.

'Yeah, and that didn't answer it either. I'm going to talk with the consultant today and hope a thunderbolt hits me with the answer!'

'Whoa!' he signs, widening his eyes. *'I prefer more low-profile assignments so you can keep your thunderbolt to yourself.'*

Blushing with a giggle and feeling inappropriately flirtatious, she replies, *'Maybe a mini one then.'*

'OK, a mini one will do,' he signs with a twinkle in his eye.

Holding each other's gaze, they stand with big fat stupid smiles across their faces. The air between them crackles. She has so much to tell him but nothing of importance, no major events or changes in her life (even though there have been some!) it's just chit chat and catching up. He's just one of those people she feels she could be happy spending time doing absolutely nothing with. Just being together is enough.

'Apart from your mum, how was your Christmas?' she asks.

'Just a quiet one with my brother. It wasn't a year for celebration. How was yours?'

She pauses. To tell him about Christmas means mentioning Olly and something inside her is resistant to do that. It might erase their smiles and ruin this moment. So, not mentioning her fiancé so she just shrugs and smiles awkwardly. *'Yeah, it was good, thanks.'*

Connor looks over her shoulder to a nurse calling something.

'Come on, you're up. Let's see if that thunderbolt strikes.' He smiles.

Seated in the office Connor places himself at the end of the desk alongside the consultant, Mr Khan. Greta takes her seat opposite them both.

'Hello Greta,' Mr Khan says. Greta looks to Connor. She doesn't want to miss one syllable of this conversation and makes the decision there and then that, no matter how easy this consultant may be to lip-read, she is going to watch Connor.

'Hello,' she replies.

'Right, you've had all the tests and I am pleased to tell you that, as we suspected, you are a suitable candidate for a unilateral cochlear implant. We would also issue you with a coupling hearing aid in the other ear to maximise your auditory perception.' He pauses to adjust his glasses. 'So, shall we talk risks?'

Greta jolts in her seat. 'Erm,' she starts. 'I'm still not one hundred percent convinced about the operation. I'm quite nervous.'

'OK.' He smiles kindly. 'That's totally understandable. I won't lie to you, it's a big operation.' He pauses to look at her squarely and she returns his gaze. Wearing hipster, heavy framed glasses and his hair in a quiff, she guesses he must be in his forties. He's both classically handsome and confidently reassured and really does seem like a person you could trust. 'You don't have to do this, Greta,' he continues. 'But I'd like to think about this: it could be the start of a whole new and exciting journey for you.' Greta watches Connor closely. 'You know how you just miss that one thing that someone has said? And then you feel like retreating from the conversation? This operation and some hard work in rehab - and believe me it is hard work - could allow you to hear that one thing. Announcements in railway stations - do they frustrate you?' Greta nods. 'Well, I can't promise you'll be able to distinguish exactly what is being said but you'll know that an announcement has been made and you might decipher enough to know that the train isn't coming or you need to move to another platform.'

'That'd beat following other people who've heard it wrong,' she jokes.

'Quite. It won't solve everything but this operation will equip you with more tools to cope in the hearing world.' He pauses.

'But - what if it goes wrong?' she asks.

'OK.' He leans back in his swivel chair. 'Of course there are risks - there are with any operation. I have a list of them here.' He leans forward and passes her a sheet of paper. 'But, Greta, I have been performing this operation for ten years - it's a tried and tested procedure. I could do it with my eyes closed. I mean I won't, but I could.'

She laughs politely.

'You need to be aware that there are certain things you won't be able to do anymore.' He pauses again. 'Are you a keen rugby player?' Greta laughs politely again and shakes her head. 'And getting through airport security is more of a bind than it should be -

you need a letter now to show the people in uniform.'

She continues to learn how this device that could radically improve her life will also inhibit it. Does it matter that she won't be able to partake in any sport that might result in a head injury? She's never really seen herself as a skier/boxer/martial arts champion anyway, so it's not really an issue. What's surfacing as more important is the whole question of identity; all her life she's been deaf - what happens when that label is taken away?

Mr Khan studies her face. 'OK, Greta, tell me, how do you feel?'

She shrugs lightly and sighs. 'I live in a world of hearing people and I'm used to being the deaf person; it's familiar to me. I'm also part of the Deaf Community, not that active in it anymore, but it's still a place I can go to when I've had enough of lip-reading. It's always there when I need it. What if, after this op, I don't need it anymore? Sorry, does that sound silly?'

'Not at all,' he says. 'All I can tell you is that I've implanted many young people like yourself and the benefits have outweighed the bad. Why not just think of this as a very powerful hearing aid?'

Hmm, other people have said that and it is an idea she could warm to. She'd still fundamentally be a deaf person, just one with a powerful hearing device inside her head. It could give her the best of both worlds.

'So,' Mr Khan continues, pushing a form across the desk towards her. 'Are you ready to sign on the dotted line?'

Greta looks from him to Connor. This isn't exactly the thunderbolt she was hoping for, but if she was forty percent sure before entering this room, she's now around sixty to seventy. Maybe life is about taking a leap of faith; jump in with both feet and an open heart and see where you end up? Connor raises his eyebrows quizzically at her. Greta turns back to the consultant.

'Have you got a pen please?'

Chapter 48

'That's it then, done deal. A cochlear implant in sexy red it is!' Connor signs with a cheeky grin, as they exit the doctor's office.

'I thought if I'm gonna do it, I might as well go all out - out and proud.' She shrugs.

'Good call,' he signs with a smile.

Greta returns his smile. *'You, er, got time for a quick coffee?'* she asks, guessing Mia won't be finished yet.

Connor looks at his watch. *'Oh damn, no, sorry, I've got another appointment.'*

'OK, no worries. Thanks for today.'

'No problem.'

'Might see you at the pre-op?' she signs.

'Hope so. Take care.' He gives a shy smile, turns on his heels and leaves.

Greta watches him disappear and finds herself yet again reasoning with her heart. What *is it* about this man? He's so opposite to Olly - softer and gentler in nature - maybe that's it? Maybe it is just the juxtaposition of the two of them that draws her both ways.

Right, Greta thinks, looking at the clock on the wall, a quick trip to the loo and then wander down to radiology to meet up with Mia. As her own appointment went well enough she hopes the same applies to her friend.

Leaving the toilet, she follows the signs to radiology, along long narrow corridors filled with people searching for departments, orderlies pushing gurneys and small children racing and skidding on the shiny floor. She eventually reaches the reception and looks around at the people waiting. Mia isn't there so, assuming she must still be in her appointment, Greta quietly takes a seat at the back of the room. It doesn't feel that long ago that she was sitting in A&E waiting to find out how her father was. She gives a small smile thinking how he's done really well. It really shook them all up, but credit must go to her mother who went way beyond the call of duty to bring her beloved dad back to full health. They really are quite a partnership, she thinks, as she stares out into the room. She'll never quite understand how her father puts up with her mother's melodramatic temperament but he does, and their relationship works. Simple as that. And that is what Greta wants too: a partnership built to weather storms.

Just then Mia appears from the side of the reception desk. Craning her neck Greta can see that she is signing to Jerry. Now *this* is definitely the benefit of a visual language, Greta thinks, as she reads their conversation from afar. Mia is smiling and telling Jerry that they can just take it *'one day at a time'*. Although he looks like he's been plugged into an electric socket, he is nodding in agreement. Greta makes her way over to them.

'So, how'd it go?' she directs to Mia.

'Hi. Good. They did this full structural scan, looking for what they call 'soft markers'. Apparently by looking at different parts of Sprogly - hands, forehead - they can pretty much tell if she has Downs. And they say they can't see any. So, the chances are she doesn't have Downs.' She looks to Jerry. *'That's right, isn't it?'*

'Yeah,' he nods.

'Didn't you have an interpreter?' Greta asks, aghast they could've gone through such an appointment without clear communication.

'Oh yeah, we did, my brother,' Jerry signs.

'Hmm,' Mia signs, giving a knowing look to Greta. *'He's just in the loo. And I think you'll find that you know hi...'* Following Mia's eye-line, Greta turns to see none other than Connor heading towards her.

What on earth?!

Her face drops as realisation hits. Oh no! What? He's the brother? The one who planted seeds of doubt in Jerry's mind? The quick-to-judge older brother who thinks that her friend is trying to hoodwink his baby brother into taking responsibility for a child that might not be his? The know-it-all hearing sibling who stuck his oar in? Connor? She did not have him pegged as *that* man!

'Hi,' Greta curtly signs. *'Again.'*

'Hi.' He frowns. *'You okay?'*

Greta pulls herself up straight. *'Come to keep an eye on your baby brother, huh? Make sure he's not being fooled, hmm?'*

'Eh?'

Her eyes are accusing. *'You don't think much of my friend, do you?'*

'To be fair I don't know her…'

'No, exactly, but you're quick to jump to conclusions though. And just who are you to point the finger, eh?' Greta keeps her signs low and sharp; an argument in any language is not good conducted in public.

'Look,' he signs. *'I didn't realise she was your friend.'*

'Clearly.'

'If I'd have known who she was…'

Greta points to her friend. *'SHE has a name!'*

With a pinched expression he tilts his head, *'Why are you so upset anyway?'*

'Because she's my friend!'

'SHE? I thought she had a name!'

Mia and Jerry look like stunned Wimbledon spectators whilst Connor and Greta, resembling alpha wolves, remain locked in a scowl.

'And anyway,' Greta signs. *'Isn't it a bit unethical to interpret for a family member?'*

Connor's face registers that she's got him; he shouldn't interpret for family members - it's considered a conflict of interest. As an interpreter he is fully aware of the power he holds as he could easily sway the outcome of an assignment just by his use of language. In fact, a couple of years ago an interpreter faced a disciplinary for requesting treatment for her dying mother when her mother hadn't specifically asked for it.

Connor holds up his hands to Greta and then turns to Jerry. *'I'll be in touch, Gerald, okay.'*

'Thanks, bro,' Jerry says and cups his brothers fist in a handshake.

As they break apart Mia signs her thanks to Connor for interpreting. Then, without another look at Greta, Connor turns and walks out of the hospital.

Chapter 49

A few days later Connor sits in the small cafe near the centre of town waiting for Maggie to join him from her local business women's breakfast meeting. For much needed courage, he's ordered three shots in his coffee - he just knows this supervision isn't going to go well. Two weeks previously he'd felt quite self-assured bypassing the usual interpreter booking system so he could 'be there' for Jerry, but now his mouth is quite dry at the prospect of having to explain it to Maggie.

She enters and signs across the room, '*Want a drink?*' He gestures to his full cup and shakes his head. A few minutes later, carrying a bowl-like cup of coffee, she joins him.

'How are you then?' she asks, taking off her coat and pulling out her laptop.

'Good thanks, Mags.'

'Sorry about meeting here - but I guess it gets us out of the office and we get a decent cup of coffee.'

'Yep, I'm not complaining.' He raises his glass.

'So,' she says, logging into her laptop. 'What's been happening?'

He exhales deeply. 'Well…'

'Uh-oh,' she says, adjusting her multi-coloured scarf. 'I don't like the sound of that.'

'Look, don't shout at me, Maggie…'

'Ha! Is that why you're happy to meet here? Safely in silence, eh?'

He rubs his face. 'OK, Jerry told me that this girl is pregnant and it looks like it's his. You know my brother, Mags, he can be so gullible, and he's my baby brother…so when he told me they'd got a scan booked, I just put it in my diary. I was at the hospital anyway for an appointment with Greta, who just happens to be the best mate of said pregnant girl…'

Maggie raises her hands to halt him. 'Whoa, OK, let me see if I've got this. You took on an interpreting assignment for a family member, on works time, and as you didn't book it in we won't even get paid for it.' She looks over rimless glasses. 'Is that about the sum of it?'

Connor nods slowly, wishing he could decipher her expression; is she angry? Frustrated? Ready to sack him? Or just, and possibly the worst option, disappointed in him?

As Maggie replaces her cup on the table, she takes her glasses off and furrows her brow.

'Why are you telling me, Connor? Surely you didn't mean me to find out?'

'There might be a complaint coming in,' he says sheepishly. 'I thought it'd be best if you were prepared.'

'Who's going to complain?'

He wriggles in his seat. 'Greta.'

'For God's sake, Connor, what happened with her this time?'

'I've been kind of advising Jerry. I think he has a right to know if the child is his before he devotes all his time and money, so I suggested a DNA test. Obviously the girl, Mia, must've told Greta that Jerry's 'interfering older brother' is a pain. Greta went for me big time. Told me I was unethical interpreting for my brother.'

'She's not wrong.' Maggie snaps. 'And you know what, Connor, you already know this stuff.'

'I know, I know.' He hangs his head. He hates upsetting Maggie; she's always been so good to him.

'OK, Connor,' Maggie takes a sharp intake of breath. 'What would you do if you were me?'

'Eh?'

'Tell me. If roles were reversed what would you say to you?'

'That I'm a dickhead?'

'Well as tempting at that is, I was thinking more along the lines of a professional point of view.' He looks blank. 'Come on, Connor!'

'I don't know.'

'OK. The first time you met Greta you came away all of a fluster - your personal feelings interfered with your professional self, etc. etc. Now, you've undertaken an unethical assignment, let's forget how you've cheated the agency out of a fee, and ended up upsetting Greta again. When it first happened I thought it was a blip - but now I think we need to look at your understanding of the role of the interpreter. It was always going to be harder coming from a deaf family - of course you have loyalty to them and want to protect them - but you can't make up the rules as you go along.' She pauses for breath. 'Think about the poor young woman who's pregnant. She knew that you were against your brother getting involved with her and the baby and then you show up to interpret. Could she trust you to be impartial? I don't know how far along this pregnancy is...'

'Twenty weeks.'

'Right, so they could've been discussing termination. How would you have interpreted IMPARTIALLY?'

'I get it, Mags, I really do.'

Maggie leans back in her chair and stares at him. She sighs deeply and takes another mouthful of coffee.

'OK, I think you do understand,' she continues. 'But I need to cover the agency's back. You need to research a course on interpreting ethics and book yourself on to it. I will let the fact that you lost us a fee slide this once.'

'Thanks, Maggie. I'll do that. It won't happen again, I promise.'

'Make sure it doesn't.'

Maggie returns to her screen and pulls up the bookings timetable for the coming weeks.

'Right, you should've received a copy of your workload. There's only one other appointment that came in last thing yesterday to add and..' She smiles wickedly. 'You are gonna love it....'

Connor cringes. 'Oh no, Greta Palmer?'

'Greta Palmer.'

'Any chance of swapping with someone?'

Maggie purses her lips. 'Not a chance.'

Chapter 50

Greta jumps off the bus and walks the tree lined road to her parents' house. It's odd enough they've invited her and Olly over mid-week, but the fact that her mother's text was slightly mysterious about *why* they were being invited, sealed the deal in favour of going. She asked and then begged Olly to attend and eventually he agreed. They arranged to meet there.

As she passes the sturdy brick built detached houses her mind rewinds to that awful argument with Connor at the hospital. Damn him for walking away! She feels like he's left her in a limbo of the worst kind, and, as is inevitable with cross words, she regrets what she said in the heat of the moment. Shortly after he'd exited, Jerry had also made his excuses and left, at which point Mia had turned to her.

'Greta! What is wrong with you?'

'I just can't believe it's Connor who stirred things up. What an arse!'

Mia had shrugged. *'It's kinda understandable, Grets; he's Jerry's brother. Wouldn't you do that for your brother?'*

Greta sniffed. *'So, are you going to have the DNA test?'*

Mia nodded. *'It's only fair.'*

Greta looked around the room before turning back to her friend. *'So, do you think I overreacted?'*

Mia had winced and held her thumb and index finger a centimetre apart.

Hmm. Maybe Greta had jumped in the deep end, feet first, maybe she was a little harsh on him - especially accusing him of being unethical. But then this isn't the first time he has pushed her buttons with such aplomb. With him it seems to be either giggles and lingering stares or pistols at dawn. No middle ground.

As she turns the corner she sees Olly's Audi in the drive. Hurrah! Olly present and correct - that's one less thing to stress about.

'Darling,' Sylvia says, opening the door. 'Come in, Oliver's in the lounge just fixing some drinks.'

'Ooh, just in time,' Greta says, smiling.

Going through to the lounge she finds her father and Olly standing at the oak drinks cabinet pouring aperitifs. She greets them and takes her glass over to the sofa as everyone sits.

'So, what's the mystery?' Greta asks. 'What're we celebrating?'

Her parents exchange furtive glances.

'Well,' her father starts. 'Your mother and I have been talking…'

'Ey-up,' Olly says to which everyone chuckles.

'And, well, as you all know I valiantly fought death this year and won…'

'A little over dramatic, dear,' her mother interjects.

'The point is,' he continues. 'I want to *live* the rest of my life. It's a bit of a cliché but I feel like I've been given a second chance and I want to grab it with both hands.'

'Blimey, Dad, what you gonna do? Sports car and toupee?' Greta teases.

He gives her a rueful look. 'No. Your mother and I are going off round the world.'

'Wow!' Greta says. 'Never realised you wanted to do that!'

He nods seriously. 'Honestly, it's made me reassess life and I don't want to spend the rest of it just playing golf and doing the same old same old. I want a bit of adventure before I shuffle off.'

Greta looks at her mother who sits proud and protective.

'So,' Olly says. 'Is it backpacks and wet wipes?'

'Hardly!' Sylvia exclaims, tapping Olly's arm in a 'don't be ridiculous' manner. 'We've booked onto H.M. Princess of the Sea. Sailing from Southampton.'

'Oh My God, Mum, when?' Greta asks, unsure if she's lip-reading correctly.

'July. We wanted to wait until you're well again after the operation.'

'Oh you didn't need to worry about that! I've got Olly here to nurse me back to health,' Greta says.

'Nevertheless,' Sylvia continues. 'We'd prefer that you're fit before we go.'

'How long are you going for?' Greta asks.

Her parents look to each other again and then back to her.

'A year,' her father says.

Greta is speechless. She lives an independent life for sure, but at the same time she always knows her parents are there, waiting in the wings if she ever needs help. She's never considered them not being there. This feels weird...

'A year,' she repeats.

'I think it's great,' Olly chirps. 'Why not? You're both free and young enough to enjoy it - good for you.'

'Thank you, Oliver,' Sylvia smiles at him. 'There was one other thing. We wondered if you both would like to move in here for a year? You could save on rent, extra money for your wedding, and you'd have the run of the place.' She looks around. 'We'd be back for your wedding, of course.'

'Move in here?' Greta says, slightly dazed.

Olly shifts in his seat. 'Oh, we couldn't do that. It's kind of you and that, but I don't think we'd want to give up the flat. It's such a reasonable rent - we wouldn't get another like it.'

Greta turns to him. 'But we'd save all that rent money. Mum's right, we'd have more money for the wedding.'

'Yeah, but long term it might not do us any favours,' he says tightly. Then turning to Sylvia and John his expression softens. 'No offence, it's a really kind offer but I don't think we can accept.'

'Olly, I think we should give it some thought,' Greta insists. She turns to her parents. 'We don't have to answer now, do we?'

'No, of course not,' her mother says a little too quickly. 'And anyway if you don't want it, we might just leave it empty and get one of those companies to keep an eye on it. Don't worry. Nothing's decided yet.'

Greta feels a pang of sympathy for her mother. It's clear that her father is the instigator of this trip and her mother has dutifully acquiesced, and now Olly has shot down her generous offer of their house.

'Anyway,' Greta says in an effort to resume the excitement. 'I think this deserves a toast.' She lifts her schooner. 'To Mum and Dad, the intrepid explorers!'

'To the intrepid explorers,' Olly echoes, half lifting his glass and then downing it in one.

Sylvia stands and smooths her skirt. 'OK, dinner will be ready in ten minutes, get your hands washed everyone.' With that she bustles out to the kitchen followed by John.

Greta and Olly turn to face each other.

'What?' Greta says with wide eyes.

'Not now,' he growls. 'We'll talk later.'

•

Once again Greta finds herself buckled into the Audi with the G Force of his erratic driving hurting her neck. Why does he have to drive like this? She surreptitiously holds the edges of her seat and braves the ride. Out of the corner of her eye she can see that he's sulking like a spoilt five-year-old and she wishes that life had a fast forward button so she could skip the inevitable conversation they're going to have.

Arriving at the flat he takes off his coat and heads for the lounge. She pulls up the footstool and sits facing him.

'Come on then, Olly, let's talk.'

'Do you really think giving up this place is a good idea?' He gestures around him.

'Yes, I do, if it saves us money.'

He shakes his head vehemently. 'No. It'd be madness. Just for a year of living in middle class suburbia. Bloody hell - those twitchy neighbours would drive me mad! It's all Volvos and golfing stories and who's holidaying where. It's total bollocks and I don't want to live there.'

'It's only for a year! And we wouldn't have to speak to the neighbours. You don't have to join their club, you know. It's just a means to an end. Think how much better off we'd be.'

'Look, babe, you've lived there before, you're used to it, but I'd feel like I can't even fart in there! What if we broke one of Sylvia's bug-ugly china pieces!'

'Lladró, they're Lladró! And I'm sure she'd understand breakages. She's not an ogre!'

'Bloody hell, Greta, you've changed your tune! Thought she drove you mad? You're so hypocritical wanting to move there. What happened to your independence?'

'What?' Greta stares at him. He's right, of course; her mother is a pain - but, when all is said and done, she is *her* pain! Greta can say what she likes about her own mother but her sense of family loyalty kicks in when Sylvia is being attacked by an outsider. And anyway, what about cutting her some slack for making a kind offer?! Greta exhales deeply. 'What has my independence got to do with this? We would be living in their house for a year whilst they're away - not moving in permanently.'

He shakes his head for a very long moment and eyes her sadly. 'I can't do it, Switch.'

Her heart palpates, unsure of what it is exactly he can't do. 'Can't do what?'

'Move into their house.'

She breathes a half sigh of relief. 'But why?'

'I'd just feel like we'd become your parents. I'm sorry.'

He nervously plays with his fingers and shifts in his seat like a trapped animal. She suddenly feels sorry for him; if it's going to cause him this much stress then maybe it's not such a good idea. Is she putting too much pressure on him? Is he seeing his life flash before him? To her it's just a place to stay for a year, a handy free residence, but to him it obviously symbolises something far more intense.

'Okay,' she says, squeezing his leg. 'I thought it was a good idea but if you don't fancy it, that's fine.'

He strokes her hair. 'Sorry.'

'I know.'

He leans forward, pulls her to him and embraces her tightly. Feeling the warmth of his body she lets any concerns about the differences between them slide away. Life would be boring if they agreed on everything, she tells herself, and with that thought she presses herself to him and nuzzles into his neck. With a small sigh, she considers how no one ever said that relationships are easy...

Chapter 51

Mia could've guessed that the news of her pregnancy would reach far and wide into the Deaf Community and that before long she'd hear from him. And that happened today. Whilst on her lunch break she'd received a text from Finn. Direct as ever, he wrote that he had heard she was pregnant and wondered whether it might be his. Mia wondered how you go about answering something like that? Especially in a text! As sure as she feels that Jerry is the rightful father, she can't dismiss out of hand that it might be the boy who's loved her since Year Seven.

They'd met at boarding school when Finn joined late in the year; apparently, he'd struggled in mainstream education and his parents had finally accepted that he needed a special school. She can remember the first time she saw him; a stocky lad with a shock of dark hair, thick lips, big smile and a permanently innocent look. Did she fancy him initially? No, probably not. But she certainly liked him. He, on the other hand, was smitten. Throughout the years he's had girlfriends, but Mia has always noted that they never last long, and always wondered if that was to do with her.

She returned his text inviting him over to her flat for a chat and he replied saying he'd be round at seven. As she now moves to put the latch on her door she finds him standing there.

'*Hi, you're early, come in,*' she signs.

He lowers his head, nods and follows her in. She gestures to a seat and he sits but then quickly stands again.

'*I forgot,*' he signs. '*For you.*' From the pocket of his leather jacket he produces a dented box of After Eights.

'*Thanks., Er, you weren't expecting dinner, were you?*'

He reddens. '*Er, well, er, no, I suppose not.*'

She tuts. '*Have you eaten?*' He shakes his head. '*Eggs and toast are about all I can offer.*' He raises his thumb and smiles. She rolls her eyes. '*Come through to the kitchen while I make it.*'

Dutifully he gets up to follow her. And that, she thinks, encapsulates their relationship perfectly: she calls and he follows. Mia has always thought that, over the years, if just once or twice he had said 'no' to her slurred suggestion of going back to hers, it might have generated a spark of interest and changed her feelings for him. What is it with people, she wonders, that they always want what they can't have? And why is it just too easy to take or leave someone who offers himself on a plate.

She cracks four eggs into the frying pan and pushes the grill pan with slightly curled slices of white bread under the heat.

'You've not eaten either?' Finn asks.

'I ate earlier, but these days,' she looks to her bump, *'I could eat a horse.'*

His eyes remain fixed on her perfectly egg-shaped stomach. She's wearing black sweat pants with the waistband below her bump and a stripy top with a neckline that hints at cleavage. He always has admired her shape and, facing her sideways, she now certainly has the rest to match her magnificent booty. He inwardly curses himself that even when she's probably carrying another man's child he could still spend time happily just staring at her. To him, she is perfect.

He shakes himself back to the moment. *'So,'* he signs. *'Is the baby definitely not mine?'*

'Blimey, Finn, you don't skirt around things, do you?' She half laughs, gouging the spatula under the eggs that are in danger of sticking.

'It's deaf culture, isn't it?' he signs, wide eyed.

'Mmm, so they say.'

'So?'

She pulls out the grill tray, turns the bread and puts it back under. *'Well, I've worked out dates and it would be highly unlikely that Sprogly is yours.'* She looks up and smiles. *'You're off the hook, matey!'* Seeing his face drop she immediately regrets her flippancy. *'Look,'* she continues. *'The likely father wants DNA testing so if it's not his...'* She trails as his moniker of 'Fall Back Finn' comes to mind. Poor Finn - he has never been her first choice and now it seems he's even second in line to father her baby. *'What I mean is...'*

'S'ok Mia, I know what you mean. That's fine.' His long eyelashes blink heavily, hiding his dark eyes. Mia hands him the knives and forks and touches his hand with a sympathetic smile.

Turning away she reaches for plates and serves the eggs and toast. She carries them through to the tiny dining table in the corner of her lounge where they sit.

She shakes salt onto her food and looks at him. *'Finn, honestly, you're dodging a bullet here. Why would you want to be the father?'*

'Who is the father?' he asks.

'Does it matter?'

'Not really.' He shrugs his shoulders. *'I'm just curious.'*

Knowing that Finn isn't the macho type who's going to hunt him down, she simply signs, *'Jerry Walsh.'*

Finn guffaws. *'Wow, Mia! Pick yourself the biggest player, why don't you?'*

Mia lowers her eyes. *'I know.'*

'Is he gonna stick around? Support you through this?'

Mia shrugs her shoulders softly. *'He says he'll help where he can. We had to go for an extra scan as they wanted to test if she has Downs - she doesn't - but he was there for that. We've agreed we'll just take it one day at a time.'*

Finn sits back in his chair, drinking her in with his eyes. He shakes his head slowly as traces of pain cross his face.

'Of all the guys you could've picked,' he signs sadly.

'I didn't plan this, Finn! You more than anyone should know that. And it totally freaked me out at first - I mean, God, me as a mother! Can you imagine?' She smooths a frizzy curl from her forehead. *'But then, day by day, having her growing inside of me, I dunno, it just changed. I changed. Everything changed. It kind of doesn't matter who the father is, this about me and my baby.'*

'You want to do this alone?'

'I'm not sure.' She pauses. *'But I know I can.'*

Finn nods and looks down at his hands. As he looks up again and leans forward, his face is filled with adoration.

'OK, right, this is a bit mad, but whoever the father is, I'll do it! I'll take on the role. I know you don't feel the same way about me, but I think, given time, you could grow to love me. We get on well enough, don't we? I'd care for you and the baby. She, you said she's a she, right?'

'Yeah,' Mia taps her belly.

'If Jerry doesn't want to be a part of this, I will! I'll stand by

you. Why do it alone when I can be there with you? So, maybe it's not the hearts and flowers you'd want, but I think love can grow. I think we can learn to love. Especially if we have such a beautiful focus.' His eyes fall to her belly and then up to hers, silently asking for permission. She nods. He reaches across and places his hand on her stomach.

She taps his shoulder and he looks at her. *'Finn, you are THE sweetest guy. I don't deserve you and I can't ask you to do this.'*

He pushes a curl from her ear. *'Yes, I am the sweetest guy, you don't deserve me and you're not asking.'* Once again, she is reminded of how he resembles an adorable yet helpless puppy. How does a grown man, who has had experience in the world, retain such an aura of innocence? Trustworthy Finn - he doesn't have a bad bone in his body; he's gentle, kind, caring and all the things a woman should want in a life partner.

His wide lips part in a shy smile. *'You don't have to answer now, Mia,'* he signs. *'Just think about it, okay?'*

Chapter 52

Half way through her working day one of Greta's hearing aid had stopped working. Conducting the normal checks: switching it on and off and taking it apart, she then blows into the tube and discovers a tiny hole. Darn it! Another trip to the hospital. Her meeting with Marcus Allbright is scheduled for the end of this week and there is no way she can attend sans aids – she'd have decreased hearing, and more importantly, decreased confidence. She'd sidled up to Rog at the coffee machine and asked if she could leave a bit early to get to the audiology department, and Rog, still basking in the glory of his brief TV appearance that he attributes to her, agreed without quibble.

She approaches the audiology reception and explains that she needs new tubing. The receptionist tells her to take a ticket and a seat and someone will be with her soon. The room is crammed and the only available seats are at the front. Figuring that she has a great view of the numbers that flip over every few minutes, she removes her coat and sits. Too far away from the magazines, and with the rule of mobiles not being allowed, Greta passes the time by testing her lip-reading skills on the two gossiping nurses standing at the desk. And pretty soon she's captivated…

The pretty dark haired one with perfect eyebrows, whom Greta has a perfect view of lip-reading has just been dumped. She is feistily recounting how this 'dog' of a man 'led her on' and has now buggered off back to his girlfriend. Although unable to catch all of what the other nurse is saying she can tell she is offering sympathetic epithets. Squinting hard, Greta is hooked: this is better than a soap opera! Perfect Eyebrows has now gone on to say that in his 'dumping' speech he also confessed that he is now engaged to his girlfriend. The other nurse puts her hand on her friend's arm. 'I wouldn't mind,' Perfect Eyebrows continues. 'But it wasn't that long ago it was all over with her.'

The other nurse turns slightly and Greta catches her lips.

'Aw, mate, you're better off without him.'

'I know.' Perfect Eyebrows pouts. 'He's messed me about. I tell you, she's welcome to him; he can keep his 'Sweet Cheeks'!'

Ha! Sweet Cheeks! Well that's funny ... Sweet Cheeks...is that what she said? Greta's spine stiffens and all feeling disappears from her fingers and toes. Her mind races back to the first time she'd mis-lip-read him and 'Sweet Cheeks' became 'Switch'. Did that nurse really just say that? No, this has to be wrong! Sweat forms on her neck. But didn't this nurse also just say it had all been over between him and his girlfriend but now they're engaged? But, no, Olly wouldn't cheat on her - would he? Whilst her heart beats wildly and every drop of saliva dries from her mouth, her body shudders with a sense of foreboding. What should she do? How can she walk away from here not knowing if her fiancé is cheating on her with this young beautiful nurse? If she just goes home and confronts him, what will he say? If he's not been unfaithful he will deny it and if he has...he will deny it! Right...shaking inside, she rises and walks towards the desk. The two nurses look up at her, questioningly.

'Hi,' she says, feeling the tremor in her voice. 'I'm sorry. I wasn't being nosy, but I couldn't help, erm, overhearing...Can I ask you a question?'

Perfect Eyebrows' eyes grow large as she nods slowly. Greta inhales deeply: she has to do this - if not she will forever wonder. Mustering every ounce of courage she has, she asks, 'What's the name of the man who's just left you?'

Perfect Eyebrows looks to her friend and then back at Greta. 'Olly, Olly Emerson.'

Greta nods and with tears filling her eyes she puts her hand on the reception to steady herself. Jumping to her side, they take her arms and steer her to some chairs in the corridor behind the desk. Their lips are moving but Greta can't take anything in. As they sit her down, the second nurse asks Greta if she'd like some water. Greta nods vaguely and the nurse leaves to get it. Perfect Eyebrows takes the chair beside her.

'Are you who I think you are?' she asks Greta, concern filling her eyes.

Greta nods, large tears running down her face. She tries to speak but the sobs drown her voice. Perfect Eyebrows puts her arm around her. Amidst the tears Greta thinks of the irony of being comforted by the woman who has been cavorting behind her back with her fiancé.

Nurse number two returns with water and tissues and, with tears subsiding a little, Greta takes both. With a deep sniff she turns to Perfect Eyebrows.

'I'd like you to tell me about it.'

The pretty nurse lowers her eyes, her feistiness long vanished. 'Yes, of course. I'm on a break in twenty minutes, shall we get a coffee?'

Greta nods and looks to the numbered ticket she's still clutching.

'Right,' Perfect Eyebrows continues. 'Maria here will see to that, okay?'

'Thanks,' Greta says and wipes her nose.

'I'll meet you by the desk afterwards, okay?'

'Okay,' Greta looks at Perfect Eyebrow's name badge, 'Bella,' she says. 'I'll wait.'

•

Maria sorts out the tubing and as it doesn't seem appropriate to engage in neither small talk nor anything in-depth, the appointment is over in a flash. Greta sits herself back down in the waiting room and mentally retraces recent times. Where and when exactly did he meet Bella? How often did he meet her? Was it those trips to the pub? Was it the nights working late? Oh God - was it that work trip away? As little pieces of his deception fall into place she's confident that she already knows many of the answers to her questions.

Eventually Bella appears at the desk and waves Greta over. They walk in silence along the long corridor that leads to the large canteen. Bella offers to get the coffees whilst Greta finds a small table near the back in the corner. Greta studies Bella as she places the two mugs on the table and pulls up a seat. There's no denying that she's very attractive: she has dark hair framing elfin-like features and eyes of bright green. Her rose coloured lips are quivering and her hand shakes a little as she holds her cup. The two women eye each other warily.

'Where do we start?' Greta asks.

Bella sighs. 'I don't know, but please just tell me that you *did* separate last year?' Her eyes plead.

'Yes, we did take a breather. But we got back together before Christmas and that was when he proposed.'

'At Christmas?' Bella's eyes shoot wide. 'He proposed to you at Christmas?'

'Yup. Christmas Day.'

'The lying scumbag,' she says, shaking her head.

'Tell me about it.'

'Sorry,' Bella says, trying to quell her anger. 'This must be really hard for you.'

'Did you know that we got back together?' Greta eyes her curiously.

Bella wriggles in her seat. 'Kind of. Look, honestly, he told me he was single when I met him. You don't know me from Adam but I would never go near someone else's fella. Honestly. Anyway, after a few weeks he said that he'd seen you and that you were begging him to return and give it another go. He also said that you have some issues and that he owed it to you to help you through it. He said it wasn't permanent, but that he couldn't leave you hanging. Said it would tip you over the edge.' She stops and expels her breath. 'What an idiot I was for believing all that! It's only now saying it out loud that I can hear what a load of old shite it is!'

Greta nods. 'I was having issues? Interesting.'

'You know I thought he was such a kind guy, such a sweetheart caring for his ex. I was prepared to wait for him,' she says, staring into the middle distance.

Greta inhales. 'So when *did* you see each other?'

'Mostly Wednesdays.'

'Ah, my art class.'

'And sometimes other week nights. He said weekends were tricky.'

'I'll bet he did,' Greta says, curling her lip.

'Hope you don't mind me being frank with you,' Bella says. 'But he made you sound a bit of a crackpot. I've only just met you, but you seem lovely.'

Greta half smiles. 'He's quite a guy, isn't he?' As she eyes this young woman her mind races with the possibilities of all the hundreds of lies he must've told to them both. Had Greta suspected that he was unfaithful to her? Somewhere deep inside? A place within her that she refused to venture to? Maybe. 'Strange question, but did you watch a Hugh Grant film with him?'

Bella's brow knits in confusion. 'Yeah, how do you know that?'

'Maybe I don't know him half as well as I thought I did, but I do know that he would never voluntarily watch a Hugh Grant film.'

'He made a right ol' fuss about it too. Who would imagine that one romantic comedy could threaten your masculinity so much?'

'That's our macho shithead!' Greta says.

'Ours? He's not mine.' Bella shivers with disgust.

'Nor mine either, anymore.' Greta takes a breath. 'Bella, I need to know, did he ever take you back to our flat?' she asks, praying with all her might that he didn't. This is painful enough but if they had been in her flat - in her bed…

Bella guiltily nods. 'I am so sorry. Honestly, I wouldn't have gone near him if I'd known…'

Greta's heart is in her mouth but looking at this slip of a woman she can't help but believe her genuine intentions. She wonders how old Bella is - twenty? Twenty-one? She's not a home wrecker; a woman who set her sights on an attached man. No, she seems like someone taken in by an experienced two-timing rat. She's someone who's been played; someone who has fallen for the lies of a man who doesn't deserve her - much like her very own self.

'Seems he's quite a piece of work, isn't he?' Greta says looking at Bella's remorseful expression.

'You do know that it's for the best, us finding out, ' Bella says. 'I know it's horrid and I do feel bad that I was still with him as he was trying to end things with you…'

'Which he wasn't…'

'What a bastard.' Bella grimaces. 'But you wouldn't want to marry a man like that, would you?'

Greta wipes her nose and shakes her head. 'To be honest I don't even know why he asked me.'

'I think in his own little world, in his own way, he loves you. But a man like that…I don't know, will he ever settle down? Isn't the grass always greener?'

Greta shrugs.

'What're you going to do?' Bella asks.

Greta voice cracks. 'Leave him and not look back.'

'Hmm, wise,' Bella says.

'Maybe I shouldn't have gone back to him,' Greta says, wondering aloud. 'But when we got back together we were so happy. I thought we were solid.' She shakes her head. 'All this time...'

Bella gives a long sympathetic look and then glances down at her watch. 'I'm so sorry, Greta, I have to get back.'

Greta wipes her nose. 'That's fine. You go.'

Bella gets up but before she leaves she turns back. 'And I am really sorry that I was any part of this. You do know that, don't you? My sin was falling for his charms and believing his bullshit.'

Greta looks up at her. 'Mine too, Bella, only I did it for a lot longer.'

Chapter 53

Greta has no idea how she arrived but she now finds herself standing in the middle of their bedroom. She stares at the bunting she'd bought and hung above the bed and the ornate Victorian framed photos of them that she'd lovingly placed on their bedside tables and tears spring to her eyes again. Where did it all go wrong? At what point did he decide that this wasn't enough for him? That she wasn't enough? When did he stray off the straight and narrow to pursue another woman? How long has he been lying? How many lies has he told? And what if Bella isn't his first transgression and there have been others? Should she have been more suspicious? All she truly knows is that right here, right now, she feels deceived, cheated on and taken for a complete mug. As she climbs on the chair to retrieve her suitcase from the top of the wardrobe, she knows that this time it's for good; she won't be coming back. Ever. Does that make her less of a mug? That she's actually leaving him? Taking her case down, she wonders if she really should be berating herself for her gullibility. Doesn't the blame lie squarely on him? It certainly wasn't hers or Bella's fault.

Clocking the time, she realises that he'll be home soon and there is no way she wants to see him. Not because she is scared, but because she doesn't want to witness his denial nor his confession. And she certainly doesn't want to endure him ending their relationship or alternatively, him begging her to stay. There is no value to be had in that.

She quickly texts her father, explaining what's happened and how she would really *really* appreciate him bringing the Volvo so she could grab as many of her belongings as possible and get away. Ever the loving parent, her father responds and is on her doorstep within minutes.

'Thanks, Dad,' she says, opening the door.

Her father cradles her in his arms. When he pulls away he

puts his hands on her shoulders and looks straight into her eyes.

'Come on, darling, let's get your stuff and get you home. You're done here.'

'Yes, OK. Thanks.' She nods.

She tells her father the items she wishes to take and those she couldn't care less about. As she wants nothing that will remind her of Olly she actually takes very little. With a couple of cases, her artwork, a footstool, her favourite cushion and the spots and stripes cutlery packed up, she's ready to leave.

'I'll see you in the car,' her father says, as he picks up the last of her belongings.

As she looks around the flat she goes to the kitchen and finds the post-it notes. Looking at the little yellow slips she thinks about the number of times he wrote one saying he was going somewhere or meeting someone when, in reality, he must have been meeting Bella. She grabs a pen. There's no point thinking through what she wants to say as she would be there all night. Instead she simply writes,

Olly,

Had to go to the hospital today. I met Bella and we talked.

Nothing else to say.

I've taken all I want and that's why I'm leaving you here.

Greta.

She sticks the note on the kitchen counter, and then freeing her door key from its keyring she places it on top. Finally, she slips off her engagement ring and places it next to the key.

Without a backward glance, she strides out of the flat.

•

Arriving at her parents' house her mother greets her with a fluster.

'Darling, darling, how dreadful. Whatever happened?' Sylvia asks, lightly putting her arm around her daughter.

Seated on the sofa, with a cup of tea, Greta relays the events of her day. Sylvia appears genuinely shocked; she obviously never had Olly pegged as a philanderer. Her mother makes 'oohs' and 'aahs' and pulls sympathetic faces as Greta fights tears to reach the end of her tale.

'Well, darling, he had us all fooled,' Sylvia says. 'He always was a bit of a Jack the Lad, but I thought that it only added to his charm. You know - a kind of rough diamond. But I always thought he treated you well enough. Do you think that other woman was the temptress?'

Greta looks to her mother incredulously. 'Mum!'

'What? You know how these young floozies can be!'

'Even if she is a floozy, which she isn't, Olly is a grown man with a brain. He can say 'no', you know!'

'But, he's a man. We know where they keep their brains.'

Her father looks up. 'Er, hello?'

'Oh, not all men, dear, not you.' Sylvia says, brushing him aside with a wave of her hand. 'Anyway, Greta, the important thing is that we hadn't put any deposit down on anywhere for the wedding. We could've spent money on invitations too, and thankfully there's not many people we have to notify that the wedding's off.'

Greta watches in silence and awe at her mother's positive spin on breaking off an engagement. Sylvia isn't even addressing how her daughter might be heartbroken, bereft for the future she should've had, hurt and bitter that the man she loved didn't love her back. No, in true Sylvia fashion, her mother is more concerned with appearances and money.

Continuing to watch her mother talk (it certainly isn't a two-way conversation) she thinks how this is the essence of Sylvia. She's a woman who has such a opposite take on life to herself. One of Greta's life gripes is that her mother doesn't accept her the way she is, but now it suddenly occurs to her that maybe *she* has to accept Sylvia the way *she* is! Her mother is never going to change; she is never going to stop covering her mouth when she talks, become proficient in sign language, stop talking *for* her daughter and start including her in all conversations, and will never stop giving unfeeling hugs whilst simultaneously talking over her shoulder.

Ever.

But, Greta thinks, she knows her mother loves her and cares for her happiness dearly. Yes, they frequent different wavelengths - but maybe that's okay. Or perhaps that just has to be okay. Maybe she should accept Sylvia, warts and all? Forgive her for what she's not capable of and then, and only then, maybe the 'mother angst' that Greta carries (and has carried for many years) can be purged.

As her mother's pink lipstick'd lips continue to flap, Greta's thoughts are filled with the theme of accepting things and people just the way they are. Her mind wanders to Olly and she questions whether he just wasn't a compatible partner. She'd always believed that love could overcome their differences - but maybe it doesn't work like that? Love happens at various levels, for sure: Sylvia would swear blind that she loves her daughter but it wouldn't be the all-consuming, tactile, deeply caring love that Greta would have for her own child. And Olly probably would say that he loved Greta - but, as Greta well knows, it's not the sort of love that can be sustained if he can't be faithful. Sorrow, hurt, anger, bitterness and disappointment all take turns to wash over Greta; there are still many tears to be shed, but, somewhere in the corner of her heart she is perplexed to find a sliver of relief. Not quite understanding why, she nevertheless decides to hold on to it like a beacon in a storm. Whatever it means and whatever happens from now on, she knows that life is going to be a whole lot different.

Chapter 54

It's early doors in The Jolly Sailor, so there's only a handful of the usual suspects there. Greta finds a table and sits patiently waiting for Mia. After unpacking and moving herself back into her childhood bedroom, she had texted Mia to tell her everything. Having always sensed Mia's disapproval of Olly, Greta was relieved that her best friend didn't feel the need to say anything damning. Instead, hasty arrangements were made to meet and have a proper face to face session.

Mia wafts into the pub, maternity cargo pants, cheesecloth top and hair bigger than ever and immediately scoops Greta up into her arms. After the longest bear hug in which Greta is actually only making contact with Mia's belly, she is finally released.

'How are you?' Mia asks, her hazel eyes soft and kind.

Greta shrugs. *'I don't know, to tell you the truth. All feels a bit unreal.'*

'Have you heard from him?'

'Yes.' Greta nods. *'He's been texting me constantly. He started off just playing dumb, saying he didn't know who Bella was. I replied, elaborating, and then he went on to accuse her of lying. Then when I told him I believed her, he got defensive. Then he got angry and then I stopped answering. I've now got…'* She picks up her phone from the table. *'Three, four, ten, twelve, fifteen messages.'*

'So he's not giving up without a fight. You gonna see him?'

Greta shakes her head. *'Nope, I'm done. You should've met her, Mia, and heard the things she said. The lies he told her to keep her in tow whilst he was obviously trying to figure out which one of us he wanted.'* Greta shudders. *'To think I was still having sex with him.'*

'You're best off out of it, Grets. If he can do this once he can do it again.'

'*And who knows if this was the first time.*' Greta's shoulders fall with a sigh.

'*Wanna drink?*' Mia signs, rubbing her friend's arm.

'*Don't worry, I'll get 'em.*' She reaches for her purse. '*What's your non-alcoholic not-so-poisonous poison?*'

'*Soda and lime, please.*'

'*Sure, hang tight.*'

Greta makes her way to the bar and as she waits for the bartender to bring her drinks she spots Jerry standing at the far end.

'*Is Mia here?*' he signs.

'*Yep, over there.*' Greta points in the direction of her friend.

'*Tell her I'll be over in a minute, okay?*'

'*Okay.*'

Making her way back to Mia she puts the drinks down and informs her of Jerry's presence. Mia stirs her drink with the straw whilst a guilty smile creeps to her lips.

'*OK, Ms. Smug, wanna tell me what's going on?*' Greta signs.

Mia looks up innocently. '*What?*' Greta pulls a 'don't come the innocent with me' face. '*Well, it's nothing really, but Finn came to see me. He'd obviously heard that I'm 'with child'.*' She comically points down to her bump. '*And wanted to know if it's his. I told him I didn't know but there'll be a DNA test and he ended up saying that Jerry is the biggest player on the planet and he will step up in his place.*'

'*Seriously? Wow, he really is 'Fall Back' Finn!*' Greta signs.

'*I know. But he was so sweet, you know.*'

'*You're not going to take him up..*'

Just then Mia breaks eye contact and looks over Greta's shoulder. Greta turns to see Jerry heading for their table.

'*Right, I'm going to leave you to it*' Greta signs. '*I need the loo. Back in a bit.*' Greta grins, gets up and smiles at Jerry as they pass.

Jerry approaches the table and putting his pint down, slides into Greta's seat.

'*Hi, how you doing?*' he signs.

Mia suppresses a small gulp as his ever-striking appearance of dreadlocks, chiselled features plus piercing blue eyes works for her every time.

'*I'm good thanks. Just getting on with it really.*' She looks to her stomach.

'*Well, you're looking good on it.*'

'*Thanks. I'm quite enjoying the eating part of being pregnant.*'

'*Cake?*' he teases.

'*Well duh!*'

They both laugh gently and then Jerry takes a deep breath.

'*Look, I've got something to tell you…*' he starts. Ah – as his beautiful eyes darken she senses she is not going to like this. What is he going to say? That he can't give up any part of his free-spirited life? That he is turning his back on her and Sprogly and continuing his life as a player? Whatever it is she can tell he's about to deliver a blow. '*…A few months ago,*' he continues. '*I was partying, having a good time, life was simple and now it's so…different.*'

'*Worse different rather than good different, huh?*' Mia signs.

He nods slowly. '*With my mum dying and the idea of being a father, I just don't recognise my life anymore.*'

Mia raises her eyebrows. '*And?*'

He inhales deeply. '*The NDO are setting up an office in Belfast. They've asked me if I want to lead on it.*'

Mia swallows hard. '*I see. So, you're going to take it?*'

'*I think so, yeah. Look,*' he adds quickly. '*I'll still support you, you know, if the test turns out…*' His hands stop in mid-air.

Yep, she knows exactly what he means; he'll dutifully shell out cash if Sprogly is his, but that's as far as his commitment goes. (And she bets he is praying to all the Gods that the baby isn't his and he'll remain commitment free.)

'*I see.*'

He looks deeply into her eyes. '*I am sorry, Mia. You know if we'd just gone out together I think this could've been something.*'

She resists sniffing the air and saying she can smell bullshit. '*Hmm, you think?*' she signs. '*Well, guess we'll never know, huh?*'

He gives her a look that borders on a smoulder and something inside her snaps. She is not going to play out this 'star crossed lovers' scene as it's just not genuine. He doesn't have to run off to Belfast and they *could* start a relationship complete with a baby. The odds would be stacked against them for sure, but if he felt enough for her they could certainly try.

'Honestly Jerry, don't sweat it. In fact,' she signs breezily. 'Do you know Finn Parker?' Jerry nods cautiously. 'He's offered to take me and Sprogly on. He wants to look after us. So, I'm kind of sorted. We're all good.'

Like she had physically slapped him, Jerry's face drops. 'What?'

'Yeah, he came to see me the other night - we've always had a good relationship and when he found out I was pregnant he said he'd look after us. In fact, if I have my dates wrong,' she signs, patting her stomach, 'she could actually be his.'

His lips curl as he squints at her. 'You bitch.'

'Says the man who's legging it off to Belfast.'

A heavy silence sits between them. She casually stirs her drink whilst watching his eyes glint with anger. Ha, she thinks, he certainly wasn't expecting that. He thought he'd play out a love scene where he's the tortured good guy who could disappear with minimal guilt.

'One question,' he eventually signs with cold eyes. 'Do you love him?'

'Who? Finn?'

'Who else?'

She shrugs. 'No - but who said anything about love?'

He frowns. 'But?'

'Maybe love isn't the answer. Maybe contentment, security, raising a child with love - maybe that's what it's all about.' She shrugs. 'I've known Finn many years - we get on really well. I can see us rubbing along quite happily. The more I think about his proposition the more I think it makes sense.'

Jerry looks at her in disbelief. 'Contentment? Rubbing along? Makes sense? Jeez, Mia, it sounds boring and, to be honest, like you're just giving up.'

'Oh really!' she signs, straightening up in her seat.

'Look Mia, what I meant is -'

At that moment they both look up to see Greta standing awkwardly at the table. Mia exhales deeply.

'Look Jerry,' she signs. 'Hope it goes well for you, I really do.'

Jerry shakes his head with a sigh before slowly getting up. 'You too, Mia.'

As he turns and walks away Mia puffs out a sigh of relief.

'What happened there?' Greta asks, sitting down.

'He's moving to Belfast to a new job.' Mia shakes her head. *'You know, a player's gotta play.'*

'What did you say?'

'Oh I told him about Finn - maybe I was cruel but I just didn't want to be the dumped little woman.' A flash of sadness crosses her face.

'I'm sorry.' Greta leans forward. *'But you're not really going to take Finn up on his offer, are you?'*

'Nah, he's sweet and all that, but no, I can do this on my own,' she signs, shaking herself. *'You know as far as Jerry's concerned I think it was a one night thing that should have been just that. He was never ready for anything more - baby or no baby. It's a shame though as I did really like him...'*

'Or really 'lusted' him,' Greta interrupts.

'Ha, you could be right. But, you know, I'll be fine, I know I will.' She turns to face Greta head on. *'We both will, eh?'*

As Greta agrees her eyes suddenly light up. *'Hey, I've just had the best idea!'*

'OK, but you'll have to hold that thought.' Mia winces, touching her belly. *'Sprogly is doing a jig on my bladder. Back in a mo.'*

As Mia walks away with the beginnings of a waddle, Greta sits back in her chair and smiles. She never used to believe that good things are born from unhappiness, but now it seems that she might have to review her thinking on that one as well.

Chapter 55

Greta skips into art class the following week, eager to tell Malcolm all about her meeting with Marcus Allbright. Turns out Marcus is quite a charming man who is extremely keen to display certain pieces from Greta's portfolio on a sale or return basis. To get such an opportunity in a prime gallery is quite a coup and the thought of it has given Greta a necessary distraction from Olly's constant texts. But, saying that, in the last day or so his messages have thankfully started to lessen. She wonders if she should meet him to gain the closure that he clearly needs - but a part of her cannot bear the thought of watching him snivel. No, it's done, over. She always knew she was that person who could be pushed and pushed but then reaches a point of no return. Meeting Bella was that point.

'Evening!' Joan smiles. 'You look happy,' she says and puts her fingers to her corners of her mouth to emphasise her point.

'I am, Joan. That art gallery wants to display my work, my ex has stopped texting so much and this morning I got the date for my cochlear implant!'

Richard's ears prick up. 'Really?'

Greta nods emphatically. 'Yep, there's been a cancellation so they've offered it to me. Next Monday.'

'Crikey, how are you feeling?'

'Ha, you know me, Richard, nervous, scared, still a little unsure...'

'Tish tosh,' he says, waving his hand. 'You're a soldier and you'll have the operation and come out better the other side.'

'Better', thinks Greta, strange how that word sticks. So she's not at her best now? She knows Richard doesn't mean it like that but...

Malcolm enters the room and calls the class to attention. The classmates excitedly tell him Greta's news and he, as supportive as ever, is extremely enthusiastic.

'Wow, Greta,' he says. 'Everything is happening for you, isn't it? All well-deserved too. If your pieces sell do we see you giving up your job at the council?'

'Actually,' Greta says. 'I'm thinking about doing that anyway. I'm going to see how the operation goes and when it's all done I'm going to keep making life changes. I read somewhere that you can't live the same year for seventy years and call it a life.'

'Oooh, very inspiring,' Joan says, eyeing her husband, Nigel, who in turn looks a little nervous.

'Who knows what the future holds,' Greta says.

'Indeed,' Malcolm says. 'But one thing I do know is that due to the overwhelmingly positive reaction to The Art of Being Disabled, Adult Ed. are putting on two more identical classes. So, you can pick you night: Monday Tuesday or Wednesday, or all three!'

Joan frowns. 'Oh no, we can't be separated!' she says, looking around at her class mates. 'We'll stick to Wednesdays, won't we?'

As everyone agrees and Nigel suggests taking a second class together, Greta smiles broadly and starts to unpack her art case.

While she begins to draw she thinks about the past two weeks back with her parents. She has to concede that it's going rather well. John is as soft and twinkly as ever and Sylvia is definitely…well, less Sylvia, and with their great trip now booked, there is much excitement in the air.

That morning, before work, over tea and toast, Greta had brought up her most recent brilliant idea.

'Mum, Dad, when you leave what do you think if I asked Mia to move in here?'

Her parents had looked to each other.

'I think that's a marvellous idea,' her mother had ventured first.

'Really?' Greta replied. 'That's great! That way I'll be on hand to help Mia, as her birthing partner and then as her right-hand woman in those early sleepless days. I want to be the coolest, most reliable and loving 'aunt' I can be.'

John and Sylvia chuckled at their daughter's enthusiasm; happy to see her smile despite still coping with all the disappointment of Olly.

'I rather like the idea of you being able to help Mia and also for Mia to be here for you. Someone to lean on is always valuable,' John said with a sideways tender look at his wife.

Full of the thrill of the moment, Greta had rushed upstairs to video-call her friend and put forward her proposition. Mia, being hormonally charged anyway, had wept uncontrollably. It was agreed. Two women and a little lady it was.

Losing herself in her drawing, Greta is just thinking how every aspect of her life seems to be radically changing when she becomes aware of Malcolm standing behind her, looking over her shoulder. He moves around the table to face her and clears his throat.

'Well what do we have here, then?' he says, a grin playing on his lips. 'Colours, Greta?'

Looking up at him, Greta blushes slightly, smiles and nods. 'It's time.'

Chapter 56

'Come on, darling,' her mother fusses as Greta descends the stairs, case in hand. 'What time did they want you there?'

'Plenty of time, Sylvia,' her father interjects.

Greta looks at her mother, hopping around near the front door, the worry of her daughter's impending operation written all over her face. Of course it's natural that a mother should worry about their child going under the knife, but Sylvia's flapping does nothing to calm Greta's nerves. Greta wishes in a way that it could have been Olly taking her today - he certainly wouldn't have made a fuss - in fact she can imagine him showing no emotion whatsoever. And talking of him, she doesn't know how he found out but he actually sent her a good luck text this morning. He's turned into 'Best Behaviour, Olly', but even that doesn't tug on her heartstrings anymore; he no longer has the power to reel her in. Despite the stress of today's operation, the one good thing is it has provided a marvellous distraction from grieving for him

'OK, Gretsy?' her father asks, putting on his shoes. 'You all set?'

'Yep, ready as I'll ever be.'

Her father drives whilst her mother twitches in the front seat. Greta looks out of the window, feeling a little like it's not really happening to her; like she's in a movie or something. Thoughts of this being the last day she'll have breakfast, a shower, brush her teeth or sit in a car without a metal implant in her head, crowd her mind. Her whole world is about to change and the thought of what tomorrow will be like is exciting and scary in equal measure.

Arriving at the ward the nurse takes them to her room. She shows Greta the ensuite bathroom and where to hang her clothes. Greta perches on the bed and the nurse invites her parents to take seats.

'I'm Julie. We have to do the pre-op, okay?' she says with a smile. Just then she turns her head to the door. 'Come in!'

Oh crap, no! It's Connor! Greta inwardly groans. Not today. Why does this man keep showing up like a bad penny? Today is already filled with anxiety; another showdown with him isn't going to help.

He eyes her nervously and nods to her parents. Her mother says something to him and they exchange smiles. He then pulls up the remaining chair, positions himself next to the nurse and lifts his hands to interpret.

Greta focuses rigidly on Julie's lips. 'Right,' she says. 'Shall we get started? Just some questions.'

Greta breathes a sigh of relief that this nurse is lip-readable and that she doesn't have to look at Connor. Guilt and remorse from their last meeting is still lingering and she doesn't want to be burdened with that today. Instead she focuses intently on the nurse who asks her the standard health questions that precede an operation. Connor waits, ready to spring into action if Greta should miss or misunderstand something. Greta feels his gaze upon her and tries in vain to block it.

'Right, now all you have to do is get changed into this,' Julie says, holding up the cotton white gown. 'And the doctor will be in to see you in a while. Do you have any questions?'

'What time will the op be?' Greta asks.

'Er.' Julie looks at a schedule on her clipboard. 'Looks like you are near the bottom of the list, so it should be...' She glances at her fob watch. 'Around four o' clock.'

'What a wait!' Sylvia pipes up.

Julie turns to Greta's parents. 'Well, you can go to the canteen and the shop. But you,' she says, turning back to Greta. 'I'm afraid you're not allowed anything to eat or drink. Not even water, okay? When you come out of surgery and as soon as you feel up to it we'll get you some tea and toast.'

'Thanks,' Greta says

'Okay, I'll leave you to it,' she says. 'Any problems please use the button and someone'll be with you.' As the nurse turns to Connor, Greta strains to catch her lips. 'Doctor will be here in a few minutes so best if you wait here, okay?' He nods and Greta's heart sinks.

As Julie bustles out of the room, John stands. 'Right,' he says to Greta. 'Hate to be thinking of myself, but I need a cuppa.' Then turning to his wife, he adds, 'Shall we head off to the canteen for a bit?' Sylvia agrees and as Greta realises she is about to be left alone with Connor, her heart sinks even further.

As the heavy door closes a nervous silence replaces her parents' upbeat chatter. Connor looks around the room until finally resting his eyes on hers.

'How you feeling?'

She shrugs. *'Nervous.'*

'Hmmm, does it help or hinder that I'm here?' She gives him a look of disbelief. *'Ok,'* he adds quickly. *'Shall we just not talk?'*

He looks at his hands. Greta gets up and picks up the stringed gown.

'I'm going to get changed, okay.'

He nods and returns to his hands. A few minutes later, emerging from the ensuite, she self-consciously crosses back to the bed.

Unable to stand the awkwardness any longer, she takes a deep breath. *'Connor, look,'* she signs. *'I was a bit harsh on you the last time we met. I'm sorry, okay?'*

He puffs out a sigh. *'No, I was in the wrong. I shouldn't've been there, interpreting for them. I'm the one that should be sorry.'* They exchange a small smile. Greta faffs with her gown, trying to make it cover everything it should.

'Very becoming,' Connor signs, with a smile.

'Why thank you, I had it made 'specially!' She half giggles and moves the material over her knees.

He laughs. Then, fixing her with a serious look, he asks, *'So how is your friend? I hear my brother is on the move.'*

'Yeah, she's fine, actually. You know it's funny how these things turn around...' she signs.

'Oh yeah?'

'Oh, long story.'

He gestures around the room and smiles. *'I'm not going anywhere!'*

'Ok, so, you know my dad had a heart attack? Well, he's decided to take life by the horns...'

'Not sure that's the right phrase.'

She pulls a face. *'Whatever! Anyway, he's off with my mum*

around the world. They're going for a year and asked me to move into the house to look after it. And then they agreed that Mia should move in. I can be there for her in the last weeks of pregnancy and the early days of Sprogly - we're gonna be the best team.'

'Oh wow! That's fantastic!' His face lights up and then his brow starts to knit. *'But what about your fella? Where does he come into it?'*

'Ah, yes, him, we split.'

'Eh?' His eyes widen in surprise.

'Yeah, let's say he wasn't the faithful person I thought he was.'

'Oh, I'm sorry.'

'Hmm.'

As Connor nods, taking in the information, a small smile dances on his lips.

'Do you want to tell me why you're looking so pleased?' Greta asks, her hackles starting to rise.

He shrugs his shoulders. *'You're single.'*

Before she can reply the door swings open and Mr Khan strides in with a student in tow.

'Hello Greta!' he says. Connor moves to his side to interpret.

Feeling stunned and with her hands still in mid-air, Greta swallows hard and gives a vague smile. 'Hello Mr. Khan.'

Chapter 57

Her mind races with Connor seemingly happy that she's single. It has completely thrown her; does he think she deserves being cheated on or is he genuinely happy that she's a free agent? And what a time to say it!

'Right, how are you feeling?' Mr Khan asks.

Truthfully? Distracted by this interpreter… 'Fine, thanks.'

'Right, so, we said we'd do the…' He looks to his notes. 'Left ear. I just need to mark it.' With that Mr Khan produces a marker pen and moving Greta's hair away from her ear, he draws an arrow. 'Don't worry it'll come off in the wash.'

'How much of my hair will be shaved?' she asks.

'Just this patch here,' he says, running his finger around the top and back of her ear. 'You have plenty of hair so it'll soon cover over. OK? Any last questions?' She shakes her head. 'Right well, I'm afraid it's just a matter of sitting and waiting now. There's the television.' He points to it on the wall. 'And there are magazines. Okay?' She nods. 'I'll see you down there later this afternoon.'

With that he sweeps out of the room closely flanked by his follower. Connor pulls up a chair next to the bed.

'Sorry,' he signs.

'What for?'

'For looking happy that you're single. You've just finished a relationship, I'm sure you're not ready. That's even if you feel the same…'

'So, hang on, back up,' She holds her palms out to him. *'You like me?'*

'Greta,' he signs. *'In case you haven't noticed I am a complete idiot around you. I say the wrong things and I usually end up offending you - yes, I really like you!'*

'Wow, hate to see you with someone you don't like!'

They both laugh.

His eyes grow dark. *'But I still don't know how you feel.'*

Just then the door flies open again and Greta rolls her eyes at the sight of her mother rushing in.

'Aaargh, I forgot my purse! I've left your father with Chelsea buns and tea, holding up a long queue!' Connor interprets and both he and Greta laugh. 'Has the doctor been round?' her mother asks.

'Yes, look,' Greta says and pushes back her hair to show the arrow.

'Oh darling,' her mother says, her hands moving to her mouth. She moves to Greta's side. 'Looks like one of those dreadful tattoos.' With genuine sadness in her eyes she touches her daughter's head. 'My little girl,' she continues. 'Perfect since the day you were born...' Her mother stops and bites her lip. 'Right, better get back to your father.'

As she leaves, Greta turns back to Connor.

'Weird, my mother is acting weird.'

'I think she had a moment there,' Connor signs.

'What do you mean?'

'Your mother loved you as this completely formed baby and, of course, still does - who wants a surgeon to rearrange perfection?'

'That's rather lovely,' Greta signs, nodding, not totally convinced they are Sylvia's feelings. *'Ok, let me ask you this, Connor, coming from a deaf family, don't you think that technological advances are there to provide deaf people with a better way of life? If this op had been around when your parents were young, wouldn't they have gone for it?'*

He thinks for a moment. *'I honestly don't know. But I do know their life was perfect in its own way. They were happy. They loved the deaf way: deaf friends who were really like family, the deaf club, their own beautiful sign language. They were part of a club that not being able to hear granted them membership to and being on that deaf club committee made them top of the pile. That was their life. Yes, maybe an operation could've helped them hear a doorbell or the sound of someone's voice - but it would never have made them hearing - and in truth I don't think they would've wanted it to.'*

'Oh wow, wish I hadn't asked,' Greta signs, fear and confusion evident on her face.

'Oh no, no no, I didn't mean to put a case forward for not

having the op!'

'The doubts are already here. I've been through it so many times, and sometimes I am so sure it's the right thing to do and then other times...' she trails off.

Connor moves to sit beside her on the bed.

'I'm not here to advise, but can I tell you one thing my mum used to say?' Greta nods. *'She used to say that if I wake up on my wedding day and I have even one doubt, I shouldn't go through with it.'*

'What? You're getting married now?'

'No! What I mean is if you have doubts, should you be doing this now? This op can be done at any time and maybe you should have it when you're one hundred per cent sure?' His eyes soften. *'You don't have to do this today, Greta.'*

Her stomach churns. Really? Just tell the hospital staff that she's not sure and leave it at that? Can she do that? Won't she be seen as a time waster? But there again, what's worse? A time waster or an unsure implantee?

Looking back into Connor's eyes she feels a new kind of calmness settle over her.

'So?' Connor signs. *'Do you want me to get the doctor back in here?'*

'No.' She gets up from the bed and heads into the ensuite. A few minutes later she appears fully clothed and moves to place the white gown on the bed. Hurriedly she goes to her handbag and pulls out her trusted pen and pad. She quickly scribbles,

So sorry, can't do this today.

Greta Palmer.

Connor reads the words she places on the bedside cabinet. *'Blimey, Greta! Hey, what about your parents?'*

'I'll text them later. Ready?'

Connor nods and they move to the door. Poking his head out he turns to Greta.

'OK, coast is clear. Let's go!'

With their heads lowered they briskly walk along the corridor and past the nurse's station. They quicken their pace as they reach the main reception and as they approach the wide automatic sliding doors they break into a slow run.

Moving out into the daylight they continue to run, each step feeling like freedom. The blue-sky air fills their lungs as they move into the rhythm of their feet on the pavement. They career out onto the country lanes and Greta throws her head back laughing at Connor's shortness of breath and bright red face. She thinks he's about to dissolve from all his sweat when she misses her step and lurches into a stumble. Connor manages to grab her hand and slowing down, panting and laughing, they fall into a comfortable walk.

An hour later, when they reach the cafe on Grafton Street, he is still holding her hand.

Chapter 58

A few months later…

Greta sees the landing light on and knows that Mia must be up. She slips on her dressing gown and wanders down the stairs to find Mia and Saffy having a midnight snack in their usual spot on Sylvia and John's beige flowered sofa.

'Hey, how you doing?' Greta asks her friend.

'Little missy here doesn't want to sleep - all she wants to do is eat.' Mia signs with a smile, readjusting her swaddled baby to her breast.

'Aw bless her. How about you? Want something to eat or drink?'

'Love a vodka,' Mia jokes.

Greta goes to the kitchen and brings back two hot chocolates, places them on the coffee table and then perches herself on the side of the large armchair. She watches her friend and the feeding baby. Weighing seven pounds and five ounces, Saffia Esme Gregory had been born a few moments after Mia had begged for every drug going. 'No time for that, lovey,' the midwife had said. 'This baby is coming.' Saffy had chosen her moment and was born in the blink of an eye. Greta's eyes had filled with tears at the sight of this olive-skinned beauty and Mia sobbed with gratitude as Saffy was placed in her arms. Greta put her arm around her friend and they gazed lovingly at this little miracle. Life since then has been nappies, insomnia, Sudocrem and giggles.

'You had any more thoughts about the DNA test?' Greta asks, taking a sip of her drink.

Mia shakes her head thoughtfully. *'Not really. Jerry's been in touch but he hasn't mentioned it once. Maybe he doesn't want to know, so I'm not going to bother. I know who the father is.'* She strokes Saffy's soft black hair that is starting to form into little tight curls. *'I think these could turn into dreadlocks, don't you?'*

Greta nods and smiles.

'Oh I meant to ask,' Mia signs. 'How did it go at work yesterday? How's the lovely Marcus?'

'I love the job, Mia. I mean, it's less pay than the council, but being around all that art, even it is just doing paperwork, I love it! It inspires me to keep doing what I love...'

Their attention is taken to Connor who strolls into the lounge, suppressing a yawn and rubbing his eyes. 'What are you two doing up at this hour? Don't you see enough of each other?'

Greta stands and puts her arm around him. 'Don't blame us, blame Saffy.' She kisses him playfully on the lips. 'Anyway, what are you doing up?'

'I missed you.' He kisses Greta.

'Oh get me a bucket,' Mia signs, rolling her eyes. Greta laughs. She loves the fact that Mia and Connor like each other; there's no tension, just good-humoured banter. And although this living arrangement won't last forever it somehow feels like a complete, albeit unconventional, family. John and Sylvia send postcards from the many destinations they travel to and on the last one they wrote that they are extending their trip by six months. Great, more time for Mia to sublet her place to Finn, (who really needed to move out of his family home), and for everyone here to just be as they are.

'You ok then?' Greta asks Mia.

Mia peers down at her baby. 'I think she's nodded off. I'll try putting her down again.'

Connor and Greta bid their goodnights and climb the stairs together. He slips his hand in hers and as they reach the top he turns to her.

'You know we said we'd take things slowly? Is this okay?'

She stifles a giggle. 'Sure, Connor, only staying over five nights out of seven is definitely taking it slowly.'

He pulls a face. 'Look, I know how you are with decisions - I don't want to pressure you.'

'Are we talking about the 'C.I.' again?' she mouths the initials as they always jokingly do. 'Because if we are, I have some news...I'm going to jump into the twenty first century and get me some digital hearing aids - after that, who knows!'

He laughs. 'Well, look at you!'

'I know! Today - digital hearing aids, tomorrow a cochlear

implant…'

'*Maybe,'* they both sign in unison and laugh.

'*When the time's right, eh?'* she signs with a small shrug.

'*Exactly,'* he replies. *'You're perfect without and you'll be perfect with.'*

Greta winds her arms around his neck and kisses him deeply. Then, pulling apart she raise her hands and points to herself: '*I*', crosses her hands over her heart: '*love,'* and points to him: '*you*'.

Connor scoops her up in his arms and spins her around before they lose balance and fall through the bedroom door. Their loud laughter echoes throughout the house as they collapse onto the bed.

And the only person who stirs is Saffy.

THE END

Huge thanks to…

Matthew Talbot who constantly helped with the details.

Isabel Reid who gave me enthusiasm, support and the value of her insight.

Jane Walton who encouraged me to write it.

MH Ferguson who edited and gave never-ending support.

Viv Wilson for the final proof read.

Laura Schlotel for constant guidance.

Phil Collins for always being the voice of reason and support.

Joyce Munton for relentless support.

Ruby and Beattie for listening to me blather on about writing.

To all the D/deaf people who have shaped my knowledge.

And finally to Malcolm for being the man I share my life with, who just happens to be Deaf. Thank you for 'taking on' a hearing wife. X

Other titles available by Maxine Sinclair:-

Snapshots

Dixbury Does Talent

Return to Dixbury

Please see the author's page